SEAL TEAM SIX:
HUNT THE SCORPION

ALSO BY DON MANN WITH RALPH PEZZULLO

SEAL Team Six: Hunt the Wolf

Inside SEAL Team Six

SEAL TEAM SIX:

HUNT THE SCORPION

DON MANN

WITH RALPH PEZZULLO

MULHOLLAND BOOKS

LITTLE, BROWN AND COMPANY

NEW YORK BOSTON LONDON

Mulholland Books / Little, Brown and Company
Hachette Book Group
237 Park Avenue
New York, NY 10017
mulhollandbooks.com

The publisher is not responsible for websites (or their content) that are not owned by the publisher.

Printed in the United States of America

Originally published in hardcover by Mulholland Books, February 2013
First Mulholland Books mass market edition, October 2013

10 9 8 7 6 5 4 3 2 1

"Courage is not the absence of fear, but rather the judgment that something is more important than fear."

—Ambrose Redmoon

This book is dedicated to the courageous Navy SEALs, past and present, who have risked their lives to protect our freedoms. And to their families.

SEAL TEAM SIX:
HUNT THE SCORPION

PROLOGUE

To those who do not know that the world is on fire,
I have nothing to say.

—Bertolt Brecht

THE FIRST thing she noticed when she walked across the deck was the case-hardened locks on every outside door. Heavy-duty solid steel. Even on the smallest hatches. Also, the skylight over the engine room was cinched tight by a stainless-steel chain and secured with a padlock.

When she asked her husband, Jake—the captain of the forty-thousand-ton cargo ship—about them, he shrugged and mumbled one of his typically short answers. "No big deal. A simple precaution."

"From what?"

"Aliens and peeping Toms."

"Oh, Jake."

They stood side by side on the navigation bridge of the MSC *Contessa* looking out at the rising moon, glowing mustard yellow. The sky was an iridescent shade of dark blue bleeding into purple. A swath of even darker clouds formed an arch above the moon like some mischievous child had smeared the sky with black ink.

"Stunning, eh?" Captain Jake McCullum offered.

"Breathtaking, darling, yes. How much longer until we reach Marseille?"

"Three days, maybe four, depending on winds and currents."

From the moment they met, Tanya had felt herself drawn to his quiet strength, his confidence. Those qualities continued to give her comfort, even if the two of them had been married for less than a year and had spent only two months of that time together.

He'd been working almost nonstop, taking all the ship captain assignments he could get, so they could cobble together a down payment for a flat in their native Melbourne.

The 450-foot *Contessa* was thirty-five miles off the east coast of Africa, approaching the island of Socotra. Not only was this a busy shipping lane, but the waters up the coast and into the Gulf of Aden were typically crowded with trawlers from Taiwan, South Korea, India, France, Saudi Arabia, Japan, and other countries. Together with local Somali fishermen in smaller dhows, they mined the seas for high-value tuna, lobster, deepwater shrimp, whitefish, and even shark.

Tonight dozens of small vessels dotted the dark sea ahead of them, which caused the CPA (Closest Point of Approach) alarm on the Furuno radar to ring and flash. Captain McCullum walked to the radar on the long console, flipped a switch, and the bridge turned quiet.

"That's better," he said, wrapping an arm around Tanya's narrow waist. "Now we can enjoy the night."

Just the hum of the engine and the sound of waves slapping the metal hull.

The navigation bridge was a spacious, somewhat sterile chamber with large reinforced windows that were tilted open on this warm night. The raw, salty musk of the ocean mixed with the faint smell of tropical flowers inspired dreams of romance and adventure in Tanya's head.

She glanced at her husband's lean, chiseled face and saw that his eyes were focused on Socotra, specifically the flashing red light on the southwest extremity.

Tanya was about to say that the island's dark shape reminded her of a sleeping elephant when the captain turned to the officer on duty and barked, "Port, thirty."

"Port, thirty, sir," the handsome young Sikh officer echoed back.

The navy-turbaned officer slowly turned the ship's wheel, causing the dial of the electric compass to click off degree by degree as the cargo ship responded to the change of course.

"Steady at twenty knots," the captain said.

"Yes, sir, full away," the first officer responded.

To see her husband in his role as captain, to watch the way the crew of twelve responded to his quiet authority, made her love him even more. To Tanya's mind, he was an old-school man of the world, a leader and adventurer. A rare species in modern society.

The constellations Orion and Pleiades glittered overhead. Nature felt close.

"Wind out of the south-southwest, sir, steady at fifteen to twenty knots. Latest report has rain squalls blowing in from the south," the Sikh officer reported.

"Tell the third mate, deck lights fore and aft, spotlights on the poop deck," the captain ordered.

"Yes, sir."

"Don't want those fishing boats to miss us. You've got the radar. And keep an ear out for the radio."

"Aye, aye, captain," the officer responded, reaching for the phone that was embedded in the long center console, along with numerous dials, gauges, readouts, and radar screens.

"Keep sharp. Call me for any reason. I'm going below."

He turned to her and smiled.

"Time to walk the plank, my lady."

"What do I have to do to get you to spare me?"

He rubbed his rugged-looking chin. "Let me think..."

Anticipation fluttering through her body, Tanya followed her husband down the metal steps and into a narrow corridor one deck below. Ever the gentleman, he stopped at a white door, turned the handle, and stepped aside so she could pass through first.

Before she did, she read the warning stenciled on the door in red: DANGEROUS SPACE, TEST AIR BEFORE ENTRY.

"What's that mean?"

"Nothing, really."

"Then why does it say 'dangerous space'?"

"Because I sleep here."

"No, really."

Her husband smiled his Marlboro Man smile and said, "We put it there to ward off uninvited visitors."

"Like who?"

He had never answered. It really didn't matter, because Tanya's mind stopped the moment Jake removed the towel from her freshly showered body and sighed in a low voice, "God, you're lovely."

"You think so?"

"Oh, yeah."

"I missed you, Jake."

"Missed you, too, sweetheart. And you smell delicious."

His strong hands touched her skin. Their lips met. Then he picked her up and lowered her to the bed as if in a movie.

"Please, Captain. Be gentle. I'm a young, inexperienced lass," she said, keeping up the game.

"Gentle, eh? Not in my nature, miss. *Grrr.*"

It was a modest twelve-by-twenty-foot cabin with small portholes that looked out to a large expanse of deck and the sea beyond. Nothing remarkable about it except for the large silver-framed wedding photo of the two of them getting pelted with rice as they emerged from St. Bartholomew.

Attached to the bedroom was a much larger captain's dayroom equipped with easy chairs, a sofa, bookshelves, a desk, a large flat-screen TV, and a refrigerator. That's where Jake spent most of his free time, surfing the Internet, reading, writing in his journal.

It didn't matter that the cabin smelled of mildew, or that the mattress felt hard against her back. Tanya was exactly where she wanted to be, feeling the ship roll from side to side beneath her as they made love. Usually an unemotional woman, she was surprised to find herself on the brink of tears.

She reached up and took her husband's face in her hands. "Oh, Jake... What is it about you that makes me so happy?"

"My bounteous gold treasure? My undying love for you?"

"The latter, darling. Ahh..."

Gazing into his eyes, she felt as though their souls were intertwining. Then she heard something that sounded like thunder. Her husband stopped moving.

"What?"

"Hold on."

"What is it?"

He placed his hand over her mouth, slid off her, and rested on his elbow. "Ssh."

More loud, muffled sounds followed—a metallic thud against the hull, a hard sound like steel barrels rolling on the deck outside.

He got to his feet quickly and picked up the phone, leaving her naked, covered with sweat.

"Jake..."

"Just a minute."

"But—"

"Sorry, sweetheart. Probably nothing. Might be some rowdiness among the crew."

For some reason, she didn't think so.

The noise increased. She heard the sound of feet running along the deck below.

"What's that?"

He dropped the phone because no one answered, held up a finger to his lips to tell her to be quiet, then ran naked to the porthole.

Along the starboard side of the ship he saw a small boat without lights motoring alongside them. Even odder, he noticed that the lights of his own ship were off.

Then a bright orange flash lit up the night sky.

Tanya gasped. "Oh, God! Have we struck something?"

"No. No. Not at all."

"Jake..."

"Don't worry."

He scooped his pants off the floor and pulled them on. "I'm going up to the bridge," he said urgently. "Lock the door behind me. Don't let anybody in under any circumstances."

"But, Jake—"

"No one! You hear me? I'll be back."

Captain McCullum climbed the steps to the navigation deck two at a time, hoping that this wasn't what he thought it was. But the moment he reached for the door to the bridge, reality flew out at him—six strange men armed with knives and guns. Pirates!

They grabbed him by the neck and started punching him and shouting like wild animals. All wore ski masks and a motley mix of jeans, shorts, T-shirts, military-style shirts, and scarves. Some had footwear; others were barefoot. All had eyes that were fierce and threatening.

Two of them dragged the young Sikh officer behind them by the hair, blood dripping from a wound in his stomach.

Jake moved toward him. "No! Dear God. He's seriously hurt. Let me tend to him. Get my medical kit. There's no need for that."

Before McCullum could get another word out, he felt a knife blade at his throat. A cacophony of voices screamed in his face in guttural, primitive English. "You fight, we kill! We cut you up! We kill everyone! Everything!"

"Alright. Okay... whatever you want."

"Whatever! What you mean?"

"Tell me what you want."

He tried to remain calm, aware that it was his primary responsibility as captain to protect his men and save the ship. He was willing to sacrifice the cash that he kept locked up in the ship's safe, and even the cargo, if necessary. The dark-skinned hooligans most likely wanted American dollars, and they were probably as frightened as he was.

Nodding as much as the blade against his skin would allow, McCullum said evenly, "No fight. No resistance from me. Tell me what you want. I'll oblige."

"Money!" the tallest of the men said emphatically. A thin black face covered with beard, eyes the color of copper.

"Much money!"

"Of course. No problem."

Another fellow, a little wiry man wearing an Ohio State T-shirt with the sleeves cut off, stepped forward and smashed Jake in the face with the butt of his pistol.

Christ!

Next thing he knew, rough hands were pulling him up, going through his pockets, tying his wrists together behind his back with a piece of rope. The men were shouting at one another in their native language. Somali, probably, which he couldn't understand.

The tall pirate was the only one who made sense. He said in broken English, "Money. You show the money. We give the mercy. No kill. No." His dark skin was streaked with grease and sweat.

"Sounds bloody good to me."

"You show."

"Yeah. I show. This way."

Jake stumbled down the metal stairs, wondering what had happened to the wounded Sikh officer and the rest of the crew. When he saw the dayroom door, his attention shifted to his wife and he stopped, felt a stab of panic. He had to find a way to protect her from these criminals.

He said, "I'll give you money, but you can't harm my crew."

"Money!" the man in the Ohio State T-shirt shouted.

"Nobody gets hurt. No hurt. That's the deal."

"What you say?"

"I give you money. You let us go."

"No kill, yes."

"No injure, either."

"Money! Give the money!"

"Where's the rest of my crew?"

The moment he unlocked the door, the pirates pushed past him so violently that he lost his footing and fell to the floor. Looking up through the fog in his head, he beheld a scene of savage frenzy. Two pirates were in the process of ripping the flat-screen TV out of the wall. Others were tearing through the drawers of his desk, the books and DVDs on the shelves, throwing papers everywhere.

Another was trying to kick in the bedroom door while holding Jake's laptop under his arm.

"Wait. Please, listen. Stop!"

They ignored him completely.

In the midst of this madness, the tall pirate stood calmly, surveying the room. He wore a webbed belt and red bandana around his neck. Stuck into the belt were a rusted machete, a coil of nylon rope, a hammer, and a screwdriver—the tools of his trade.

As the others ripped the room apart, he walked to the walnut cabinet behind the captain's desk, opened it, and found the safe. Then, stepping back with his hands on his hips, he screamed, *"SHEEL! SHEEL!!!!"* in a voice so shrill it hurt Jake's ears.

The other five pirates stopped.

The tall man pointed to the safe and said, *"Arkid!"*

Now they picked up the captain and dragged him to the cabinet like a rag doll, shouting, "Money! You open! Now! FAST!!!!"

He decided that he was ready to sacrifice his own life if it meant saving Tanya, who was only a few feet away in the adjoining room. In the chaos he had forgotten to ask if anyone was manning the bridge. If not, his ship was charging down a major shipping lane unattended, out of control.

"If there's no one on the bridge, the ship will crash," he said to the tall pirate.

"No."

"Yes, it will. Believe me."

The pirates cut the rope around his hands and danced at his sides like a pack of hungry wolves.

"Someone needs to steer the ship," he repeated. "Do you understand what I'm saying?"

"You open!"

"The ship will crash into the rocks, and we'll all drown!"

"Open. Now!"

Like a bloody broken record. Better to get this over quickly and return to the bridge.

McCullum lowered himself to his knees and turned the dial of the safe, praying he could recall the combination.

Twenty-one right, two spins left to five, then right to sixteen.

He pulled the handle, but the door didn't budge.

Shit!

One of the pirates kicked him in the back so hard he fell forward and his face hit the door of the safe. Blood trickled from his mouth.

"No open, you die!"

"Fuck you, mate."

"We kill now."

"Hold on. I'll give it another go."

Stars spinning in his head, the captain righted himself and, fighting through the pain in his face, spun the dial once more. This time when he pulled the handle, the heavy door swung open and the pirates screamed with delight. One of them started singing in a high voice. Others joined in.

Bloody hands reached into the dark space and pulled out three stacks of bills bound together with rubber bands. Jake estimated that it came to roughly twelve hundred dollars. It had been fifty thousand at the outset of the voyage, but he'd paid the crew in cash.

"There's the money. Now I've got to return to the bridge," he said, standing.

The tall pirate stopped him. "No."

"That's all we've got. The ship will veer off course and crash."

"No go!"

As the pirates huddled together counting, McCullum wondered what had happened to the other members of his crew. The pounding he heard from a lower deck indicated that at least some of them had been locked in one of the lower cabins.

Several pirates grabbed him by the hair and yanked his head toward them. "More! More money!" they shouted.

"That's all there is. Everything."

"More money? Where?"

"That's the whole lot. I promise."

To the captain's alarm, their attention now turned to the bedroom door. Several of them were kicking at it and trying to force it open. Another lifted a fire axe that had been affixed to the wall outside the dayroom.

"There's nothing in there!" the captain shouted. "No money!"

The axe smashed into the door, releasing a shower of sparks.

"I said, there's nothing in there, dammit. It's my bedroom. I... sleep. You might find jewelry and watches in the crew's quarters, one deck down."

"No."

"Yes! Go down. Downstairs."

The pirate pointed at the cabin door. "Open!!!!"

"I can't."

The pirate responded with a fist to the captain's mouth. Another pirate dragged his long knife along his forehead, causing warm blood to drip into his eyes.

"You open or you die!"

He shook his head, which produced a frenzy of kicks and punches from the pirates.

Through the pain he heard Tanya sobbing, "Jake, darling! Jake, oh my God, are you alright?"

He winced at the sound of her voice and quickly shouted back, "Don't unlock the door. Whatever happens. Don't! You hear me?"

Someone stabbed him in the back of the neck. The shock caused him to shout in pain. “Bloody…fuck!”

Now he had trouble raising his head. He heard a lock turning, and managed to twist his body sideways to look.

Pirates were rushing through the bedroom door, howling. Seconds later two of them came out pulling Tanya by her strawberry-blond hair.

“God…no!”

Their eyes met, and he saw the panic in hers as the men pawed her skin and ripped away the shorts, T-shirt, and bra she was wearing. One of them cupped her pale white breast and pointed to the little blue heart tattoo she had gotten during their honeymoon.

“No, please…”

He heard the pirates’ shouts and his wife’s pleas for mercy. In her horrible distress he loved her more than ever, and wanted to tell her that this was his fault. He should have been a better captain and a smarter husband. It was his job to protect her. He should never have invited her on what he knew was a dangerous voyage.

If he ever got another chance, he’d make it right.

Please God. Spare her. She’s a good woman. She doesn’t deserve this. She’s never done anyone any harm.

A sharp noise reverberated in the tight metal space. His ears rang. His head hurt. Everything seemed to stop. Ignoring the excruciating pain from the back of his neck, he turned to see where the sound had come from.

Standing in the door were three men—all Middle Eastern–looking, all dressed in black. They held automatic weapons.

Who the bloody fuck are they?

It was the short one in the middle with the blazing

black eyes who seemed to be in charge. He shouted at the pirates in a foreign language—Arabic maybe, or Farsi or Urdu.

The pirates cowered and backed against the wall. They let go of McCullum's terrified, half-naked wife and lifted him into a chair.

"What's... what's going on here?" he asked in a daze.

The Middle Eastern man with the dark eyes and short black beard walked over to the wounded captain and addressed him in broken English: "We take over now. We navy."

"Which navy?" the captain asked, trying to remember which Arab country was nearby. Egypt maybe.

"You safe now. Very safe."

"Thank you. God bless you. But who are you, exactly?"

Tanya ran to his side and crouched beside him. He held her trembling body.

"If you cooperate, your woman and crew will be free. But we need see cargo first."

"The cargo? What country did you say you were from?" McCullum asked, relieved.

"Your cargo, yes."

"Are you Egyptian?" he asked.

The little man smiled. "Egyptian, yes."

"Then be my guest."

CHAPTER ONE

Act in the valley so that you need not fear those who stand on the hill.

—Danish proverb

CHIEF WARRANT Officer Tom Crocker of SEAL Team Six looked up at the moon rising over the mud-walled compound, which was roughly two hundred feet in front of him. Then he turned to Davis, the blond-haired comms man to his right, and asked, "Any news?"

"The drone is on its way."

"How much longer?"

"Ten minutes max."

"Ten additional minutes?"

"That's what HQ said."

The SEAL Team Six assault leader looked down at his watch. It was 2202 hours local time, which meant that they'd been waiting for nearly an hour behind the dry scrub that grew around an outcropping of rocks on a hill in South Yemen.

It was a minor miracle they hadn't been discovered. They sat smack in the middle of al-Qaeda territory only a dozen miles south of the city of Jaar, which had been seized by the terrorists in March 2011.

The lights of a little Yemeni village sparkled in the distance to his right.

This was supposed to be a simple insert-and-destroy, the target a Sunni mullah named Ahmed, formerly a citizen of the UK and currently a vocal leader of al-Qaeda in South Yemen.

Because of U.S. political considerations the target had to be ID'd first, which involved an elaborate trail of digital connections that began with the SEAL team on the ground and ended in a trailer in the parking lot of CIA headquarters, where an officer from the CIA Directorate of Operations had to peer into a video monitor connected by satellite feed to a camera on the drone and confirm that the image on the screen likely corresponded to the intended target. Then, and only then, could he give the order to Crocker and his team to take out the target.

How was the officer in Langley supposed to establish Mullah Ahmed's identity with any degree of certainty when he was probably bearded and wore a black turban like all the other al-Qaeda terrorists? Why was the Agency being so careful?

These were questions of DC bureaucratic politics Crocker had learned to avoid, as much as they seemed to want to drive him crazy.

Instead of complaining, which he knew would do no good, he focused on applying his extensive training, experience, expertise, and instincts to the mission at hand.

Surveying the area around him through AN/PVS helmet-mounted night-vision goggles, he confirmed that all the pieces of the op were in place. Ritchie (his explosives expert and breacher) and Mancini (equipment and weapons) were in position outside the back of the compound. They were ready to detonate the explosives that would initiate the assault and cover anybody retreating out the back. Akil (maps and logistics), Davis (communications), and Calvin (the Asian American SEAL sniper he had brought with him) hugged the ground to Crocker's immediate right.

They were positioned on a hill that looked directly into the front of the compound, which was rectangular and approximately eighty by eighty feet and contained three structures—a main house and two smaller sheds or garages. The second and third stories of the house were visible above the ten-foot-high wall. Low yellow lights shone in some of the windows, creating an eerie effect.

"This is Tango two-five. You guys fall asleep? What's the good word?" Ritchie's voice came through the earphones built into Crocker's helmet.

"We're still waiting for the order."

"Manny's getting hungry. He's looking at me funny. What's taking so long?"

"We're waiting for the drone. Stand by."

Crocker understood their frustration. He and his men liked to strike fast and extract. Cooling their heels in enemy territory only invited trouble.

He hoped that once they got the go-ahead, they could overwhelm the compound quickly and finish the job. First, a big explosion along the back wall, then Akil would run forward and attach C5 to the front gate. Blow it in. Then they'd rush in, taking preplanned routes and firing positions. Should the terrorists show themselves in any of the compound windows, Cal would pick them off.

Once the mullah was down, Mancini and Ritchie could cover their retreat to the helicopter extraction point, which was approximately half a mile behind them.

His team was also prepared for other contingencies, should they occur.

Approximately eight feet ahead and three feet to his right, Cal was completing the setup of the MK11 Mod 0 sniper weapons system, which consisted of an MK11 precision semiautomatic rifle, twenty-round magazine box, QD scope rings, Leupold Vari-X Mil-Dot riflescope, Harris swivel-base bipod on a Knights mount, and QD sound suppressor. The weapon fired a 7.62 NATO round with a muzzle velocity of 2,951.5 feet per second and an effective range of 1,500 yards.

Cal—who looked Polynesian, but was a mixture of Japanese, German, and Irish—carefully adjusted the Leupold scope to factor in the wind blowing in from the southeast. Four clicks moved the point of impact one inch at approximately one hundred yards.

Crocker had relied on Cal before in similar circumstances and knew him to be a deadly shot. He was also an avid conspiracy theorist, hunter, and Texas hold 'em enthusiast in his spare time. A somewhat odd but friendly fellow who claimed to have won over half a million dollars playing poker. Unmarried, unattached. Almost never spoke about his personal life. His eyes and mouth upturned in a seemingly perpetual smile.

Having adjusted his weapon, Cal turned and flashed a thumbs-up.

"See anything?" Crocker asked.

"Got one of the camel jockeys in my crosshairs through the upstairs window. Can I take the shot?"

"Any minute now."

"I'm ready. More than ready."

"Hold on."

"I'll make this easy. Pop. Pop. One dead mullah. We go home, listen to some music."

"Negative, Cal. We're waiting for the drone."

Crocker glanced at his watch. More than ten minutes had passed since the last time he'd looked. He crouched behind a car-sized rock listening for the hum of an approaching drone, but all he heard was the low whistle of the wind over the mostly barren hills and goats braying in the distance.

He turned to Davis and asked, "What the fuck is taking so long?"

"Apparently the Predator got lost."

"What?"

"The Predator got lost."

"How does a drone get lost?"

"Some doofus entered the wrong coordinates into the computer."

"Fuck that."

"Human error dinks us one more time."

Crocker started to think about all the SEALs he knew who had lost their lives because of bad intelligence or some careless screwup—a helicopter full of them in southern Afghanistan, at least half a dozen outside of Fallujah, Iraq. He stopped.

Akil, the tall, barrel-chested Egyptian American maps and logistics expert, leaned in and said, "I think we ought to set off the explosions now."

Crocker wanted to bark *Don't think, just follow instructions*. But he was a better, more restrained leader than that. He valued and welcomed the input of his men. Six disciplined, combat-tested brains were better than one.

He said, "First, we'll find out if the drone can see through the windows up front using its infrared camera. Apparently it's also equipped with some new camera gizmo that can deploy inside buildings."

"Sweet."

"But don't ask me how it works."

"I won't. You still haven't figured out how to change the oil in your car."

Akil was referring to a recent mishap Crocker had had at home, in which he had failed to fully tighten a gasket after an oil change on his wife's Subaru Outback, which caused her engine to lock up on the highway.

Again he heard Ritchie's voice through his earphones. "Tango two-five here. Looks like we got something moving in from the southwest."

Crocker's calves and knees were starting to ache. "What?"

"Appears to be a vehicle."

"Only one?"

"I'm gonna say one, yes."

"What do you see, exactly?"

"Two headlights approaching, slowly winding down out of the hills to our right, your left. Direction northwest."

"Roger, Tango. Heads down. Weapons ready."

"Roger and out."

He turned to Davis manning the radio and said, "Tell HQ we've got a vehicle approaching."

"Yes, sir."

From somewhere in the hills beyond the compound, he heard an engine. Then the grind of tires on a dirt road. Saw what looked like a light-colored extended-cab pickup swing into the half light.

Crocker readied his MP5, then spoke into his headset: "Tango two-five. Report a white truck. Looks to be at least two individuals inside. Approaching the compound."

"Correct that. I see three, sir. Two in the cab. One in back."

"Three, then."

"Roger."

Crocker watched the gate to the compound open and a bearded man wearing a black turban wave the battered Toyota pickup in. He made out a man with a long beard sitting in back with an AK-47 held between his knees.

He saw Cal to his right, peering through the scope of the MK11 Mod 0 sniper weapons system, ready to take a shot. Felt a rush of excitement.

God, he wanted to give the order now. Now was the time to attack—while the gate was open. But discipline held him back.

He heard Davis's urgent voice to his right. "Boss. Boss?"

"What? You spot the Predator?"

"No, headquarters says abort."

"Abort, now?" He thought it had to be a joke.

"Abort. That's correct."

"What do they mean, abort? Tell 'em we've got the terrorists in our sights."

"I did already. They want us to pull back to the extraction site."

"Now?"

"Yes."

Feeling like the wind had been kicked out of him, he asked, "Why?"

"No reason given. It's a simple abort."

Twenty-two minutes later, Crocker and his team had strapped themselves onto the benches of a Black Hawk helicopter and were cradling their weapons as it lifted off the desert ground.

Ritchie, his dark eyes blazing, sat to Crocker's right.

"Boss?"

"Yeah." Shouting over the helo's engines.

"What just happened?"

"Beats the shit out of me."

"Were we at the wrong compound?"

"Not as far as I know."

"SOS, huh, boss?" Meaning same old shit.

"Yeah, SOS."

"Crazy-ass way to fight a war."

This wasn't the first time this had happened. They'd spent the last five weeks on the Arabian Peninsula training, collecting intel, practicing for different ops, then being told to abort at the last minute. Adding to their annoyance was the fact that they missed their families and needed a break from the 24/7 pressure of being deployed.

Davis's wife had a young baby and was expecting another. Ritchie's new girlfriend was threatening to start dating other men if he didn't return home soon. Crocker's wife wanted some relief in dealing with his daughter, her stepdaughter, who had been living with them for a year. Mancini's wife was looking after his younger, wheelchair-bound brother, who was suffering through the final stages of pancreatic cancer and about to die. Akil's Egyptian-born father's jewelry repair business was losing money.

Every one of them had myriad problems and concerns outside their jobs.

As Crocker unbuckled his helmet the copilot, in a camouflage flight suit and helmet, walked over and tapped him on the shoulder.

"Sir?"

"Yeah." Holding on to the bench as the copter banked sharply.

"You Chief Warrant Officer Tom Crocker?"

"That's correct."

"Orders to fly you and your men to USS *Carl Vinson* in the Gulf of Aden."

"What for?"

"We're operating on a need-to-know basis here, sir. Those are my orders."

"Received. Thanks."

Fifteen minutes later they had safely landed on the deck of the *Carl Vinson*. A landing signal officer handed Crocker a bottle of water with the ship's seal stenciled on it and underneath it the Latin motto *Vis Per Mare*—"Strength from the Sea." She was strong, all right. A metal beast measuring 1,092 feet long with a capacity to hold up to ninety fixed-wing aircraft and helicopters, she carried a crew of over six thousand, including airmen. She was one of a fleet of ten Nimitz-class supercarriers—the largest, most lethal warships on the planet.

He'd been up twenty-four hours and would have preferred something with a little kick, like black coffee, Red Bull, or a can of Diet Mountain Dew. But water was better than nothing, especially with the taste of the desert still in his mouth.

The last time Crocker had stood on the deck of the *Carl Vinson* was the morning of May 2, 2011, when he and his team watched the corpse of Osama bin Laden being disposed of in the ocean. As much as they'd wanted to kick and piss on that piece-of-shit terrorist, they weren't permitted to. But they had cheered as his white-shrouded body was slipped overboard and devoured by sharks.

It seemed like a lifetime ago now. Since the death of the notorious al-Qaeda leader, Crocker and his team had been running ops almost nonstop. Over fifty in the last year, to places like Pakistan, Afghanistan, Yemen, Sudan, and Somalia.

Still, Crocker managed to squeeze in a few races. Like the 150-mile, six-stage marathon across the Sahara in Morocco (called the Marathon des Sables) that he and his men were scheduled to compete in next week. They had been trying to build up to it with at least sixty miles a week, plus a thirty-mile run on their day off. Which explained why both his Achilles were tight and his knee and lower back were barking. Crocker was used to dealing with pain. He thought of it as weakness leaving his body.

The lean, white-shirted LSO led him briskly along the flight deck past one of the steam catapults (known as a Fat Cat) that was capable of accelerating a thirty-seven-ton jet from zero to 180 miles per hour in less than three seconds. The marvels of technology. As much as Crocker admired engineers and scientists, they still hadn't invented anything that could replace the versatility and ingenuity of men on the ground. He and his men were arguably the most highly trained, battle-tested, and lethal fighting force in the world, prepared to deal with anything on sea, air, or land. Raids behind enemy lines, commandeering ships or airliners, rescuing hostages, assassinations, sensitive intel-gathering ops—all in a day's work.

A wise man named Friedrich Nietzsche once said, "Many are stubborn in pursuit of the path they have chosen; few in pursuit of the goal." Crocker had committed those words to memory. They were his mantra. Don't worry about the fuckups and bumps in the road, focus on your goal.

The goal was to protect his countrymen from people who wanted to destroy their way of life, take away their freedoms, shred the Constitution and the Bill of Rights.

That wasn't going to happen as long as Tom Crocker was alive. No way. He hadn't earned his reputation as Chief Warrant Officer Manslaughter for nothing. People oohed and aahed over high-tech drones, listening systems, heat imaging. But when real nasty, difficult shit needed getting done, it was sheepdogs like him and his men who had to step in to protect the sheep from the wolves.

Crocker followed the LSO down steep metal steps and through a tight corridor that led to the captain's quarters. Photos of the ship's namesake, Congressman Carl Vinson—the only man to serve more than fifty years in the U.S. House of Representatives—lined the walls. Another bald-headed, sharp-eyed man in a suit. All Crocker wanted when he grew old was a shack in the woods, his wife—hopefully—and a means of securing food and water.

The LSO stopped and opened the door to a state-of-the-art conference room. The captain—an energetic man with a lantern jaw and short-cropped gray hair—stood and squeezed Crocker's hand.

"Welcome aboard, Warrant. Glad you could make it."

"It's good to be back, sir."

"Take a seat and we'll drop the disco ball."

Crocker, still dressed in his desert cammies, barely got out a question—"Sir, what's going on?"—before the lights dimmed and a panel of four large color LED monitors descended from the ceiling and lit up. On one of them he recognized the gaunt face of his CO back at SEAL headquarters in Virginia, which caused him to sit up at attention. Instinctively, he started to wonder what he had done wrong.

"Crocker, is that you?" His CO, Captain Alan Sutter, was squinting through wire-rimmed glasses.

"Affirmative, sir." Crocker focused on the bump where the captain's nose had been smashed during Operation Urgent Fury in Grenada, 1983, when his chute had failed to open and he crashed into a tree. Lost a mouthful of teeth, too.

"Can you hear me?"

"See and hear you clear as day, sir." His CO was damn lucky to be alive. So was he.

"Good."

"How are things back at headquarters?"

His CO didn't answer, cutting the small talk. "A critical situation has come up. Somewhat of a strategic emergency. Demands a swift response."

"My men and I are ready, sir, to do whatever's needed."

"We need someone we can trust with a very difficult scenario who's deployed in the area," Sutter continued.

Crocker was going to say "Difficult is my call sign," but bravado didn't go over well in SEAL teams. Operators were expected to be humble, do their jobs, and limit the chest pounding.

"I appreciate that, sir," Crocker said instead, fighting through his exhaustion. He wasn't twenty years old anymore but in his midforties. And even though he was in incredible shape, his body needed time to recover.

He could probably forget about resting tonight.

From the video monitor, his CO continued: "Involves a pirated cargo ship off the Somali coast."

The word "pirated" intrigued Crocker. He'd heard stories of local gangs stopping cargo ships and even supertankers off the coast of East Africa and the Malacca Straits in Indonesia.

An aide slipped a pad and pencil in front of him, and Crocker took notes as his CO and two officers from the Agency's Counterterrorism Center related the ship's position and various details, including info gleaned from the vessel's emergency signal and satellite surveillance.

Crocker was wondering why a cargo ship of Australian registry was getting so much attention when his CO mentioned that it was transporting "sensitive nuclear material" from Melbourne to Marseille.

Among Crocker's various duties, he happened to be the WMD officer at SEAL Team Six. "You referring to yellowcake, sir, or something else?" he asked. Yellowcake was uranium ore concentrate. Once it was enriched in a process that involved turning it into a gas called uranium hexafluoride, it could be used to fuel nuclear bombs.

"The exact nature of the material is classified. It's not dangerous in its current state. But it's important. Very goddamn important."

"I understand, sir."

"The White House wants this handled immediately."

"Yes, sir."

"Get your men geared up and ready to deploy."

"You can count on us, sir."

"There's no time to fly in another team or the cigarette boats. You think you and your men can handle this situation alone?"

"Absolutely. We'll take care of it, sir, as long as someone can get us there."

Typically pirates operating off the coast of Somalia held ships and their crews hostage while they negotiated five- and six-figure ransoms. So Crocker asked, "Have there been any communications from the pirates, sir? Have they made any demands?"

"None so far."

Strange, he thought.

"Approximate number of pirates?"

"Expect six to ten. Secure the sensitive material because the White House would like to use it as evidence."

Evidence of what?

"Deploy as quickly as you can," his CO said.

"Yes, sir."

As soon as the room's lights illuminated, the supercarrier's operations officer appeared at Crocker's side. A big man with a shaved head, dressed in a khaki uniform, he said, "Give me a list of what you need and I'll turn this carrier upside down to find it."

Crocker thought quickly and answered, "A helicopter that can get us there fast, two Zodiacs with twin outboards, wet suits and skin suits, fins, Dräger LAR V rebreathers, twelve frag grenades, a telescopic pole and caving ladder if you have one, flares, TUFF-TIES, comms, SMGs, and pistols."

The op officer scribbled everything down. "That all?"

"A cutlass and eye patch, if you can find them."

"What?"

"It's a joke."

"I should find most of this in one of the Conex boxes from the last SEAL platoon on board."

"Works for me."

"Be on the flight deck in fifteen minutes with your men."

"Yes, sir."

Crocker was thinking about his wife, Holly, as a tall navy officer led him through a maze of corridors, past a gym, commissary, and barbershop. She worked for State Department Security and was about to deploy overseas any day, too. He wanted to call her, but there was no time.

They entered the ship's mess, where he found his men feasting on Szechuan chicken and chow mein noodles. Moving them over to a corner table out of earshot, he briefed them as more aides arrived with nautical charts and satellite photos.

According to the latest intel, an unmarked assault boat appeared to be towing the MSC *Contessa* to the Somalia coast, which was highly unusual. What were primitive pirates doing with a launch that was powerful enough to tow a forty-thousand-ton ship?

Crocker and his men would soon find out.

Still chewing a mouthful of chicken, he helped his men carry their gear and weapons up past the ship's hangars to the flight deck. There they were greeted by a fresh ocean breeze, a welcome relief from the stale air and claustrophobic atmosphere below.

Crocker didn't like the confined feeling of ships, particularly the submarines he and his men had deployed from a dozen or so times over the years, which seemed like sardine cans filled with pasty-faced men. He especially disliked Swimmer Delivery Vehicles (SDVs), which were basically mini-subs.

He covered his ears as an F-18 Super Hornet approached the *Vinson*'s flight deck, its engines screaming, its tailhook deployed. The F-18 hit the deck, sending a tremendous shower of sparks into the night sky. The fighter jet was slightly off track and missed the ship's arrest wire, so it quickly zoomed up to full throttle and took off again with a roar.

Crocker noted that the sky was cloudy and the sea choppy, which caused the carrier to rock side to side.

"That can't be easy," Akil remarked.

"Flying in at a hundred and seventy-five miles an hour and trying to hit a wire. You try it sometime."

"No thanks."

The LSO who was escorting them shouted into Crocker's ear, "Be careful where you walk. A year ago one of our maintainers got his cranial matter sucked right out of his head when he stood too close to the intake of an A-6E."

"Good to know."

Right under the ship's superstructure, known as the island, they met the pilots and copilots of the two MH-60 Knighthawk helicopters that had been tasked with flying them in. Each helo was equipped with M240 machine guns and Hellfire missiles. The four stood in a huddle studying weather charts as Crocker's men loaded their gear. One of the pilots—a lanky-haired man with gray eyes and a Fu Manchu mustache—turned to Crocker and said, "Expect the flight to be a little rough. We got some weather blowing in from the south."

"What have you got in terms of in-flight entertainment?"

"If you watch carefully you might be able to see a pelican taking a crap."

"Just get us close. We'll be fine."

"You planning to fast-rope onto the deck?"

"No, I'd rather take the bastards by surprise," Crocker answered.

"How far away you want us to drop you?"

"You'll need to approach lights-out. Drop us about a mile behind the stern so we can't be seen."

The lead pilot nodded. "We can do that."

"Then what are we waiting for?"

CHAPTER TWO

Only the dead have seen the end of war.

—George Santayana

FIFTY MINUTES of bouncing around in the sky later, the six SEALs were in their black skin suits, ready to jump. Crocker leaned out the side door of the Knighthawk, trying to locate the MSC *Contessa* ahead. The light mist that fell dampened his face and hair. That and the cloud cover made visibility problematic, which meant that they had to rely on the helo's radar.

The pilot kept his eyes focused on two green blips on the screen that appeared practically on top of each other east of the coastal town of Eyl—part of Puntland, the northeast corner of Somalia, which had declared itself an autonomous state in 1998.

When the helicopter got within two miles of the vessels, the pilot spoke into his headset. "Looks like they've both anchored off the coast."

"They've stopped moving?"

"Correct."

"Two vessels?" Crocker asked.

"Yeah, the cargo ship and the launch."

"At what location?"

"Approximately fifteen miles off the coast. Direction... east."

"Interesting."

Crocker could understand the pirates commandeering the ship and anchoring it in friendly waters while they negotiated ransom. That was SOP in such cases. But what was the launch doing there?

The pilot's voice interrupted his train of thought. "Signal when you're ready for extraction."

"Will do. And thanks for the lift."

"Godspeed."

The pilot lowered the helo within forty feet of the ocean and flipped a switch, which changed the light inside the starboard door from red to green. Crocker gave his men the signal to go. They pushed out the two Zodiacs and then the men fast-roped down—Ritchie first, followed by Akil, Davis, Mancini, Cal, and Crocker.

Lastly the copilot lowered their equipment—engines, paddles, Drägers and related dive equipment, fuel bladders, watertight weapons bags, telescopic pole with caving ladder attached.

Each three-man squad moved expertly, Davis, Akil, and Crocker in Zodiac 1 and Mancini, Ritchie, and Cal in 2. Each man knew what he was supposed to do: connect the engines and get them started, establish direction, comm. Check gear and weapons.

Within three minutes they had the motors running and were on their way, water slapping the bows, the boats twisting violently from side to side.

Crocker felt the adrenaline slam into his veins—that welcome burst of energy that produced a sense of invincibility. He lived for moments like this.

The warm air and faint scent of rot and tropical flowers reminded him of the times he'd operated in Somalia before. All hair-raising and life-threatening. Each time he left injured or sick. It was a country that had come apart at the seams in the early '80s and never managed to pull itself back together. An anarchic mess of young gangs and drug lords armed with AKs and rocket-propelled grenades. Somalia seemed many centuries away from the social norms and political stability enjoyed in the U.S. and even other African countries. Much of which, he thought, people back home took for granted as they sat in their easy chairs watching TV.

He'd save that thought for another time.

Now he was trying to locate a dark shape ahead, which was difficult through the clouds, the spray from the bow, and especially the pitching of the Zodiac.

"You see anything?" he shouted at Davis.

"Fuck, no!"

Be a real shame if we can't even find it.

"There it is!" Akil exclaimed from behind them. "Eleven o'clock."

Crocker wiped the moisture off the lens of his night-vision goggles and looked again. This time he located a triangular-shaped blotch with a smaller, indistinct form beside it.

"Bingo! Good eyes."

Akil quickly adjusted the direction of the Zodiac until Davis held up a hand and shouted, "Now we're on course!"

"Nice work, huh?"

"That's what you get paid the big money for."

"Sit back and enjoy the ride!"

The view through Crocker's NVGs was anything but steady. The rubber duckie climbed up the crest of an oncoming wave, then dropped and slammed hard at the bottom, tossing the contents of his stomach up and down. The swells seemed to be growing bigger, which indicated that they were approaching the coast.

He turned back and spoke to Akil—more like shouted into his ear. "When I give the signal, cut the engines." They needed to go in undetected.

Akil: "You need me to hold your hand, too?"

"We'll dive from about a thousand meters."

"Nice night for a swim."

"Get an exact bearing."

"I did that already, boss. What kind of fucking navigator do you think I am?"

"A wiseass one I've got to constantly check on."

"Ha. Ha!"

He'd done hundreds of VBSSs (Visit, Board, Search and Seizure operations) in his career, in the Middle East and Central and South America. He'd also been on dozens of hostage-rescue ops—Christian missionaries in Afghanistan, kidnapped oil company execs in Colombia.

Crocker waited until the ship grew bigger in his NVGs, then held up his fist. "Kill it here. Stop!"

Akil cut the engine on Zodiac 1. Ritchie, piloting Zodiac 2 behind them, did the same. As the current tossed them up and down, side to side, the SEALs in both boats quickly donned masks and Drägers, grabbed gear and waterproof weapons bags, then slid into the Indian Ocean.

They swam in order, Akil, Crocker, Mancini, Davis, Cal, Ritchie, all holding on to the five-foot telescopic pole with its attached caving ladder. They moved at the same speed, same depth—approximately twenty feet under the surface—the way they'd been trained when they were part of Green Team, the four-month training course required to get onto an assault team and ST-6.

The water was cool and dark. Visibility was terrible, barely enough to see the luminescent dials on their depth gauges, compasses, and Tudor dive watches. The German Drägers strapped to their chests fed them pure oxygen so no bubbles would escape to the surface to give away their position.

Akil, the primary navigator, focused on his dive compass. Crocker kept time and counted kicks. He knew exactly how many kicks it took to swim one hundred yards. Because they were swimming against the current, they had to kick harder than normal. Thirty minutes, forty, fifty, until Crocker figured they were getting close.

Although visibility was limited, the last thing he wanted to do was surface and be seen. He had planned the dive for four legs, but it was awkward turning and stopping with three men on each side of the pole, maintaining a depth of twenty feet.

They proceeded at a forty-five-degree bearing for six minutes, then Crocker squeezed Akil's arm, which was the signal to reset their compasses and watches before starting the next leg at seventy-two degrees for twenty-two minutes.

Less than a minute into their fourth leg, Akil stopped abruptly and pointed to the dark shape literally two feet in front of him. He signaled to Crocker, then swam away from the pole to establish their position. Returning, he signaled that they were on the ship's starboard side, approximately fifteen feet from the stern, which put them beside the ship's superstructure. Realizing that it would be easier to climb aboard near the cargo bays, Crocker ordered his men to swim another twenty feet along the hull.

They surfaced one at a time, the sky a welcome sight.

Light rain continued to fall as Akil and Crocker raised the telescopic pole with its caving ladder. The others removed their MP5 submachine guns from the waterproof bags—safeties off, straight fingers as always.

After a couple of attempts they managed to hook the pole on a deck railing. Then Crocker signaled to Akil to pull down sharply, which released the caving ladder from the rubber tubing that held it to the pole. The ladder rolled down the side of the hull approximately fifteen feet to the ocean.

Crocker, as lead climber, was the first man up, his MP5-N equipped with a three-inch silencer slung over his shoulder. He placed his weight on each rung carefully because he didn't know how securely the ladder was hooked. Attached to his web belt was a holster with an MK23 Mod 0 .45-caliber pistol, extra ammo, and a climber carabiner with three tubular runners. He made it look effortless. After climbing over the rail he hitched a two-foot tubular nylon runner to it and carabinered that to one of the ladder's rungs. Now it was secure for the rest of his team.

Then he crouched behind a hatch cover and conducted a quick survey of the ship. All the deck lights were off, except for several around one of the cargo bays near the bow. That bay was open, and the foremost cargo crane seemed to be in use.

Interesting, he thought.

Not one pirate in sight, so he signaled the rest of his team to climb up.

They had already secured their Drägers, masks, fins, and weight belts to the rungs of the ladder below the surface. Now they climbed up quickly and took up preassigned firing positions that gave them a 360-degree security perimeter. Dressed in black suits with camo face paint, they looked like ninjas.

Crocker raised his hand and tapped his head twice, which was the signal to deploy they'd worked out during their abbreviated PLO, or Patrol Leader's Order—Ritchie, Mancini, and Cal toward the stern and the ship's superstructure; Crocker and the other two in the direction of the bow, always staying in visual contact with one another.

Seeing someone climb out of the forward cargo bay, Crocker extended his right arm and lowered it. Akil and Davis behind him quickly knelt down out of sight. He pointed to Akil, then placed his hand on his KA-BAR knife.

Akil nodded, then ran in a crouch along the centerline bulkhead to the forecastle bulkhead. Crocker, meanwhile, took two steps to his right. Past the forward mast, he saw a man in black standing with his back to him on the forecastle deck. He watched him push a button that lowered the crane into the cargo bay. A few seconds later the man punched another button and the crane rose, bearing a fifty-gallon orange barrel with a triangular yellow deadly-materials symbol on its side.

The question that flashed through Crocker's mind was *Why were pirates unloading sensitive nuclear material from a ship?*

That's when he realized that the man operating the crane looked too well dressed to be a pirate. And when he turned sideways, Crocker saw that he was somewhat light skinned and had a close-cropped beard.

The SEAL team leader watched Akil spring from the foredeck and grab the man from behind. His left hand covered the man's mouth while his right dragged the blade of the KA-BAR across his neck.

Textbook, Crocker thought, until Akil let go and the slumping man slipped off the wet bulkhead and pitched forward into the open cargo bay.

Mistake!

Shouts and exclamations echoed out of the bay, then someone started firing up at Akil, who hid behind the foremast. Sparks were flying everywhere from bullets ricocheting off metal as weapons discharged.

"We've been compromised. Let's go!" Crocker shouted.

He and Davis followed the path Akil had taken forward. Halfway there, he heard an engine start up on the port side of the *Contessa.* Detouring left, away from the bulkhead to the port rail, he caught a glimpse of the launch.

It wasn't a funky pirate vessel, but rather a clean, military-type fast attack boat painted gray. No markings, no name. Seventy to eighty feet long, armed with deck-mounted .50-caliber guns fore and aft.

"Watch out!" Davis shouted.

Seeing a bearded man on the deck aiming an AK-47 at

him, Crocker jumped back and ducked behind a ventilator. He was joined by Davis, who reported seeing orange barrels stacked along the bow of the launch.

"How many?" Crocker asked.

"Half a dozen."

"Pirates, my ass."

An explosion went off near the top of the *Contessa*'s superstructure, where Ritchie, Cal, and Mancini had deployed. It pushed Crocker and Davis into a round metal ventilator and sent shards of glass and hot metal flying through the air, smacking the deck and mast. Crocker felt something embed itself into his left forearm, more painful than disabling.

I'll deal with it later, he thought.

Men shouted at one another from the boat below while others continued to fire from near the bow of the *Contessa* toward where he and Davis hid on the deck. The shouting sounded more like Persian than Arabic.

Iranians? he asked himself.

It made sense. The Iranians needed parts and nuclear fuel for their atomic weapons development program. And they'd been hit by a series of UN embargoes that made it almost impossible for them to import uranium legally.

So they'd hired pirates to hijack a vessel transporting the things they needed.

Kind of clever.

"We've gotta stop that launch!" Crocker shouted as bullets smashed into the metal in front of them.

"What about Akil?"

A teammate in a firefight was always a priority. "We're going to save his ass first."

Not only was Akil pinned down near the *Contessa*'s

foremast, but pirates firing automatic weapons had climbed out of the cargo bay and were attacking him from two sides.

On Crocker's hand signal, he and Davis moved to the bulkhead at the center of the deck. From a position twenty feet forward, they fired their MP5s and caught two pirates by surprise—one in the chest, another raked from his knees to his sternum.

Akil took out a third with his 9-millimeter handgun. All those years of daily live-fire practice had paid off.

The foremost deck became quiet.

"Dammit to hell," Akil groaned, holding up his right hand. "I got stung!"

"Where?"

"Back of my hand."

Although it was a bitch to see in the minimal light, Crocker did the best he could, feeling through warm blood along the palm to the knuckles and fingers, ascertaining the extent of the damage.

Akil gritted his teeth. "What the fuck..."

Crocker said, "Appears to be a gash. Not serious. You're one lucky motherfucker."

"I don't feel lucky."

He turned to Davis. "Give him something to cry into while I wrap this baby up."

Opening the emergency medical kit he wore on his back, Crocker first wiped away the blood, then sprayed the wound with disinfectant. Next he wrapped the whole hand in a bandage that he secured with tape.

All the time he was aware that the launch was getting away.

With the wounded man providing cover with his automatic pistol held in his left hand, Crocker and Davis took the grenades Akil was carrying and got into position to toss them at the target, which was approximately forty feet off the *Contessa*'s port side and slightly in front.

"Aim for the stern," Crocker said. "We don't want to damage the barrels up front. Might be yellowcake."

"Okay, boss."

On the count of three they stood together and threw. Once, twice, three times in succession.

Seeing the Americans, the guy manning the .50-cal on the launch's deck opened up. *Whack-a, whack-a, whack-a*… Fortunately his aim sucked, and Crocker and Davis had time to crouch behind the foremast. Hot, angry rounds glanced off the metal around them. Then a series of six explosions ripped into the air and lit up the night sky.

The .50-cal paused for a few seconds, then started firing again.

A seventh blast stopped it altogether.

"What was that?" Davis asked.

Crocker hazarded a look. It appeared that one of the grenades had hit a barrel of extra fuel, because flames were rising from the attack boat's stern. Seeing dark figures scurrying around the deck, he leveled his MP5 and started firing. Then another blast lit up the deck, throwing a burning man into the ocean.

The concussion was strong enough to kick Crocker and Davis back, too. By the time Crocker righted himself enough to steal another look, the launch's stern was almost completely engulfed in flames. If they reached the dozen barrels of what could be yellowcake along the bow, it could set off an explosion that would be the equivalent of a dirty bomb, releasing dangerous radiation that, depending on the wind's direction, could kill many thousands of people.

Crocker turned to Davis and shouted, "Cover me. I'm going down."

"Where?"

"Into the water. After the launch."

"But—"

Before Davis could get the rest of his words out, Crocker handed him his weapon, flung off his pack, and was diving off the *Contessa*'s port rail.

He sliced into the water, came up to take a quick breath and establish direction, then started swimming underwater using the combat swimmer stroke he'd been taught in Basic Underwater Demolition/SEAL (BUD/S) and had practiced with his team once a week when not deployed. He'd progressed thirty-five feet when his lungs felt like they were going to explode. Crocker knew that the carbon dioxide receptors in his brain were telling him it was time to exhale because he had too much CO_2 in his system. So he breathed out a little, releasing some of the air in his lungs.

This enabled him to swim the last ten feet or so without too much discomfort. Coming up near the launch's stern, he breathed in the smoke-filled air but held back a cough. Immediately he was confronted with another challenge—the fire made it too hot to board at the stern. So he dove under the boat's hull and, following the stem, where the two planes of the hull had been welded together, surfaced near the bow.

The boat was moving slowly, at 1.5 knots, so boarding was relatively easy. He simply grabbed the anchor port and pulled himself up to the windlass and deck, where he crouched with the rain pelting his back and head.

On closer inspection the launch reminded him of an old navy PT boat or a British motor torpedo boat—light and simple, with a displacement-type hull and a small superstructure pitched toward the stern.

No one had spotted him so far. In fact he didn't see anyone, except for a badly burned man he stepped over as he headed for the wheelhouse. Much of it had been destroyed—the windshield completely shattered and many of the gauges in the console cracked.

Crocker pulled back the throttle to idle, then looked for the switch to cut the engine.

The rain picked up, propelled by strong gusts of wind. He wasn't sure if these conditions would extinguish the flames or fan them. It all depended on whether the fire was oil based, which was something he had no time to determine.

His immediate concern was the barrels along the bow. He had descended three steps into the cabin in search of a fire extinguisher when he ran into two men starting up, then saw a third, shorter man behind them. All three had soot-covered faces. One was holding his right arm, which appeared to be injured near the shoulder. A piece of bone protruded.

The man behind them had fierce eyes, deep set like a falcon's.

When the man to Crocker's right reached for something in his belt, Crocker reared his right leg back and kicked him hard in the face. Then, brandishing his KA-BAR knife, he threw himself at the group. Teeth sank into his arm.

Fucking savage!

The pain didn't stop him from grappling with arms and legs on the wet floor and slashing his knife blindly in the dark; it only added to his determination. Less than a minute later two men lay bleeding to death, grunting. Crocker couldn't find the third one. Possibly he'd escaped up the stairs.

The cabin was a smoke-filled mess, disgusting-smelling. The fire from above had started to burn through the deck in the forecastle bunks. It was only a matter of minutes before the flames would reach the fuel tank and the whole damn boat would explode. He did the only thing he could think of, which was to reset the vessel's engine and turn the wheel so it was headed away from the *Contessa*.

Then he ran to the bow and tried to push the orange barrels overboard. This required using his bloody knife to cut through the ropes that secured them, then angling one at a time against the low railing, pushing the top enough to wedge an empty ammo box he found on the deck under it, then lifting the barrel from the bottom until it flipped over the railing into the ocean.

It was hard work, but the hundreds of thousands of squats and dead lifts he'd done in the gym helped.

With the muscles in his arms and upper body burning, Crocker dove into the water and swam back to the *Contessa.* He was reminded of the summer nights he'd spent with his brother, sneaking into the neighborhood pool, fireflies creating magic around them. The sea was dark and turbulent, pulling him in one direction, then another. Instead of calling to Davis to throw him a line, he swam to the starboard side and came up the caving ladder, which was still in place.

Wiping ocean scum from his face, he noticed that a

small fire was burning on the ship's bridge, lending the radar mast and funnel an eerie red-orange glow.

Davis called from behind him, "Boss, you okay?"

"Good. And you?"

"Fine."

"Where's the rest of the team?"

"They're all inside."

"Where?" he asked, trying to catch his breath.

"Mancini's trying to extinguish the fire and get the bridge in order."

He recovered his MP5 and reloaded as they talked. "Has anyone seen the captain?"

"Don't know. It's real ugly in there."

"How come?"

"The pirates hacked up some of the crew. At least one man is still alive but badly injured."

"Get on the horn. Tell the folks on the *Vinson* to send a medical team and a helicopter to take us out of here. We're also going to need a salvage team and some divers. There are six barrels of some kind of sensitive nuclear material sitting on the bottom of the ocean at eleven o'clock off the *Contessa*'s bow."

"A medical team, a rescue helicopter, and a salvage crew. You got it."

"Then meet me inside."

He hurried to the superstructure and climbed the steps two at a time, his MP5 at his side. On the first deck he ran into Ritchie standing over three pirates bound with TUFF-TIES at their wrists and ankles.

"Where are the rest?" he asked.

"At least two of them are holding the captain and his wife hostage."

"Where?"

"In the captain's dayroom, two decks up."

"Show me."

Ritchie led the way up the narrow steps. On the next deck they ran into Mancini, whose face was black with soot.

Crocker asked, "What have we got?"

"Five crew dead, another two injured, two survivors."

"How bad are the injured?"

"One's barely alive; had his head bashed in. The other's got a bullet wound. They're both in the hallway one deck up."

"Cal?"

"He's with Akil."

"Where?"

"Outside the captain's quarters. That's where some pirates are holding the captain and his wife."

"Show me!"

One more flight up, Crocker stopped to examine one of the ship's officers, who had been shot. A bullet had entered his lower back and appeared to have fractured the right side of his pelvis. His breathing was normal and his pulse steady, so Crocker smeared QuikClot around the entry and exit points, then wrapped them tightly with a bandage and gave the officer 800 milligrams of Extra Strength Tylenol.

"Swallow these. You'll be fine. Medevac is on its way."

On the next deck, Ritchie led him down a narrow hallway where they found Akil standing outside a door marked DANGEROUS SPACE, TEST AIR BEFORE ENTRY.

"What's that mean?"

"Unclear."

"What's the situation?"

"Two armed pirates, possibly three, claim to be holding hostages."

"Have you spoken to the hostages?"

"No."

"So you don't know if they're alive?"

"That's correct."

"Have you tried talking to the pirates?" Crocker asked Akil, who spoke both Arabic and Urdu, which is close to Persian.

"They only speak some local Somali dialect. Some of the words are similar. I understood enough to know they're threatening to kill the captain and his wife and blow up the ship."

"Where's Cal?"

"He's with one of the crew members on the deck above, looking for access through the ceiling."

"Where?"

Akil pointed over his head. "The chart room, I believe, behind the wheelhouse, upstairs."

"Okay." Crocker turned to Ritchie.

"Boss, I can breach through this sucker if you want me to."

"Can you do that without killing everyone inside?"

"Since I don't know the position of the hostages, there's no guarantee."

"Alright, then, look... Check your watches. Give me five minutes. If you don't hear me shoot off a couple of rounds, that means I'm going in through the ceiling. You guys create as much of a diversion as you can, starting now. Shout, pound on the door like you're trying to break through."

"Copy, boss."

The bridge, one flight up, was hot and thick with smoke. He found Mancini, Cal, and a Filipino crew member in a little room behind the wheelhouse. Mancini was using a screwdriver to remove a metal panel in the wall.

"What you got?"

"Access, hopefully."

When the panel was pulled aside, Crocker saw an opening to an aluminum vent that looked too small to squeeze through. Mancini quickly enlarged it, removing a metal flange, then carefully cutting around the vent with his knife to expose its full width, roughly four feet in diameter.

Crocker looked down at his Suunto watch. Four minutes exactly.

Mancini stuck his head inside and illuminated the space with a small flashlight.

The crewman whispered, "See where the vent makes a sharp turn? Right after that, the first opening should be directly above the dayroom."

"That's where they are?"

"The captain and pirates. Correct."

Crocker tapped Cal on the shoulder and whispered, "Follow me."

Navigating through the vent with their MP5s would be too awkward, so they took their handguns instead. Each man carried a smoke grenade and an extra magazine of ammo.

Crocker had to squeeze his shoulders together to get through. The bend at the bottom was tight, but after he twisted past, it was only five feet to a rectangular vent cover.

He stopped and pointed. Cal nodded.

The vent, which was approximately three and a half feet by one and a half, presented another challenge—namely, the noise they would create by trying to remove it.

He waited and listened, with Cal behind him. No discernible sound from the room below, just muffled pounding in the distance and the low hum of the ship's engine.

Crocker indicated that he was going to cross to the other side of the vent and wanted Cal to position himself where he was now. Cal nodded. Assuming a catcher's crouch, he turned sideways and reached his leg across. Then, lying on his stomach, he peered through the opening.

All he saw was a pair of bare feet that looked to belong to a woman, the legs of a chair, and a blood-covered shirt on the floor.

He took a series of deep breaths, knowing he had one chance to dislodge the metal vent opening before attracting the pirates' attention and getting them all killed. Checking his watch and seeing that he was within ten seconds of his five-minute limit, he pulled himself up into a crouch, readied his pistol, signaled to Cal, then sprang sideways onto the aluminum vent. His weight immediately dislodged one side, causing his right leg and arm to slide through the ceiling. But his entire left side and torso were stuck. So he twisted his shoulder and reached with his right hand, grabbing the edge of the hanging vent cover with his fingers and pulling it free.

When it came away, he had nothing to hold on to and fell, hitting the floor awkwardly so that his right leg slipped out from under him. The impact stunned him.

He heard shouting and pulled himself up onto his right elbow. Saw the woman tied to the chair, another man bound and gagged, lying on a bed.

He wasn't in the dayroom. It was the captain's cabin.

Two pirates rushed through the door and charged. One of them held a machete.

Crocker didn't have his weapon. It had dislodged from his hand and was pinned under his left shoulder. He turned to grab it, and as he did he looked directly up into the pirate's face and saw the machete.

There was nothing he could do but shield himself with his right arm and hope he didn't lose it. He heard four pops in succession and watched the top of the pirate's head explode.

Cal!

The pirate crumpled midscream and fell on top of Crocker, who remained focused on the blade of the machete. He managed to twist away to avoid it. Blood and brain matter sprayed everywhere.

The other pirate screamed and reached for his pistol. Crocker saw his sneakered foot out of the corner of his right eye. Pushing the other man off him, he grabbed the foot and yanked it with all his might.

As the second pirate tumbled, Cal quickly finished him off with a head shot from his 9-millimeter.

No time to catch their breath. The two SEALs freed the prisoners and carried them down to the main deck. The captain slipped in and out of consciousness. His wife kept sobbing and talking to herself, something about church steps and the smell of orchids.

Twenty minutes later they were helping them and the injured crew members onto a medevac helicopter. And then they were all off into the inky night, the burning vessel getting smaller behind them.

Crocker turned to Akil and asked, “How’s your hand?”

“The bleeding has stopped. I’ll be fine.”

“Glad to hear it.”

He looked at the bite mark on his wrist and sighed.

It hadn’t been pretty, but they had prevailed.

CHAPTER THREE

Without pain, without sacrifice, we would have nothing.

—Fight Club

CROCKER DREAMT he was surfing off the west coast of Maui with his teenage daughter. She wore a bright orange bikini and a big smile as she waved to him from the water. He didn't see the huge wave building up behind her until it was practically right over her head.

He shouted, "Jenny, watch out!" as the wave came crashing down—hundreds of tons of water.

And then he awoke.

His surroundings weren't immediately recognizable. The bunk he lay in was tight and the air around it stifling hot. To his right he saw a blue wall with a framed photo of a blue whale bursting out of the water.

He sat up, read the name printed on the bed's top sheet—USS *Carl Vinson*—and relaxed.

As he scanned the contents of the eight-by-ten room—a chair and a counter built into the wall that served as a desk, his gear and clothes stacked neatly on the bunk below—the events of the previous night came rushing back at him, increasing his anxiety. He sensed that he'd left something undone.

What? He'd never called his wife, who was scheduled to leave for Cairo, Egypt, sometime soon. He had wanted to reach out to her before she left. Their friends jokingly called them Mr. and Mrs. Smith, like the married CIA assassins in the Brad Pitt–Angelina Jolie movie.

He pulled on a freshly laundered shirt and pants, found an office with a satellite connection, and, not knowing his wife's time of departure or the time difference between the Gulf of Aden and Virginia Beach, Virginia, called home.

No one answered, so he tried his daughter's cell phone.

"Hey, Daddy, what's up?" Jenny answered brightly on the third ring, sounding as if she was only a few blocks away.

He loved it when she called him daddy. "Where are you?"

"I'm staying with my friend Francesca."

"Francesca?"

"Yeah. Remember Francesca?"

He did, vaguely. Another tall girl with long brown hair. "Yeah, sure."

"I'm watching her dad make paella in a special pot Francesca bought for his birthday. Have you ever had it?"

"Paella, yeah. It's good." Memories of one of his favorite cities, Barcelona, flooded back, along with an image of a Spanish girl he'd dated before he was married—dark hair, dark eyes, magnificent body.

"Where's your stepmother?" he asked.

"She left for the airport early this morning. I guess she's in the air somewhere over the Atlantic Ocean by now."

Jenny was the product of his first marriage—a clever girl, charming, pretty, full of energy and mischief like he'd been at her age. No, he'd been far worse.

Still, she had her own mind and never listened to anyone, especially her mother, who couldn't deal with her. Reminded him too much of himself, which made him worry. She needed direction, goals. Like Crocker had before he joined the navy at nineteen.

He knew there wasn't much he could do now except tell her he loved her and hoped to see her soon.

"Sure, Dad. When do you think that will be?"

"Probably in two weeks, when the race is over."

"What race is that?"

ST-6 operators weren't allowed to tell their families where they were or what they were doing. But in addition to his SEAL commitments, Crocker competed in long-distance endurance events. So he told her, "I'm running in an ultramarathon, the Sahara, that starts in a few days."

"Isn't that, like, in the desert?"

"It is a desert."

"You're running in a race in the Sahara desert?"

"That's right."

"Won't everyone just, like, burn up and die?"

He laughed. "I hope not."

"You're so crazy, Dad."

He'd considered the possibility sometimes. Yes, the choices he made were extreme. Even abnormal. But he blamed that on his thirst for adventure and the wild energy he'd possessed since he was a little boy. During different phases in his life that energy had been both a blessing and a curse.

"Everything okay with you?" he asked.

"Fine, Dad."

"When did Holly say she's getting back?"

"A week from Friday."

He remembered Francesca's last name. "Say hi to the Novaks and thank them again for me. Be good."

"You, too, Dad. And one more thing."

"What's that?"

"I hope you win!"

He hung up and asked for directions to the ship's mess. Noticing photos of famous visitors, including his favorite NFL quarterback, Joe Montana, as he entered, Crocker found Ritchie and Mancini sitting at a corner table chowing down on eggs, ham, and hash browns.

He filled a plate, grabbed a cup of coffee, and sat. Mancini—the combination weight lifter and tech geek—was talking about a whole new generation of drones the air force was developing, some of which were the size of insects and birds.

"Insects and birds? You're exaggerating like a motherfucker," Ritchie said.

Bull-necked, crew-cut Mancini held his ground. "In another five to ten years max, war is gonna be fought by geeks at video screens."

"No way."

"Yeah." Mancini sniffed at a slice of bacon on his plate and pushed it aside. His wife, Carmen, had him on a strict diet to keep his cholesterol down.

"I've seen photos of one they're testing now that looks

like a hummingbird. Flapping wings and all. Flies at about twelve miles per hour and can perch on a windowsill."

"You hear this, boss?"

Crocker listened as he filled his stomach.

"In the future, the government wants to take out some terrorist leader, they dispatch one of these little suckers equipped with a camera and a weapon. Flies in the window, IDs the bad guy, then puts a bullet in his head. Maybe even tickles him first."

Ritchie, part Cherokee, ex-rodeo rider, shook his head. "That's when I'm retiring to Montana to raise horses."

"You ever see a Raven?" Mancini asked.

Crocker had, near the western border of Pakistan. He nodded.

Mancini continued. "It's about three feet long. Right, boss? You want to see something on the other side of a hill, you toss this thing like a model airplane that's equipped with an electric engine and an infrared camera. It beams images back."

Crocker was thinking that change was a law of the universe. Even the planet was shifting as they spoke. He cleared his throat. "Where's Akil?"

"In the infirmary getting his hand attended to. Davis is getting his hair cut."

"Soon as I'm done here, I'll call the CO."

"Oh, and the captain wants to see you. He's in his office on the bridge."

Crocker finished his breakfast and hurried up the seven flights of steps. Whereas the bridge of the MSC *Contessa* had been cramped, blood-splattered, and chaotic, this one was vast, orderly, and serene. Alert clean-cut officers manned various stations—the wheel, radar, sonar, weather. Everything seemingly under control.

An ensign in navy dress blues took him to see the captain, who sat in an office with his feet up on his desk. He and a half dozen other officers had their heads turned to a flat-screen monitor tuned to CNN.

The captain said, “Welcome, Warrant Officer Crocker. You still intact?”

“More or less.”

“Nice piece of work you and your men pulled off.”

“Thanks.”

“Pull up a chair. Take a load off. The commander in chief is making a statement.”

As Crocker watched, the president of the United States stood behind a lectern in the White House and talked about the rescue of Captain McCullum and his wife by commandos from the Joint Special Operations Command. No mention was made of the fact that they were navy SEALs from Team Six, or of the Middle Eastern men, or that the MSC *Contessa* had been carrying sensitive nuclear material.

But that was no surprise to Crocker. He and his men had carried out many daring missions all over the world that never made the news.

“Did the salvage team find the barrels?” Crocker asked after the president had finished.

“Yes, they’re bringing them up now,” the captain answered, as if it was no big deal.

Another officer with commander stripes on his uniform said, “They’ve also recovered the bodies of some of the men on the launch.”

Crocker sat up. "Any idea who they were and who they were working for?"

"The Agency is keeping that to themselves."

The sun was setting red over the desert when the Gulfstream IV carrying Crocker and his team landed at NSA Bahrain, a U.S. Navy base on the island of Bahrain, home of the U.S. Naval Forces Central Command and the Fifth Fleet. The Persian Gulf base occupied over sixty acres in the Juffair suburb of the capital city, Manama. Like other American military bases around the world, it seemed like a little piece of home—complete with fast food joints, a miniature golf course, and a bowling alley—far away from the continental United States.

After dropping their gear off at the Central Command barracks the six SEALs set out on a slow and easy run that took them along the perimeter of the base, beside the coast. It felt like months since they'd last trained.

As they ran, Mancini filled them in on local history. He was blessed with a near-photographic memory and could tell you what he'd eaten for dinner on any given night three years ago. "The Kingdom of Bahrain is actually a chain of thirty islands in the Persian Gulf, just east of the Kingdom of Saudi Arabia. The ancient Sumerians considered it an island paradise where wise, brave men could enjoy eternal life."

"The Sumerians?" Davis asked.

"Yeah, the Sumerians."

"I read a book about how the Sumerians described having contact with aliens," Davis offered. "They were the first great culture and spawned the Babylonians, Persians, and Assyrians."

Davis, who looked like a California surfer, was the other reader in the group. His tastes included science fiction, New Age, and philosophy—everything from Russian literature to American history, and from Nietzsche to William Gibson and Edgar Cayce.

Akil changed the subject—sort of. "Let's talk about Kim Kardashian's booty."

Ritchie: "What about it?"

Akil: "I read that it's been invaded by aliens."

Ritchie: "Thousands of times!"

Akil, Crocker, and Cal cracked up.

Mancini, who didn't find this funny, continued, "Like Saudi Arabia, Bahrain is ruled by a Sunni royal family. But in Bahrain's case about seventy percent of the native population of seven hundred thousand are from the Shia sect of Islam, which creates political problems. The remaining half million of the country's 1.2 million population are guest workers from places like India, Pakistan, and Asia. Many of them work in the oil and gas fields and in Manama's financial center."

"Boring," Akil said.

Ritchie: "Let's talk about what we're doing tonight."

They were passing the harbor, with the Marina Club (filled with luxurious yachts) and the Bahrain National Museum on their right. The lights of modern office towers sparkled in the clear night. Even though the city was relatively small, with a population of less than two hundred thousand, the skyline was impressive and featured two of the tallest buildings in the world—the Bahrain Financial Harbour at 853 feet and the Bahrain World Trade Center at 787.

"We might want to explore the city," Mancini said.

"It's active and lively. All kinds of restaurants and nightclubs. Last time I was here I went to a place called BJs that had a killer DJ and loads of beautiful young women."

Akil: "Now you're speaking my language."

"Foreign workers mostly, looking for a good time."

"You hook up?"

"None of your fucking business."

"You tell Carmen about that?" Davis asked.

"Do I look stupid?"

"Now that I think about it..." but Akil stopped. Nobody really wanted to piss Mancini off. He was a teddy-bear-type guy with a keen sense of justice who didn't react well when certain boundaries were crossed.

Crocker had read that during demonstrations in February 2011 in support of the Arab Spring, five people had been killed by Manama police. This sparked further protests by the Shia majority, which were eventually quelled with the help of troops from Saudi Arabia and the United Arab Emirates.

There were no signs of unrest now as they crossed the island and jogged down Al Shabab Avenue in the suburb of Juffair, which featured local franchises of McDonald's, Dairy Queen, and Chili's.

"I know a great Indian restaurant we can go to," Mancini said. "Best chicken masala and spinach *bindi* I've ever tasted."

Crocker was less interested in which restaurant they ate at than in getting his team ready for the grueling Marathon des Sables next week. As the team's lead trainer, it was his job to keep them in shape and prepare them to deal with any contingency—arctic mountains, rough seas, jungles. He was concerned because, compared to their competition, he figured they were behind in training, mileage, and long-distance desert runs.

He had led his team on climbs in the Rockies, on Mount Washington, the Devil's Tower, Grand Teton, the Himalayas, K2. They had done parachute drops from thirty thousand feet in Germany, winter training outside Juneau, jungle training in the Philippines and Borneo.

Now it was time to beat them to shit in the desert. His motto was "Blood from any orifice," and he lived it over and over.

When they returned to the barracks, a civilian aide stood waiting beside a black SUV.

"Chief Warrant Officer Crocker?"

"Who wants to know?"

"The embassy political counselor. He wants to see you."

That likely meant CIA.

Ten minutes later, showered and dressed in black cotton pants and a black polo, he entered an air-conditioned room in a utilitarian four-story building. The local CIA chief, Ed Wolfson, a medium-height, sandy-haired man with gray eyes, rose to greet him. Judging by his paunch and stooped shoulders, Crocker pegged him as an analyst type.

Sitting at the table behind him was Crocker's old nemesis, Lou Donaldson.

The last time he'd seen Donaldson, he was serving as the CIA deputy in Pakistan. He had since been promoted to an important job with CTC, the CIA's Counterterrorism Center.

"Congratulations, Lou," Crocker said, extending a

hand. "I heard you were promoted. What brings you to Bahrain?"

Donaldson ignored his hand and responded with a curt "Sit down."

His manner hadn't changed. Still an asshole.

They were joined by Donaldson's broad-shouldered deputy, Jim Anders, carrying plastic-wrapped sandwiches and Diet Cokes. Anders explained that they'd driven five hours from Saudi Arabia and were delayed because of repairs to the sixteen-mile King Fahd Causeway, which linked the two countries and also happened to be one of the longest bridges in the world. They hadn't had time to stop for dinner.

Instead of enjoying chicken masala, Crocker bit into a stale turkey sandwich. And he hated Diet Coke.

Donaldson spoke as he chewed. "That launch was completely destroyed, and with it a trove of potentially valuable intel. Were you aware of that, Crocker?"

"No, sir."

"Blew up and sank to the bottom of the bay."

"I suspected that might happen."

"You couldn't put out the fire?"

"No time, sir, and nothing to do it with."

"Fucking shame. The White House is disappointed. Could have bolstered their case at the UN."

"What case is that?"

Donaldson had dripped some mustard on the front of his blue shirt. Instead of answering Crocker's question, he used a handkerchief and water from a plastic bottle to blot it. This only seemed to make a bigger mess.

"The salvage team recovered some scraps, pieces of documents, one man's body."

"Have you been able to ID him?" Crocker asked.

"You interview the crew?" Donaldson asked back, sidestepping Crocker's question.

"The crew of the *Contessa*?"

"No, the crew of the fucking Starship *Enterprise*."

Crocker clenched his jaw, fighting back an urge to reach across the table and punch him in the mouth. "Didn't have time, sir."

"How many of them were there?"

"We recovered six dead. There were another five men injured, plus the captain."

"For a grand total of twelve, including the captain."

"And the captain's wife. That's correct."

Donaldson slapped the table. "Wrong."

"Sir?"

"Captain McCullum says he set sail from Melbourne with a crew of twelve, which means thirteen, including him."

"He sure of that?"

"Yes, he is. One of them apparently got away."

"Got away?"

"Yes, goddammit. Escaped."

"Maybe he fell overboard and drowned."

"Wrong again, Crocker. I suppose you weren't aware that one of the *Contessa*'s lifeboats was missing, too."

"No, I wasn't."

"Then there's your answer."

What answer? Crocker asked himself. *Why is this important?* He was going to explain that he and his men had been under attack and that the action aboard and around the *Contessa* was unrelenting, but he realized there was no point.

"Where did this crewman go?" he asked instead.

"Unclear."

"Then why is his disappearance such a big deal?"

"It is, Crocker. That's all you need to know."

Trying to understand what had been going on with the *Contessa,* Crocker asked, "Were you able to ascertain the nationality of the men on the launch?"

Donaldson nodded at Anders, who reached for a folder. "You ever hear of the Qods Force, Crocker?"

Of course he had. The Qods Force was the external intelligence apparatus of the Islamic Revolutionary Guards of Iran—essentially state-sponsored terrorists linked to assassinations and bombings in countries all over the world, including Lebanon, Israel, Saudi Arabia, Argentina, Thailand, and France.

Crocker nodded. "They're only the nastiest motherfuckers on the planet."

"Among the cleverest, too." Donaldson grunted and turned to Anders. "Show him the photo."

The image was of a middle-aged man with intense black eyes, a broken nose, and acne-scarred skin partially covered by a short black beard.

"Recognize him?"

The eyes looked familiar. He thought they belonged to the third man in the launch cabin, the one who had slipped away while he was grappling on the floor with the two others.

"Maybe."

"His name is Colonel Farhed Alizadeh, also known as Colonel D, member of the Iranian Revolutionary Corps and an engineer linked to Iran's nuclear program."

Crocker had never heard of him. "Did the divers find his body?"

"Not yet."

"I hope they find him."

"That would be a huge relief."

Back at the barracks, Crocker tossed and turned throughout the night. He kept waking up and thinking about a museum he had visited in Nagasaki when he was a young navy corpsman stationed with the marines, and about the horrors of nuclear weapons.

On the morning of August 9, 1945, a U.S. B-29 bomber veered away from its intended target—Kokura—because of thick cloud cover and instead dropped a 10,200-pound nuclear bomb, known as Fat Man, on Nagasaki. The resulting 21-kiloton explosion—the equivalent of 75 million sticks of dynamite—destroyed almost all of the city's buildings and killed roughly 39,000 people. Another 25,000 were horribly burned. Over the following weeks and months another 40,000 residents died from radiation exposure and other injuries.

According to one observer, "A huge fireball formed in the sky.... Together with the flash came the heat rays and the blast, which destroyed everything on earth. When the fire itself burned out, there appeared a completely changed, vast, colorless world that made you think it was the end of life on earth. The whole city became extinct."

It was the pictures of the burn victims, and the deformed children born to survivors from outside the city who were exposed to radiation, that gave Crocker the chills. He knew that the Fat Man plutonium bomb dropped on Nagasaki was primitive and limited in firepower compared to some of the bombs built today, ten kilotons compared to as high as ten megatons—approximately a thousand times bigger.

As the WMD officer at ST-6, he also understood the dangers of nuclear proliferation and on more than one occasion had risked his life to stop it. After the fall of the Soviet Union, when approximately two hundred nuclear warheads were either sold or stolen, he had launched spectacular missions into Belarus, Uzbekistan, and caves in North Korea to recover them.

The idea of an aggressive country like Iran, run by a group of religious zealots, getting its hands on nuclear weapons that were even more lethal than the ones dropped on Japan filled him with dread. And the more he thought about Farhed Alizadeh and the incident on the *Contessa,* the more he was plagued by questions.

They were still screaming for his attention as he ran his team thirty-five miles around the island that morning. Even after they had stretched and he had reminded his men about the importance of hydration, electrolyte replacement, bringing extra shoes, and race tactics, he kept asking himself what the Iranians were up to.

He'd learned not to shy away from things that nagged him. They always came around to bite him in the ass. So despite the fact that he had a number of things to do that afternoon to prepare for the race in Morocco, he arranged to meet Ed Wolfson in a coffee shop near the U.S. embassy.

After they sat down, he said, "I hate being made to feel responsible for an outcome that I don't really understand."

"Likewise, I'm sure. What's on your mind?"

"What do you know about Farhed Alizadeh's mission on the *Contessa*?" Crocker asked.

"Enough to tell you that from my perspective the whole thing was planned ahead of time. More precisely, the crew member who disappeared was working for the Iranians. The whole pirating incident was staged."

"Do you know what was in the barrels?"

"I do, but you didn't hear it from me."

Crocker nodded.

"High-strength aluminum alloy. Component parts for L-2 centrifuges manufactured by Scomi Precision Engineering in Malaysia. High-speed triggers made in China."

"So Iran really is trying to build nuclear weapons."

Wolfson folded his hands on the table and said, "Correct. And they've been playing a double game. Holding talks to stall the international community and playing up to China, which is secretly supplying them with parts, while working pedal-to-the-floor to build a bomb."

"How close are they?"

"That depends on who you talk to."

"What do you think?" Crocker asked.

"Most experts agree that they lack two things: some of the high-tech parts needed to build one, and enough enriched uranium."

"Hence the high-speed triggers and parts in the barrels on the *Contessa*."

"Exactly."

CHAPTER FOUR

It isn't the mountain ahead that wears you out; it's the grain of sand in your shoe.

—Robert W. Service

IT TOOK approximately two days for Seal Team Six to reach southern Morocco. First they flew ten hours to Gatwick Airport in London, then after a three-hour layover caught a charter to Ouarzazate, Morocco, known as the door of the desert—a quiet, dusty Berber town of fifty thousand built around a central street. Back in the early '60s it had served as the location for the desert scenes in *Lawrence of Arabia.*

African traders had been using it as a crossroads for centuries. For many modern Europeans, it was a holiday destination and a launching point for excursions into the Sahara. Features included palm groves and kasbahs, earthen structures with high walls and tiny windows.

They chose an old man with a white wisp of beard to escort them to the hotel. As they drove through the dusty, sleepy streets, Akil, the handsome, single Egyptian American on the team, regaled them with stories of his sexual adventures with a beautiful blond runner from Norway whom he had met on a trip to Patagonia.

"She kept me up all night. Couldn't get enough."

"Of what?" Ritchie asked. "The bullshit stories you were feeding her?"

"Don't expect that to happen here," Crocker said. "The few female entrants registered for this event will be too exhausted to do anything but ask you to massage their feet. So will you."

Akil: "Envy is a green-eyed monster."

Mancini: "Maybe one day when you drop the BS you'll find a woman you love who loves you back."

Ritchie: "Unlikely."

Cal sat in the back, plugged into his iPod.

"What are you listening to?" Davis asked.

"Gotye."

"What's that?"

"You don't know 'Somebody That I Used to Know?' "

"Never heard of it."

Cal passed his earbuds to Davis.

Crocker said, "Instead of dicking around and playing music, you guys might want to start thinking about the race."

Akil: "After what we went through last time in the Himalayas, this will be a piece of cake."

"You think so? We're looking at running the equivalent of five and a half marathons in hundred-and-twenty-degree heat. And we have to carry everything we need, except water, in rucksacks on our backs."

"That's why it's considered the toughest footrace on the planet," Mancini added.

"I'll take the heat over the freezing cold anytime," Akil said.

Ritchie: "And you'll probably be the first one to pussy out."

"I never backed out of fucking anything."

"We'll see how long you last."

They stayed at a hotel inside the medina with a view of the valley and nearby reservoir. After a dinner of Berber spiced chicken and goat-cheese fritters, they sat in the lounge on the roof, sipped local bottled beer, and went over the plans for the race.

Crocker had put Mancini in charge of procuring and shipping all equipment and supplies. Besides running shoes big enough to comfortably accommodate swollen feet, shorts, tees, Adidas Explorer sunglasses, Cobbers, Skins compression vests, RailRiders Adventure shirts with front pockets, CW-X three-quarter-length compression tights, Injinji bamboo liners and SmartWool cushioned socks, Inov-8 390 boots, Sandbaggers gaiters, Buff headbands, RaidLight trekking poles, PHD Minimus sleeping bags, Platypus hot water bag with lid, ProLite 3 sleeping mat, titanium Esbit Wing Stove combination 900-milliliter cooking pot, titanium spork, disposable lighters with disco lights, toilet paper, alcohol hand gel, iPod, Suunto watches with heart-rate monitors, scarves, and hats, each man had to carry a rucksack packed with 14,000 calories of food—M&Ms, instant noodles, expedition meals, muesli, Honey Stinger Gel—extra clothing, gaffer's tape, antivenom pump, compass, sunscreen, head torch with spare battery, disinfectant, Endurolytes, electrolytes, knives, safety pins, signaling mirror, space blanket, rehydration sachets, and whistle.

The backpacks were lightweight OMM 32-liter models. Also RaidLight pouches for their front belts that were big enough to hold snacks, lip salve, sunscreen. RaidLight bottle holders for each shoulder. Crocker preferred the CamelBak Podium bottles over the RaidLights because they were easier to suck water out of.

And there were medical kits—including lots of painkillers (Solpadeine, Diclofenac, Tramadol), zinc oxide, sterile padding, tape, needles, syringes, erythromycin for infections.

Everything was in order, except that two cases of the Datrex 3600-calorie survival food bars were past their expiration date.

Mancini was irate. “I’ll make ’em send back our money.”

Crocker said, “Don’t worry. We’ve got plenty of MREs, Clif Bars, and beef jerky. Besides, most ultramarathon organizers bring sponsored supplies like gels and energy bars.”

“Last time we use *that* supplier.”

“Let’s focus on the race.”

The next morning after breakfast, the six SEALs packed into a bus with registrants from the UK, Australia, Israel, New Zealand, and France for a five-hour drive into the desert. When they arrived at the staging area in the early afternoon, all they could see out the window were endless sand dunes, a vivid blue sky, and the brilliant sun. A painted sign read in English: ANY IDIOT CAN RUN A MARATHON, BUT IT TAKES A SPECIAL KIND OF IDIOT TO RUN THE MARATHON DES SABLES.

“They’re kidding, right?” Akil asked as he stretched. “We’re supposed to run in this?”

“What the hell did you expect?”

That night they slept in a tent with two competitors

from Worcester, England. One of them, who called himself Perks, said he was planning to run the entire six-day race with an ironing board strapped to his back to raise money for a cancer hospice back home. Why he was making the already very difficult race even harder for himself was unclear.

In the morning they lined up for medical checks and registration. Crocker—a veteran of many ultramarathons, including Double and Triple Ironman races and four Raid World Championships—ran into several competitors he knew, including the Moroccan Ahansal brothers, Lahcen and Mohammed, who between them had won the race thirteen out of the twenty-two times it had been staged.

Later, approximately seven hundred runners from all over the world set off into the desert to the sound of AC/DC's "Highway to Hell." The atmosphere among the competitors was jovial, bordering on euphoric.

A group of French runners yelled, *"Vive la France!"*

Some Australians countered with "Stick a ferret up yer clacker!"

Some Brits: "Hail Britannia!"

Ritchie shouted, "USA, baby, all the way!"

The excitement quickly drained out of all of them as they realized there were approximately 150 very difficult miles between them and the finish line.

The first couple of miles were relatively easy. The racers ran the flats and downhills. Most walked the uphills. Then they reached the dunes, a landscape of seemingly endless mountains of rolling sand. They sank down with each step, pushed by the weight of their full backpacks. Crocker told his men to try walking in the footsteps of the man in front to help prevent them from slipping and sliding on the way up.

The afternoon had started with a cool breeze, but as the hours dragged past, the heat grew increasingly intense, moving from the mid-90s up to 124 degrees Fahrenheit. When the wind whipped up, contestants struggled to protect every inch of their skin from the savage stinging sand.

The more difficult conditions became, the more Crocker's focus narrowed—drink some water, check your compass, concentrate intently on reaching your next checkpoint. The incredible beauty of the landscape made the discomfort bearable. No shadows for miles. Just the subtly shifting colors and undulating shapes of the dunes, interrupted occasionally by a perfectly rounded boulder or ridge of marble protruding from the sand.

He'd learned that if you didn't push yourself beyond your limits, you never understood what your limits were. Most people yielded to the voices in their heads that told them they were too tired, hungry, thirsty, or old, or that conditions were too dangerous to continue. So they stopped.

Special operators and endurance athletes learned to push past warnings like that and trust that they would pull through. If you urinated blood after a long race, as Crocker had many times, you'd recover. If you passed out, your teammates would revive you.

At the nineteen-kilometer mark they came to a checkpoint, where they filled their water bottles and waited for Akil to catch up. Ten minutes passed before they saw a blurry shape hobbling over a hill.

"What's wrong?" Crocker asked.

"It's my feet."

They'd barely started, and he'd already developed blisters on the sides of the little toes of both feet. This surprised Crocker, since Akil had run many long-distance training runs in the same shoes. He treated the blisters with Super Glue and duct tape. Then they set out again, climbing, running downhill, stopping to rest, refuel, and rehydrate, until the sun started to set. As usually happened at sundown, the temperature dropped and the wind picked up.

They reached another flat stretch of about ten kilometers, which Crocker, Ritchie, and Davis ran together, following blue, yellow, and red glow sticks that marked the route. Crocker felt a strange sense of euphoria; he heard the Doors' "Spanish Caravan" playing in his head and imagined they were following the footsteps of ancient traders.

Up ahead he saw an outcropping of flags representing the countries of the various competitors and banners championing the causes many were running for that marked the makeshift camp—a circle of tents with no toilets. Men and women were too tired to bother with modesty. They walked around half naked—men in shorts, women in skimpy sport bras and bikini-type bottoms. Thirty or so feet from the tents they squatted or stood and did their business. No big deal.

Crocker, Davis, and Ritchie waited almost twenty minutes there for Akil, Cal, and Mancini to catch up. Akil's feet were a bloody mess, and Mancini's right knee was barking—the same one he'd injured when they were climbing in Pakistan.

Crocker was attending to both when an Aussie on his

right washing his feet said, "They feel drier than a nun's nasty."

"Put some sesame oil on those puppies," Crocker said, pointing to a bottle that was being passed along the line.

"Much obliged, mate."

Mancini started complaining. "I thought we agreed we were going to run this together, as a team."

"My bad," Crocker answered. "Tomorrow we'll try to stick together."

Despite the myriad injuries, ranging from heat cramps, to heat exhaustion and heat stroke, to troubled bowels, twisted knees and ankles, and swollen feet, most contestants were determined to continue. They were doing this for a purpose—raising money for a cause, trying to achieve a personal goal.

About three dozen dropped out. Crocker watched as Berber volunteers loaded them into a truck for the ride back to Ouarzazate.

The mood among the remaining competitors was good. Someone passed a big bar of chocolate. An Aussie whipped up a vat of something called Miracle Beer—a beer made from powder he said he had purchased in the UK. One of the Brits played a harmonica and sang. Others joined in. Verses of "Maggie May," "Wild Rover," and "Satisfaction" floated through the dry night air.

Crocker had just fallen asleep when a sandstorm blew in and swept away their tent. He and the others crawled inside their sleeping bags, zipped them up, and tried to sleep through the storm. But sand managed to find its way into everything—teeth, noses, and ears.

When he did fall asleep, he dreamt he was at the controls of a huge jetliner flying over a city at dusk. Barely skimming over telephone poles and the tops of buildings, looking for a runway.

He still had enough liquid in his body to wake up in a sweat.

The morning sun was scorching from the start, which slowed their progress. Up and down, up and down. Monotonous and taxing. The sun seemed to draw every last drop of water out of them, resulting in constant thirst. Reminded Crocker of his days as a young SEAL with ST-1, training at Camp Niland in the California desert. Forty-mile hikes with seventy-pound packs in 114-degree heat. This had to be easy in comparison.

After about twenty kilometers they reached a flat stretch that they welcomed at first. But after a while the featureless terrain and the heaviness of the heat started to wear them down. The soles of their feet felt on fire.

Crocker started dreaming about summers on the beaches of New England as a kid. He and his younger brother catching sand crabs, body surfing, eating ice cream. He could taste it in his mouth—rich, creamy, cold, chocolate, strawberry, pistachio.

Beside him he heard Davis talking to his wife. He spoke as though she were walking beside him, telling her about the roof he was planning to build over their deck and how it was going to shade the back of the house. How he was going to plant fruit trees, too. Davis even started to argue, saying he wanted them to be cherry trees even though he knew she preferred peaches.

Crocker thought he saw a group of camels ahead but when he looked closer realized they were only swirls of heat.

After refreshing themselves at Checkpoint Three they

faced a monstrous thousand-meter sand dune that took over an hour to climb. Crocker blacked out a couple of times but managed to keep walking.

The camp that night was overrun with happy Berber children willing to fetch water, wash clothes, and even sing and dance for a couple of ten-santimat coins. They lightened the mood considerably. The sky glittered with thousands of stars, many of which were rarely visible to the naked eye.

Crocker learned that his team, Eagle Bravo, was currently ranked thirty-fifth out of the 120 teams in competition. They would have been even higher if not for Akil, who was still suffering but refused to quit.

They exchanged stories with some of the Aussies and told filthy jokes. Akil managed to find a Frenchwoman who massaged his feet and calves.

Day three was a bitch, with endless dunes as far as the eye could see. The sand somehow seemed softer and deeper than before. It crumpled as soon as you touched it and caused them to sink halfway up to their knees with each footfall. Crocker felt he was about to hit a wall but refused to stop. He had to set an example for his men.

The sun burned through his Adidas Explorer sunglasses. The heat pounded his shoulders and neck.

He started to feel light-headed, then felt something touch his hand. It was a blond girl in a blue bikini. Her stride was strong and sure. They were walking down the beach together. He felt water lapping at his feet.

He turned to kiss her. "Kim?"

His first wife smiled and pushed back her hair.

"Hey, Kim."

"You okay, boss?"

It was Ritchie, with his head and face wrapped in a white scarf.

Crocker thought he heard music as they approached the day's destination, a little desert town called Tazzarine. Turned out the music was real. A local band played enthusiastically as girls danced in circles and shook tambourines. They ate lamb couscous for dinner and immediately passed out.

The next morning the sky was cloudy, and one of the organizers warned him that a storm was approaching. Crocker told his men to stick together. "They can blow in quickly, so stay alert."

Fortunately, the first set of dunes wasn't as high as those of the previous day, and the sun wasn't as strong.

After an hour of trekking they stopped at a water hole to wash their faces and refill their bottles. Cal was leaning back in the sand, looking up at the clouds, when he ripped out the earbuds of his iPod and shouted, "That fucking hurt!"

"What?"

Crocker saw that a yellow sand scorpion (*Opistophthalmus*) about two inches long had bitten the palm of his right hand. He washed the area with water and noted that the site of the sting was becoming red and swollen.

Even after he applied a local anesthetic, Cal continued to complain about the pain. He also reported a tingling, twitchy sensation up his right arm.

"It's my trigger hand," Cal said, grimacing. "Maybe it's karma."

"What are you talking about?"

"Payback for all the people I've killed."

"I don't know about that."

Crocker knew that in some cases scorpion poisoning could cause shock and even death. He wished he had some tetanus toxoid with him, but he'd have to make do, because they wouldn't reach the next medical aid and communications point until evening. So he wrapped his Buff headband around Cal's right wrist to restrict the poison.

Meanwhile the sky had darkened and the wind had picked up. A cloud of fine red dust enveloped them. Huge balls of desert brambles raced across the sand.

"Where'd they come from?" Akil shouted.

"Seek cover, but stay away from the leeward side of the dunes. Keep your scarves secured over your nose, ears, and mouth. Make sure you keep your sunglasses on. Goggles, if you have them!" Crocker yelled back.

Within minutes visibility was zero. The temperature dropped twenty degrees. Each gust of wind carried with it a blast of highly abrasive sand that felt like it could rip the skin right off your body.

Crocker wrapped the thin Tyvek sheet he carried in his backpack around Cal and led him over to the water hole, where they knelt behind the stump of an old palm tree. It was hard to breathe.

Cal started to shiver. "How long is this likely to last?"

"Don't think about that."

After half an hour Crocker released the headband around Cal's wrist, held his arm in the water for approximately five minutes, then secured the headband again, just tight enough to slow the flow of blood. He repeated the process a half hour later. Then the wind abated and the air started to clear. Within five minutes the sky overhead was blue and the sun was beating down strongly.

"Amazing," Cal said.

"You feeling better?"

"My arm is killing me, and the rest of my body feels like shit."

Five men were accounted for, but Akil was missing. They found him on the other side of a dune, wrapped in a blanket and covered with sand, and helped him dig out.

"You enjoy that, desert rat?"

"I think I dozed off."

Or maybe he'd lost consciousness from sheer exhaustion. But as they walked he seemed to be his same happy-go-lucky self, talking about the movie *The Mummy* and one of his favorite actresses, Rachel Weisz. He was convinced that she'd fall for him if they ever met, and the others were too exhausted to tell him he was full of shit. Crocker helped Cal, who was slipping in and out of a fever. Hot one minute, freezing cold the next.

When they reached the night's camp, the nurse there gave Cal a shot of tetanus toxoid, and he started to improve. His hand hurt, but his temperature and pulse returned to normal.

Akil's mouth was still working, but his feet were beat to shit. And even though Mancini didn't complain, he appeared to be favoring his left leg.

One more day, Crocker said to himself as he poured hot water into a cupful of noodles. One of the Aussies shook a bucket of sand out of his long brown hair.

Someone tapped the SEAL chief on the shoulder. "Mr. Crocker?" the man asked. He was dressed head to toe in khaki and wore a bristling black mustache.

"Yeah." Wondering if he was seeing a mirage.

"You're Mr. Crocker?"

"That's correct."

The man bowed from the waist and handed Crocker a folded piece of paper. He read it quickly in the mottled light of the various lamps. At the end he saw the name Lou Donaldson, and he felt his sphincters tighten.

"Now?"

"Yes, sir."

"He wants us to withdraw from this race?"

"Affirmative, sir."

"Does he realize that we're half a day away from completing this sucker?"

"I believe he does, sir. Yes."

Focusing on the typed instructions, he read them again carefully. Ritchie saw him reading and knelt beside him.

"What's up, boss?"

Crocker folded the letter and handed it back to the waiting man. "Give us ten minutes to pack everything."

"We're leaving?"

"Seems like."

The man in khaki pointed past a mud wall to a dirt road. "The vehicles are waiting over there, sir."

"Ten-four."

Ritchie again, at his elbow. "Boss, what is it? What's he want?"

"We're going to Rabat. We've got orders. Tell the others. Help them organize the gear."

CHAPTER FIVE

From the halls of Montezuma,
To the shores of Tripoli;
We fight our country's battles;
In the air, on land, and sea…
—U.S. Marine Corps hymn

CROCKER, LIMPING on sore legs, followed Jim Anders through the gate of the U.S. embassy in Rabat, Morocco, muttering a silent prayer for the marine guards and other embassy personnel who had died there less than a year ago, victims of an al-Qaeda truck bomb.

He'd slept a few hours on the Gulfstream jet that had transported them from the heat of Ouarzazate to the Moroccan capital, where it was cool and green. Even though he'd just showered and shaved, he still smelled the desert on his skin.

So far he'd been given no reason why he and his men had had to quit the race. A part of him was hoping they were being ordered home.

He proceeded into the embassy building, where a marine behind ballistic glass instructed him to step around the body scanner and enter.

"Welcome, sir." Cordial and correct. Marine security

guards like him were on duty at 150 embassies and consulates around the world.

Into an elevator to the fourth floor. Crocker was somewhat disoriented. Instead of endless desert, he was walking through a narrow hall, past a blonde in a tight white skirt. The sound of her high heels clicking against the tiled floor reminded him of a scene from an old British movie with a youngish Michael Caine.

Sometimes he missed the chase, especially when he'd been away from home more than a month.

Their destination was a windowless room on the fourth floor that they accessed only after passing through a vault door, which meant they had entered the CIA station. There, Jim Anders asked a female officer to pull up some files from the server.

"Which ones?"

"Scorpion."

"Yes, sir." She had short brown hair and a wide face with small features. On her wrist she wore a Timex Adventure Tech Digital Compass watch like the one he'd given Holly for her fortieth birthday.

Scorpion? Crocker repeated in his head. The word intrigued him.

They sat in a room with a half dozen serious-looking men and one woman. The lights went out and images danced on a screen. Crocker recognized the puffy face of Colonel Muammar Gaddafi, former dictator of Libya. He had previously seen footage of Gaddafi's capture, sodomization, and murder, and he was familiar with some of the highlights, or low points, of his career—namely his connection to Pan Am Flight 103, which had been blown up over Lockerbie, Scotland, and other acts of terror; his vanity and extravagant personal spending; and more recently his attempted rapprochement with the U.S. and his infatuation with Secretary of State Condoleezza Rice.

He had always regarded the Libyan strongman as a very dangerous buffoon. A madman.

What he was watching now on the large monitor at the front of the room was grainy black-and-white footage of Gaddafi made in early 2011, toward the end of his forty-year reign. He knew this because of the time stamp at the bottom of the image.

"Clandestine tape of an internal meeting," Anders remarked.

Gaddafi was dressed in a tribal robe and cap, sitting behind a big desk. He was speaking to a group of military officers in the Libyan dialect of Arabic, which Crocker couldn't understand. He knew a few words of Arabic, enough to get by in a pinch, but this was different and delivered too fast for him to decipher.

At one point Gaddafi slapped the desk and shouted a word that sounded like *ala-kurab.* Even though Crocker didn't know what the word meant, he understood it to be a threat. When Gaddafi spit out the word again, Anders punched a button on the remote control he was holding and paused the disc.

"Scorpion," Anders said, turning to Crocker.

"What?"

"He's threatening his enemies with *ala-kurab,* which means 'scorpion.' "

"What enemies?"

"Anyone who opposes him—the Libyan opposition, al-Qaeda, even NATO."

"What is Scorpion, exactly?"

"The name of Gaddafi's WMD program, which supposedly shut down in 2004."

"Oh."

"He's telling his military commanders that if NATO continues its bombing campaign and the Libyan people continue to turn against him, he'll unleash Scorpion."

"Which he never did."

"No. In the end he turned out to be a romantic like Che Guevara instead of a psychopath like Stalin."

Crocker wasn't sure about the comparison to Che Guevara, but he got the point.

"But he's dead, right?" he said. "So, end of story."

"Not necessarily. If the WMDs exist, we might have a problem," Anders countered.

"Why?"

"Because our chief there thinks that the country is about to come apart. The ambassador doesn't agree. But we don't want to take a chance."

Anders pressed another button and the blurry image of a different man filled the screen—scruffy dark beard and intense eyes. At first Crocker thought he was looking at a picture of a young Gaddafi, but the nose and hair were different.

"Who we looking at?" Crocker asked.

"Anaruz Mohammed, one of Gaddafi's illegitimate sons. He seems to have had many. Anaruz has reentered the country and has been organizing militant Gaddafi loyalists in the south."

"What about him?"

"He's just one of the potential threats against the Libyan transitional government, known as the National Transitional Council, which we and our allies support."

"There are others?"

"Yes. But we think this kid is particularly dangerous."

"Why?"

"He's a chip off the old block."

"In other words a delusional nut case with charisma," one of the other officers added.

"And his mother is a Tuareg, part of a group of nomadic warriors that lives in southern Libya in a swath of desert that also runs through Niger, Chad, and Algeria. They've been a problem since the French colonized the area in the twenties."

Crocker had heard of them and knew they were one of the many Berber tribes that dominated southern Libya.

A map appeared on the screen highlighting the area.

"The Tuaregs were intensely loyal to Gaddafi, because he rescued them in the early seventies when they were starving. Saved their butts. In return, they fought for him like tigers during the recent war. At least two thousand served in his army. Now they're a concern."

"Why?" Crocker asked.

"The NTC has been trying to wipe them out. In January there were a couple of serious battles near the village of Menaka, not far from the border with Niger."

He pointed to a spot on the map that Crocker considered one of the most forgotten, desolate places in the world.

He asked himself, *Who cares?*

"The Tuaregs are under siege, so they've formed alliances," Anders continued. "One is with the terrorist organization called al-Qaeda Maghreb. Another is with the Chinese. A third is with Iran."

The mention of China and Iran got Crocker's attention.

"Why are the Chinese and Iranians interested in a nomadic tribe in the Sahara desert?" he asked.

Anders turned and looked him in the eye. "Uranium."

"Uranium?"

"Lots of it. Specifically, mines in northern Niger. For the last forty years they've been controlled by the French. But now the Chinese and their Iranian buddies want them, and they're using the Tuaregs and al-Qaeda to extend their influence in the area."

Crocker felt somewhat overwhelmed by all the information and wasn't sure what Anders was getting at.

The CIA officer said, "That's the larger strategic picture. Africa is where the terrorist action is today. Al-Qaeda sees all kinds of opportunities because of the Arab Spring and the fall of regimes in Tunisia, Egypt, and Libya."

"I get it."

"The Libyan coalition government has been effective so far. For a number of reasons involving oil, uranium, and other strategic interests, we don't want it to come apart."

"I understand."

"Recently there's been a marked uptick in bombings, kidnappings, and reprisals in Benghazi and Tripoli. We're not sure who's behind them. Some people say it's the Tuaregs, others al-Qaeda Maghreb. Maybe it's the two of them working together. Could be that the Chinese and Iranians are stirring up trouble. There are lots of interests competing for power and a piece of the pie."

"There always are."

"The immediate concern for us is Scorpion, the WMDs. We want to know, one, if they do exist. And two, if they exist, we want to make sure we secure them so they don't fall into the wrong hands."

"Got it."

"NATO claims to have inspected all the sites and secured the few old mustard-gas shells they found. But our chief there doesn't believe they were thorough. The whole NATO command thing is sensitive. We don't want to look like we're second-guessing them or stepping on anyone's toes."

"Naturally."

"But given the possible stakes, Al thinks it's too important. And Donaldson and I agree."

"I thought Donaldson didn't like us," Crocker said.

"Where'd you get that impression?"

"From him, primarily."

"He thinks you guys are great."

Crocker had another question. "You mentioned Al. Al who?"

"Al Cowens. He's our station chief in Tripoli. You'll be working closely with him. You might have to coordinate with the NATO commander there, who is a Brit. But we're leaving that up to Al. He's no-nonsense, like you, Crocker. I think you'll like him."

"I know Al," Crocker said. "He's a stud."

"Oh, and one other thing. You'll be going in undercover as American civil engineers doing a study of the city's electrical grid."

"Perfect."

"Al's idea."

"When do you want us there?"

"Tonight, tomorrow. As soon as possible."

* * *

Crocker's only previous trip to Libya had occurred roughly sixteen years before, when he had run a training program for a group of anti-Gaddafi rebels, Berber tribesmen all from one extended family. They were two dozen brave men ranging in age from seventeen to seventy. After hot days showing them how to disassemble, clean, and fire AK-47s, Crocker and the two Special Forces operatives he had been sent with would sit around a fire and listen through their translator as the men told gruesome stories about tribe members who had run afoul of the Gaddafi regime.

One man had refused to sell his farmland to one of the strongman's cronies. He and his entire family were rounded up and tortured. As Gaddafi's friends watched, men and women were raped, then the men's genitals were hacked off and the women were blinded.

After Crocker left he learned that the entire clan he'd worked with had been captured and killed. The memory left a bad taste in his mouth.

The Libyan Arab Airlines jet he and his men rode in banked over the Mediterranean. Tripoli, a sparkling gold crescent of concrete and glass in the light of the setting sun, glittered below.

Mancini, in the seat behind him, leaned forward and recited some facts. "It's a city of almost two million. Founded way back in the seventh century BC by the Phoenicians. They were essentially an alliance of city-states that controlled the area around Lebanon and Israel from about 1200 to 800 BC. Big traders. Loved the color purple, which they considered royal, and they got it from the mucus of the murex sea snail."

"The murex sea snail?" Akil groaned. "Too much information."

"Ignorance is dangerous, Akil," Mancini retorted. "Remember that."

"So is clogging up your brain with trivial crap."

The old DC-727's landing gear groaned into place as the female flight attendants tied scarves around their heads.

"History isn't trivial," Mancini said. "Those who don't learn from it are destined to repeat it."

"Thanks, professor. Now shut the fuck up."

The plane hit the runway like a bag of bolts and jerked right.

"Check this out," Davis said, lifting the carpet and pointing to a six-inch-diameter hole in the floor near his seat. Through it they could see the runway flying by.

"Nice."

Stepping off the plane, they were hit by a blast of fresh Mediterranean air pungent with spices and mixed with jet fuel.

Ritchie asked, "Didn't we bomb this shithole in the eighties?"

"That was Mitiga Airport, east of the city, near Gaddafi's former stronghold," Mancini interjected. "Nineteen eighty-six, to be exact. Part of Operation El Dorado Canyon launched by President Ronald Reagan."

"Bombed his tent, too," Ritchie added.

"That's right. Gaddafi barely escaped. Turned out he was forewarned by some Italian politician."

"Fucking asshole."

Shifting loyalties. The Libyans were now our friends. They were also one of the top oil-producing countries in the world, exporting approximately 1.2 million barrels of crude a day, 80 percent of which went to Europe. Violence and instability there meant an increase in gas and heating oil prices back home.

The terminal was dark and relatively empty. All the green flags once flown by Gaddafi's Great Socialist People's Libyan Arab Jamahiriya had been replaced with the black, red, and green of the NTC. Soldiers in green camouflage uniforms holding AK-47s patrolled the building. Some were wearing sneakers and sandals; others were equipped with boots. They looked more like gang members than members of a disciplined army.

After a period of contemplation, Gaddafi proclaimed the Socialist People's Libyan Arab Jamahiriya and released the first volume of *The Green Book,* which outlined his concept of direct democracy with no political parties. The country thereafter would be governed by its populace through local popular councils and communes. A General People's Committee (GPCO) would serve as the country's executive cabinet.

Gaddafi resigned as the head of the General People's Congress (GPC) and was thereafter known as the Leader of the Revolution. But it was really all a ruse. Absolute power still rested with him as supreme commander of the armed forces and the embodiment of what Gaddafi called direct people's power. The popular councils (also known as revolutionary committees) were used to spy on the population and repress any opposition to Gaddafi's autocratic rule.

Eventually the truth caught up with him, as it had with other despots.

When the six Americans reached Immigration, a young man with a wispy beard and thinning hair stepped forward and said, "*Salaam alaikum.*"

Because he had an olive complexion and was casually dressed in a tan shirt and wrinkled brown pants, Crocker assumed he was a local. "*Salaam alaikum* to you."

The man squinted through gold-rimmed glasses and smiled. "You're Tom Crocker, right? I'm Douglas Volman from the U.S. embassy."

"Hey, Doug. Nice to meet you."

"Welcome to Tripoli. Follow me."

The six casually dressed "engineers" followed Volman and his driver, whom Volman introduced as Mustafa, out the arched terminal entrance to a large black SUV parked at the curb.

Mustafa wore a green baseball cap with a Playboy Bunny logo embroidered on it. This struck Crocker as too casual for a local employee of the CIA.

"Who'd you say you work for again?" he asked Volman as they started loading their luggage in back.

Volman flashed his diplomatic ID. "I'm a political counselor at the U.S. embassy."

"State Department?"

"Yeah, Foreign Service."

Made sense. He seemed smart, well educated—and soft.

They sped through the city on a highway littered with abandoned, stripped cars and garbage. Traffic was chaotic and moved extremely fast. From the passenger seat, Volman turned to face them. He chewed a piece of gum as he spoke.

"Libyans are the friendliest, warmest people in the world. But everyone's on edge now that Gaddafi is gone."

"I thought they'd be happy."

"Some are. Many aren't. He remained a popular figure with a large segment of the population even until the end. He created a standard of living here that's higher than that of Brazil."

"No kidding."

Approaching the sea, they passed a modern complex made up of five eighteen-story buildings. "Those are the El Emad towers, built by Gaddafi in 1990. They house most of the foreign companies doing business here—oil, telecommunications, construction."

The skyline boasted a few other modern office towers. The rest of the city seemed to be made up of two- to four-story concrete structures painted white and beige. Domes and minarets marked the locations of the numerous mosques. Slogans in Arabic had been painted on many walls. Some of them depicted a cartoonish Gaddafi asking, "Who am I?"—a reference to one of his last televised speeches, in which he vowed to fight house to house, alley to alley, and taunted the rebels with the question "Who are you?" Others, directed at the interim government, asked, "Where are you?"

Akil translated another that said: "Because the price was the blood of our children, let's unify, let's show some tolerance and let's live together."

Crocker saw black flags stenciled everywhere—on doors, on the sides of cars, on sidewalks.

"What's with the black flags?" he asked.

"They stand for al-Qaeda," Volman said. "The Arab inscription under them is the *shahada,* the Islamic creed, which states, 'There is no god but Allah, and Mohammed is the messenger.' "

"They seem to have a strong presence here."

Volman said, "Tonight you're staying at the Bab al Sahr Hotel." He screwed up his mouth in a sour expression.

"Nasty, huh?"

"It's one of the top hotels in town. The owners claim it's a five-star. Could be, if they mean five out of fifty."

"We'll be fine." As long as it had a bed, Crocker didn't care. Unless it was infested with rats and the roof leaked, he'd been in worse.

The Bab al Sahr didn't look bad from outside—a sand-colored semimodern fifteen-story tower with weird, eye-shaped windows. It faced the Mediterranean, which stank of dead fish and rubbish. To get in they had to pass through a metal detector manned by two young men holding automatic weapons.

"Nice touch," observed Crocker.

The lobby reeked of cigarette smoke and BO. The decor reminded Crocker of an office waiting room from the sixties—one that had never been aired out. Functional chairs, sofas, and lamps were arranged around plain coffee tables. A few groups of dark-suited Middle Eastern men sat huddled together, talking in whispers.

At the front desk, Mancini pointed to a comment a former guest had written in the guest book: "Come back, Basil Fawlty. All is forgiven."

Crocker, a fan of the British sitcom *Fawlty Towers*, laughed out loud.

Volman said, "I'll give you time to get settled. At eight p.m. I'll take you to see Al Cowens. He's attending an event tonight at the Sheraton. It's the NATO coordinator's good-bye party. "

As the CIA station chief, Cowens would be coordinating their mission. Crocker considered him old school, which meant that he wasn't an analyst or an academic. He was a hard-drinking, hard-working, hands-on guy who loved running operations. He and Crocker had briefly worked together tracking down a group of narco-terrorists in the jungles of Peru. One night they were awakened by the screams of a woman in a hut nearby. By candlelight, they had helped her through a very difficult breech birth.

"How far's the Sheraton?" Crocker asked.

"It's a new place near the marina, a couple of clicks west."

The six SEALs were sharing three rooms on the eighth floor with views of a broken-down playground and the sea. Crocker and Akil followed a little old man with bowed legs who was wearing a faded green tunic. After explaining to Akil that he was a state employee and hadn't been paid in four months, he opened a door with a key and stepped aside.

"Bathroom on right," he said in accented English.

"Thanks."

Crocker set down his bag and heard running water. Thought maybe the toilet was broken. Turning his head toward the shower door, he saw a naked woman. Dark-haired. Attractive.

Seeing him, she screamed and attempted to cover herself.

"Excuse me," he said, backing out. "Wrong room."

After two more attempts the bellhop found an empty

one—empty except for the half-eaten chicken someone had left behind in the wastebasket. The bellhop took care of that, for which he was tipped five U.S. dollars.

"At your service, sir. At your very excellent service," he repeated bowing and backing out the door.

Thirty minutes later they were sitting outside by the pool, drinking warm sodas. The bartender explained that the ice maker wasn't working, and beer and other alcoholic beverages weren't permitted in the hotel. In fact, the consumption, production, and importation of alcohol was illegal in Libya.

As he stared at the pool, which was filled with dark, dirty water, Crocker wondered how Holly was getting along in Egypt, which shared a border with Libya to the east. He remembered the first time they had met, when they were both married to other people, their first date at a little Italian restaurant in Virginia Beach, the dress she was wearing, her lustrous dark eyes and hair, her strength of character in dealing with various family tragedies, and the vacations they'd been on together—cave diving in Mexico, whitewater rafting on the Colorado River, surfing in Hawaii, climbing Mount Kilimanjaro.

Even after a decade of marriage, it lifted his spirits to think of her.

"You think they clean it for the summer?" Davis asked, jerking Crocker out of his thoughts.

"Clean what?"

"The pool."

"Beats me."

Mancini reported that the restaurants and nightlife in Tripoli were reputed to be less than great. And since the war they were probably a notch lower. He, Cal, and

Ritchie decided to follow Akil to the old section of the city, which was within walking distance, where they figured they'd find some decent local dishes—*utshu* (a ball of dough in a bowl of sauce), couscous, *m'batten* (a fried potato stuffed with meat and herbs).

"Stay out of trouble," Crocker warned.

"Fat chance."

Davis chose to accompany Crocker. They were in the same black SUV, with Mustafa at the wheel and Doug Volman in the passenger seat, racing through the city at breakneck speed, screeching down narrow streets. Most of the traffic lights at the intersections didn't seem to be working, so each time they approached one it was like playing a game of chicken.

The Sheraton was just a few miles down the Corniche, the highway that paralleled the shore, but Volman took this opportunity to give them a quick tour of downtown—the old quarter, the medina, Green Square—the center of the anti-Gaddafi protests, now renamed Martyrs' Square—the Ottoman clock tower, the Roman arch of Marcus Aurelius, the Italianate cathedral.

As they cruised the mostly empty streets, Volman offered up a running commentary from the front seat. "The whole country's stuck in this weird form of suspended animation. No one knows what's going to happen next. Take this city, for example. There are over two hundred different militias controlling various neighborhoods, claiming they're trying to enforce order. Some are small neighborhood committees, others are bigger and more aggressive. You've got the Zintan, which controls the airport, the Misurata managing most of the refugee camps to the south."

"They fight?" Crocker asked.

"Sometimes. NATO commanders and most U.S. embassy officials will tell you that violence is under control and the NTC is getting its act together. But most of our reps here only talk to the top guys in the NTC, who tell them what they want to hear. The reality is different. The NTC is basically trying to figure out how to divide up the revenue from the oil exports. The whole country is walking on eggshells. More and more people are showing up dead and tortured. The security situation sucks."

"Thanks, Doug," Davis said, "for painting such a rosy picture."

"My parents were refugees from Hungary. They taught me to call things the way I see them, no matter how unpleasant they might be."

Seconds after Volman said this, a peal of automatic fire echoed through the narrow streets to their left. Mustafa turned into an alley as more gunfire erupted in front of them, lighting up the night sky.

Crocker said, "It's probably better to keep moving."

Volman nodded. "Yeah. Let's head back to the coast."

Mustafa backed up and turned right, burning rubber. Volman crouched down in the passenger seat and pointed out a dark building surrounded by a high metal fence on their left.

"That used to be the women's military academy."

Crocker saw no women on the streets, only a handful of men who ducked into buildings and vehicles seeking cover. Storeowners quickly pulled their wares inside and closed up their shops.

The gunfire, which seemed to be coming from the south, grew closer.

"How far are we from the Sheraton?" Crocker asked. He and Davis were unarmed.

Volman's hands trembled as he spoke. "I'm getting tired of this shit."

"How far away are we?"

"Maybe a quarter mile."

A huge explosion illuminated the street in front of them and lifted up the front of the SUV. It came down with a crash, tossing the four men up and down like bouncing toys.

Mustafa and Volman both lurched forward and smacked the windshield. The former started bleeding from his nose; the latter held his head and moaned. Crocker climbed over the seat to check them out. Neither wound looked serious.

"Hold your head back," he told Mustafa. "Squeeze here," showing him where to pinch his fingers near the bridge of his nose.

Volman complained that he couldn't find his glasses and couldn't see without them. Crocker pushed Mustafa to the back seat, got behind the wheel, shut off the headlights, and gunned the engine.

"Direct me to the hotel," he shouted.

"I told you, I can't see."

"Help me out, Mustafa."

"Straight ahead, sir."

He tried several times, but couldn't shift the vehicle out of second gear. Secondary explosions lit up the sky.

"What's the problem?" Davis asked.

"The clutch is fucked. Keep your heads down."

Volman said, "The Japanese embassy is nearby. We can find shelter there."

"Forget the Japanese embassy. Direct me to the hotel."

"Stay on this road, sir."

Closing in on the Mediterranean, they entered a cloud of orange-gray smoke. Directly ahead of them a fire was burning. Flames shot up above the buildings and turned the sea beyond a sinister shade of red.

Off the Corniche, down a side street, Crocker saw the shattered front of what looked like a modern eight-story hotel. Three high marble arches formed what remained of the entrance.

"I smell smoke," Volman said, poking his head up over the dashboard.

"It's the Sheraton, sir," Mustafa offered. "Looks like it's been attacked."

To the right, past smaller white guesthouses and palms, Crocker saw a marina.

"Turn this thing around and get us out of here!" Volman shouted.

Crocker drove within a hundred feet of the hotel entrance and stopped. Cars were fleeing the hotel, steering wildly. A Mercedes with a shattered windshield crashed into another Mercedes in front of it. Crocker pulled up on the sidewalk and parked. "Let's get out here, Davis. Stick together."

"What are you doing? What about us?"

"Wait here," Crocker said to Volman and Mustafa. "We'll be back."

They ran, squeezing past cars and frenzied people streaming past. Flames rose to the left around some palm trees near the entrance. Crocker saw the burning carcass of what looked like it had once been a delivery truck near a checkpoint at the end of the block. Flames rose from several other overturned cars nearby. One had landed hood-first in a fountain.

The explosion had left a gaping hole in one corner of the building. The place looked like some huge creature had taken a bite out of it. There was shattered glass everywhere. People moaning, screaming, calling out names, asking for help in various languages—English, Dutch, Arabic, French.

Dozens poured out of the smoking structure, stepping over burnt bodies, walking, stumbling, and running in all directions. Some were injured, others looked perfectly fine except for the horrified looks on their faces. Others stared ahead blankly, like the man in a suit who staggered by with blood running down his face, calmly smoking a cigarette.

The torso of a uniformed man lay in the street. His arms and legs had been blown off. His head was a gory mess of brains and shattered bone.

Crocker expected sirens but heard none.

As they approached the entrance, gunfire rang out. People jumped behind trees and walls or threw themselves to the pavement. Crocker and Davis crouched behind a planter overflowing with red bougainvillea.

"Sounds like the shots are coming from inside," Davis shouted.

"That's odd," Crocker said, looking for soldiers or security guards and finding none.

"Real odd."

"Maybe we should circle around back."

They rose together and almost tripped over a stout middle-aged woman holding up a bleeding man. The man's face was injured.

The woman screamed in a language Crocker didn't understand. The man stumbled and grabbed his neck.

With Davis's help, Crocker sat the man down on the ground, against the wall of the entrance. Then he started to reach down his throat.

The woman shouted, "No! No!" shaking her head, slipping into hysteria.

Crocker nodded at Davis, who held her back.

The man's windpipe was blocked with blood and broken teeth. Crocker swept them free and fished them out of his mouth. The man coughed and started to breathe normally. The gash across his cheek and mouth was serious but not life threatening.

With no medical kit available, Crocker removed his own black polo shirt and held it against the man's face. Then he grabbed the woman's hand. "Hold this here and wait for an ambulance. Your husband will be okay."

"Wait?"

"*Attendez,*" Crocker said, remembering one of the few words he knew in French.

"*Attendez, oui.*" She nodded her head, then kissed his cheek.

The firing from inside had picked up. More people were running out in panic. Some wore uniforms; some men, suits. Women were clothed in cocktail gowns and dresses. Many of them abandoned their high heels, which littered the tile floor.

Crocker saw someone who looked American and stopped him.

"Where's the party for the NATO chief?"

"The party?"

"Yeah. Where's Al Cowens?"

"Out of my way!"

Crocker grabbed him firmly by the shoulders. "Al Cowens from the U.S. embassy? You know him?"

"Don't go in there! Men are shooting. Lots of dead. It's fucked."

He entered the building with Davis at his side. The lobby was littered with the injured and bleeding. Blood was smeared everywhere. A lot of the lights were out. Smoke. A Muzak version of "Copacabana" by Barry Manilow played over the PA, adding a surreal element.

People were screaming, moaning, crashing into things, asking for help.

The two SEALs followed the sound of gunfire past the lobby, down a hall to the other end of the building. Turning left, they entered what looked to be a brasserie-type restaurant that faced a pool and, beyond that, the beach.

Because it stood at the back of the building, the restaurant seemed to have escaped damage from the explosion, but tables had been overturned and people were hiding behind them. He saw bodies in the corners.

"What the—"

Before he could complete his question, an explosion threw Crocker against the back wall.

He landed on his right shoulder, picked himself up, and found Davis near a banquette, holding his head, looking woozy.

"You okay?"

No answer.

"Davis, can you hear me?"

He couldn't. So Crocker did a quick inspection of his head and neck. Saw no external injuries, but his eyes were dilated and unfocused, indicating that he might have suffered a concussion.

There wasn't anything Crocker could do for him now. He said, "Wait here."

Gunshots went off and ricocheted off the walls and floor. Glass flew everywhere. People screamed. He ducked behind a table and slithered on his belly through air thick with the smell of cordite and smoke.

Reaching two NATO soldiers in light blue uniforms who lay in a heap along the right wall, he discovered that neither was breathing or had a pulse. He relieved them of their weapons—some sort of automatic pistol from one, an MP5 with a collapsible stock from the other. Both were loaded and seemingly in working order.

He peered through the shattered windows facing the back and saw men by the pool spraying the brasserie with bullets from automatic weapons held at their hips. Rambo-style, he thought. Black turbans, scarves hiding their faces.

Fucking cowards!

He watched a bearded man in a black T-shirt remove the pin of a grenade with his teeth. Before he had a chance to throw it, Crocker took aim and cut him down at the knees. The man fell backward as the grenade exploded, throwing him into the pool.

When the smoke cleared, he saw the man's legless body floating next to a woman who was facedown in the blue water. Her dress billowed out like large pink fins.

Holly's image flashed in his head, reminding him that the dead woman in the pool was someone's wife or girlfriend. This added to his rage.

Sons of bitches!

Spotting the shadows of the armed men retreating, he aimed and fired. One man stumbled and slid. Crocker ran across the patio to the far side of the pool, knelt on the terra-cotta tiles, and fired again. A group of attackers had turned right and were running in the direction of the marina. Crocker suspected that a boat or truck was waiting to pick them up and help them escape. He wasn't going to let that happen.

Smoke rising from the fire behind him, he brought down two of them with bursts from the MP5. A little dark-skinned teenager in a sleeveless T-shirt crouched beside him and toppled another. The scrawny teenager turned to Crocker, smiled with a mouthful of jumbled and broken teeth, and flashed a thumbs-up. He had big eyes that caught the light. Beside him were three other young men, all dressed in T-shirts and jeans. The black tee of one had SURFER printed on it. They were holding AKs that looked almost as big as they were.

Crocker had no time to ask them who they were and which group they were affiliated with. He was glad that, like him, they were trying to stop the terrorists, who probably outnumbered them three to one.

A helicopter circled around the hotel tower and swooped over the water. Its spotlight illuminated roughly a dozen men armed with automatic weapons and rocket-propelled grenades escaping down the beach. One of them stopped, took aim at the helicopter, and fired his RPG before Crocker could take him down. The rocket whooshed and smashed into the copter's side. The resulting explosion splashed everything with white light and numbed Crocker's ears. The copter's rear rotor continued spinning in the sky as the cockpit plummeted into the sea.

Pieces of hot shrapnel screamed through the air, stuck in the sand around them. One of the teenagers fell. He started moaning and kicking wildly.

"Where was he hit?" Crocker asked.

One of the other teens ran over to help his injured friend and was struck in the back by a volley of bullets.

Crocker shouted, "Stay down! Stay down!" as he lay facedown in the sand and returned fire. He asked himself, "Where is security? Where the fuck is NATO? How come we're the only ones shooting back?"

The attackers fired rockets in their direction, then retreated. One exploded in the sand in front of Crocker. Others screeched over his head.

He got up, spit out the grit in his mouth, and gave chase. But when he stopped to fire, the mag in the MP5 ran out. He didn't have another. When he tried to fire the pistol, it jammed.

"Piece of shit!"

Still he gave chase. Reaching the first fallen attacker, he kicked him in the face, then relieved him of his AK, which was still hot.

The sand was a bitch to run in. Made him remember his younger brother and how they used to play on the beach when they were kids. His brother now owned several car dealerships north of Boston. Meanwhile, he was halfway around the world getting shot at by terrorists.

Nearing the marina, he sensed someone running beside him. It was the kid in the sleeveless T-shirt with the big eyes and uneven teeth.

Who is he?

Sounds of chaos continued beyond his shoulder. He knelt and fired at the attackers ahead who were jumping on motorcycles and climbing into the back of a pickup parked alongside the marina. Bullets skidded off the pavement and slammed into the cab of the truck. The kid beside him hit the rider of one of the motorcycles in the chest.

"Good shot!"

The bike spun, hit the curb with an eruption of sparks, and threw its rider into the bushes along the canal.

Crocker ran over and righted the bike. Jumped on and gunned the engine.

The kid sprinted to the canal, shot the rider again, then jumped on the back. A smooth customer.

Pointing the motorcycle toward the Corniche, Crocker pulled back on the throttle. The bike roared and took off.

For the first time he heard sirens approaching, which pleased him.

Finally!

But the bike wouldn't pick up speed. He heard scraping from the back wheel.

Maybe the axle is messed up.

He got about fifty yards down the Corniche and stopped, his heart pounding.

"Motherfuckers!"

He looked at the kid with the big eyes and the tangle of dark hair that stood straight up.

The kid grinned and repeated, "Mutha-fukka."

They knelt on the pavement and fired until they ran out of ammo. Then hurried together back across the beach to where the kid's two buddies were lying. The one who was shot in the back had bled out and was dead, but the other was still breathing. Crocker removed the kid's SURFER T-shirt and pressed it against two bullet holes near his hip.

"Hold it there until we can get him to a hospital. He'll be okay."

The kid with the big eyes grinned and raised his thumb. He was a brave little guy, whoever he was.

Pointing to his chest, he said, "Farag."

"Tom Crocker. I'm going to help the people inside."

"Very good. Good man."

"Good luck, Farag. And thanks."

Back in the brasserie, Crocker spent the next hour giving CPR and trying to clear airways and stop bleeding, using towels and pillows and the pathetically meager emergency medical supplies on hand. People were missing hands, parts of legs. They'd been shot in every place imaginable, struck with shrapnel, burned.

His hands and arms were covered with blood, and he was wrapping a sock around a man's arm as a tourniquet when someone tapped him on the shoulder. Turning, he saw a NATO doctor and nurse standing behind him, light blue masks over their faces.

Emergency lights were now burning, powered by a portable generator, and he saw the room clearly for the first time. The scene was gruesome. Blood smeared everywhere. Piles of bodies. Reminded him of a documentary he'd once watched about a slaughterhouse in Chicago.

At least the wounded were being carried out on stretchers. Nurses, paramedics, and doctors were taking charge, directing armor-clad NATO soldiers.

"Have you seen Al Cowens?" he asked.

Someone pointed to a pile of bodies near the far wall.

"Really?"

"I'm sorry."

"Which one?"

The man shrugged.

He searched and found Cowens near the bottom, the top left side of his head and face missing, and his tongue hanging out. Crocker sat on the floor, rested his back against the wall, and covered his face with his hands, exhausted. Completely spent. "It isn't Al," he mumbled to himself. "It's just his body. Al, rest his soul, has hopefully gone to a better place. God bless him."

CHAPTER SIX

The wound that bleedeth inwardly is the most dangerous.

—Arab proverb

HE DREAMT that he was bleeding from a hole in his stomach and trying to get it to stop. His blood kept pouring out. It flowed into a clear hose that led to a fountain. Buzzards drank from it.

He woke up in a sweat, lying on a single bed in an unfamiliar room. An African mask staring at him from the opposite wall. Alicia Keys singing from a stereo in another room.

While he was washing his face in the bathroom, a woman with a blue scarf tied around her head entered the bedroom with food and fresh tangerine juice on a tray. Sunlight created a sharp angle on the floor. Through the doorway he saw a courtyard with a lemon tree.

"Where am I?" he asked her.

Smiling, she said, "Palm City."

"Palm City. Where's that?"

"It's in Janzour."

"Oh..." He remembered the woman in the hotel shower, Doug Volman crouched in the front seat of the SUV, flames rising from the front of the Sheraton.

He'd forgotten about Volman and Mustafa. And he hadn't seen Davis since leaving him in the brasserie.

What the hell happened to them? he asked himself.

"This home of...Mr. Remington," the local woman said.

"Remington?"

"Yes."

Crocker didn't know the name. He felt disoriented, perplexed.

"Mr. Remington is American?"

She nodded. "Yes."

She returned a minute later with clean boxers, a T-shirt, a dark green polo shirt, black workout pants. "For you."

"Thanks."

Standing under a warm shower, he felt sharp pains in his back. His whole right side was sore and bruised. The muscles in both arms were tired and tight. Otherwise, he seemed intact. Alive.

Not like Al Cowens, with his tongue hanging out of his mouth.

He dressed and entered the courtyard, where an orange cat was stalking a little bird with an orange beak—a finch maybe. Looked up at the sky above and saw the sun at approximately 9 a.m. The angle of the light reminded him of Southern California, when he was a young member of SEAL Team One living in a double-wide trailer with his first wife. She'd kept spice finches as pets.

A tall African American man in khaki pants and a white shirt entered. The lines in his face were deep.

"Crocker," he said. "My name's Jaime Remington. I'm Al's deputy. Rather, I *was* his deputy. I'm running the station now."

"Al."

"Yeah…It's terrible. I just got off the phone with his wife. She's in California. They were living apart."

"Children?"

"Two daughters. One married; the other a junior at Fresno State."

The image of his dead body flashed before Crocker's eyes.

"Fucking tragic. I saw him last night at the Sheraton."

"I heard you were there in the middle of everything."

"Yeah."

"We're all in shock…How did you sleep?"

"So-so."

"I'm kind of in a fog myself. But here's the situation…You were brought to my house last night."

"I don't remember."

"Your men are being moved to a guesthouse near the embassy. You'll meet them there later."

"What about Davis?"

"Who's he?"

"A member of my team. He was with me at the Sheraton last night, in the brasserie."

"What about him?"

"He was hurt. I want to know if he's alright."

"I'll ask. What's his last name?"

"Davis. John Davis. I left two more people in an SUV out front. Doug Volman and a driver named Mustafa."

"Volman's resting. The embassy doctor said he'll be fine. Mustafa is back at work."

"What's wrong with Volman?"

"High blood pressure and heart palpitations. Look, I'm about to leave for NATO headquarters. I'd like you to come with me, if you feel up to it."

"I'm fine."

"Finish your breakfast."

"No appetite. Let's go."

A weird calm hung over the city. Crocker had no idea in which direction they were headed. All he was aware of was movement, the sunlight, and the automatic pistol Remington held in his hand as they sat in the backseat. A bodyguard with an Uzi and sunglasses sat in the passenger seat. A backup car behind them held more armed guards.

They were speeding; tires screeched around turns. Everyone seemed tense. The muscles around Remington's mouth twitched.

A thousand thoughts were flying through Crocker's head—Davis, Al Cowens, the attackers, the kid who had helped him, the helicopter that blew up in the sky.

He noticed that the safety on Remington's pistol was off. He was about to say something but stopped.

He tried to think clearly. *First I have to find out if Davis is alright. Then I have to ascertain if what happened last night affects our mission.*

His head felt thick and heavy on his shoulders.

"How many casualties?" he asked.

"We counted twenty, but more bodies are still being recovered. Another fifty-seven spent the night in various local hospitals. We've got doctors and nurses out checking on them now."

"How many Americans?"

"Five, including Cowens."

They were speeding east along the coast, which was mostly barren. It reminded him of the desert. The majority of the nearby buildings were ravaged—bombed out, burned, pockmarked with bullets. Arabic graffiti scrawled over everything. More black flags.

They turned and stopped at a heavily fortified gate. The blue-and-white NATO flag flew at half mast. Soldiers in battle fatigues and blue helmets leaned into the windows of the SUV, anxiously scanned their faces, checked a clipboard, then waved them in.

Through the waves of heat rising from the sand he saw a runway, a control tower, and several badly damaged buildings. Tall palm trees in the distance. They stopped at a long three-story building that was under repair. Men on scaffolds were painting it a funny mustard color that seemed to clash with the vivid blue sky.

Crocker wondered if the local construction workers could be trusted, which reminded him a little of Iraq, where you couldn't distinguish your enemies from your friends.

That sense of uncertainty put him on edge.

"This is it," Remington announced, stashing his pistol in the SUV door's pocket and grabbing his briefcase.

"This is what?"

Remington was already bounding ahead, sunglasses reflecting the strong sun. Crocker had to move fast to catch up.

Tall, good-looking African soldiers in dark green uniforms stood at attention and saluted as they entered.

Asian soldiers on duty inside wore odd-colored camouflage and maroon berets. On the chest of one, Crocker read MONGOLIA.

"What are we doing here?" Crocker asked. "What's the agenda?"

"The absolute disaster last night," Remington said out of the side of his mouth.

He had the long legs and stride of a runner. Crocker followed him up a flight of stairs and into a crowded conference room. The table was covered with papers, cups, half-empty water bottles. A mélange of nationalities and uniforms.

Three dozen weary-looking men and one woman were focused on a tall man at the head of the table. His face was grim and creased with concern. He wore frameless oval glasses and an ironed khaki shirt with red bars on the collar. On his epaulets shone three gold stars.

"Communication," he said in a British accent as he kneaded his hands. "The lack of it, primarily. That's what we're dealing with here. We've spoken about this problem week after week for months. Now we're faced with a tragedy. A terrible tragedy. Is this what had to happen before we learn this basic lesson?"

His tone and words didn't seem to fit the situation. Way too scholarly and intellectual, Crocker thought.

One of the men at the table said, with tears in his eyes, "We had no warning, general. None at all."

Then several of them started speaking at once. They were all excited, emotional, and stressed. A stocky Italian officer with close-cropped gray hair stood and tried to shout down the others.

"It's an insult to all of us! A kick in the nuts!"

Someone else shouted, "We can't operate like this... like stupid sitting ducks! What's our role here, general? Define the mission."

The British general clapped his hands and said, "First, we need to cooperate. Communication works for those who work at it. This isn't communication. It's shouting."

"And accusations!" the Italian added.

"What happened to the Italians who were supposed to establish an outer perimeter around the hotel?" the only woman in the room asked.

The Italian waved a sheet of paper and threw it on the table. "Read the order! We were scheduled to relieve the Dutch at 2200 hours. The outer perimeter was the responsibility of the French."

A French officer stood up. "That's false! The order says, and I quote, 'Platoon Henri IV will be deployed at the discretion of the watch commander.' We never received a call from the commander."

"Untrue."

"Gentlemen, please!" the general said, trying to establish order.

Crocker had a hard time keeping the faces straight.

"Clearly, we have considerable work to do," the general added.

"That's an understatement."

Someone disagreed. "The problem's not communication, it's cooperation. And how can we cooperate if members of the alliance have different goals?"

It was a good question, but Crocker didn't know enough about the situation there to know what the speaker meant.

The British general cleared his throat. "Let's talk for

a minute about the specifics of what happened last night. My executive officer, Colonel Anthony Hollins, has drafted a damage and assessment report. Listen carefully."

He nodded to a thin, sandy-haired man with a pinched face, who pushed his hair off his forehead and spoke in a high, officious voice. "Last night we experienced a massive breakdown in security."

No shit.

"Instead of six squadrons of soldiers patrolling the streets around the hotel, we had two on duty. The Dutch who were there fought like heroes."

The men at the table turned to a tall Dutch lieutenant colonel and nodded.

The British general said, "Thank you, colonel, and my condolences to your fallen and their families."

Hollins continued, "The Dutch suffered the greatest number of casualties. Ten dead, four others severely wounded."

The general cut in. "I want to say that the men who were there fought valiantly. We should all be extremely proud of them."

Men slapped the table and exclaimed, "Hear! Hear!"

The British general lowered his head in silent prayer. When he was finished, the people around the table started murmuring again all at once.

Hollins raised his voice. "Ladies and gentlemen, if it weren't for the swift action of our soldiers on the scene, the results could have been much worse. Let's keep that in mind as we look at how this tragedy unfolded."

A diagram of the streets in front of the Sheraton appeared on the wall behind Hollins. With the aid of a laser pointer, he explained how at approximately 2015 hours the previous night a truck carrying explosives had tried to back up to the front entrance of the hotel.

Crocker knew that once a suicide bomber got into proximity to a target there wasn't much you could do but pray.

Hollins described how a NATO jeep with two Dutch soldiers inside had quickly moved behind the truck to block its access. That's when the driver of the truck ignited the thousand pounds of ANFO, ammonium nitrate/fuel oil, he was carrying.

Crocker found it painful to sit and listen. He'd attended hundreds of such meetings following terrorist bombings, raids, and other operations—in SPECWAR (Naval Special Warfare) they called them hot washes. But this one was particularly difficult as he kept flashing back to the carnage from the night before.

He had no appetite for the grilled chicken and hummus sandwiches that were served. Nor was he interested in the bottles of wine the Italian passed around.

After lunch Jaime Remington spoke. According to the CIA's analysis, terrorists had attacked in four directions. Forty to fifty men took part, armed with AK-47s, RPGs, explosives, and grenades. They had escaped in two directions, east and west, and left behind seven dead. None of the dead men were carrying personal items or wallets. No group had so far issued a statement taking credit.

Several of the dead attackers had the features of Tuareg tribesmen.

"Can you describe those features specifically?" the British general asked.

"They're generally taller, solidly built, copper complexions, large black eyes, finely shaped noses."

No mention of Anaruz Mohammed, the Chinese, Iranians, or al-Qaeda.

"You know what Tuareg means?" the Italian asked.

"People of the blue veil?"

"Abandoned by God."

"You'd feel abandoned by God, too, if you lived in that bloody desert."

Crocker sat with his hands folded on the table in front of him, wondering when this meeting was going to end. The most important thing he learned was that the terrorists had fled approximately fifteen kilometers east of the city, near the site of a major refugee camp.

As the hours dragged by he realized that although he was the only one in the room who had actually been at the hotel, no one was going to bother to ask him anything. He left confused and pissed off.

The sky to their right was turning bright red by the time they arrived at the U.S. embassy compound, which looked more like a house than an office building. Remington explained that these were temporary quarters. The original embassy had been ransacked by pro-Gaddafi mobs on May 2, 2011 (the same day Bin Laden was taken out in Pakistan), after the strongman's son Saif al-Arab and three of his grandchildren were killed in a NATO air strike. Remington described how the embassy had been completely totaled—balustrades ripped off, photocopiers and air-conditioning units smashed to smithereens, cabinets wrenched open and overturned. Whole floors were doused in gasoline and burned.

The temporary compound was crammed with armed men wearing body armor. As he stepped out of the SUV, Crocker glimpsed a sign that listed all the items visitors were prohibited from carrying onto the property, including lighters, matches, radios, mobile phones, laptop computers, MP3 players, and flash drives.

They sat in a small first-floor conference room—Crocker, Remington, and a dozen other men. The air was thick with humidity. Crocker reached for the bottle of water in front of him, then saw a short man with red hair lean toward Remington and whisper into his ear. Remington turned to Crocker and nodded.

"What's up?"

Remington said, "I need to talk to you outside."

"Sure."

Remington pointed to the man who had followed them into the corridor and said, "This is John Lasher. He works for us and has compiled a list of former Gaddafi bases and chemical plants that Cowens wanted you to survey."

Lasher had piercing blue eyes.

"I thought maybe our priorities had shifted," Crocker said.

Remington nodded. "You mean in terms of what happened last night?"

"My men and I would be more than happy to go after the attackers and nail their asses."

"You mean bring them to justice, right?"

"Bring them to justice, or shoot them in the head. Same thing."

It was the first time he'd seen Remington smile. He said, "I like your attitude, Crocker. But NATO's going to want to handle that."

Based on what he'd just seen and heard, he figured it would take the NATO command weeks to get their act together. By that time the perpetrators would have vanished—or, worse, carried out other attacks.

Remington said, "Given your experience as a SPECWAR WMD officer, I want you to work with John here and check the list. But you need to do it discreetly. The ambassador is wary of doing anything that makes it seem that we don't trust or might be usurping authority from the interim government."

"Of course."

Back in the meeting room, Crocker listened to more distressed reports from frustrated, embarrassed, angry men. The only difference this time was that all of them were Americans—CIA case officers, military attachés, members of the embassy political section. He spotted Doug Volman in the corner, looking pale and worried.

Still no mention of Anaruz Mohammed.

The men described again how security at the Sheraton was lax. How reports about the effectiveness of the NTC were overblown. Its weak and disorganized central security apparatus still wasn't willing or able to stop reprisals against former Gaddafi loyalists. Looting continued throughout the country. Cars were robbed; houses were broken into; women raped. Rival militias controlled different sectors of the city. All of them were basically looking after their own interests—namely, money and power in the new government.

The embassy was reluctant to put pressure on the NTC because they were competing with the French for influence with the new Libyan government. Their primary focus seemed to be the political maneuvering going on behind the scenes. The prize: the lucrative contracts that would be handed out to service and maintain Libya's substantial oil industry.

Internal security, though troublesome, was less of a concern. Nobody wanted to alienate the leaders of the NTC.

Crocker left two hours later, angry, tired, and depressed. Doug Volman, smelling like he needed a shower and a change of clothes, joined him in the hall.

"Didn't I tell you?" Volman asked.

"You did."

"Nobody wants to talk about the political vacuum that was created when we helped force out Gaddafi. Or the opportunity we've created for al-Qaeda, or other Islamic fundamentalists, or countries like Iran and China."

"What about Anaruz Mohammed?" Crocker asked. "Would you include him, too?"

Volman, seeing John Lasher approaching, lowered his voice to a whisper. "Anaruz is a simple kid who's garnered a lot of media attention because of his background. He hasn't proved that he can generate much of anything on his own."

"Take everything he tells you with a big grain of salt," Lasher muttered after Volman left. Then he informed Crocker that Remington was going to take him to meet the ambassador. Crocker said he wanted to meet the embassy security chief first.

"Make it quick," Lasher answered. "I'll be waiting outside the ambassador's office on the second floor."

The head of security was Leo Debray, a huge man with a smashed-in nose and a big, sunburned face. He had a marine flag on the wall of his little office and pictures of himself as a fighter standing in various boxing rings and gyms.

"What can I do you for?" he asked with a crooked smile. Although friendly, he radiated violence.

"I'm trying to connect with my wife, Holly Crocker. I heard she's in Cairo conducting a security survey."

Debray leaned back in his chair with his hands behind his head and howled, "Holy shit! You mean to tell me Holly is your wife?"

"That's right."

"Well, ain't that something. Great gal. She's been a big help. You're one of the civil engineers, right?"

"That's correct."

"She know you're here?"

"As a matter of fact, she doesn't."

"Holy shit! You undercover?" He lowered his voice. "Is she not supposed to know?"

Crocker: "I didn't plan to be here, and didn't have a chance to inform her. Can you tell me where she's located now?"

"Holly, let's see..." He leaned back again. "Well, I assume you know she was staying at the Sheraton the night before last."

Crocker's blood turned cold. "No!"

"Jesus, man, I'm sorry. I should have told you first, she's fine! She wasn't even there at the time of the attack."

"Thank God."

"She and her colleague finished up early in Cairo and stopped here on their way to Tunisia. They're due back in Libya to eyeball our consulate in Benghazi any day now. That puppy's in pretty ragged shape."

Crocker felt relieved. "The consulate in Benghazi?"

"Yup. Whole town had the shit kicked out of it by the colonel's hooligans and mercenaries. The uprising started there, so when the colonel's forces retook the city, they punished the joint. Sacked our consulate in the process. Nice touch, huh?"

Crocker had had his fill of Libyan history for one day. "When is she expected back?"

"Holly and Brian? I thought they were coming back today. Wait here. I'll check."

Debray returned a few minutes later with a short woman in her thirties. Dirty blond hair cut short, blue slacks, blue oxford shirt, a tattoo of a rose covering the back of her hand.

"Kat Hamilton."

"Hi, Kat. Tom Crocker."

She bounced from one side to another, and spoke with a Pittsburgh accent, turning "ows" into "ahs." "Yeah, Holly's great," she said. "Flew to Tunisia yesterday morning. With Brian. You know Brian?"

"Brian Shaw?"

"Yeah. You know him?"

"Sure do." Brian Shaw was a good-looking guy in State Department Security, about ten years younger than Crocker and a couple of inches taller. A former major league pitcher, he'd been going through a bad divorce. Holly was giving him advice and support.

Kat said, "Everybody talks about the friggin' Arab Spring and how wonderful it was, and all that. They forget to mention that most of our facilities got trashed in the process. It's gonna cost us a fortune."

"She's okay?"

"Holly? Oh, yeah. I spoke to her about an hour ago.

She and Brian were at the Carlton Hotel drinking mint tea. They're finishing up in Tunis today, then flying from there to Benghazi."

"After that she's returning here?"

"To good ol' Tripoli, that's right. We've scheduled a regional meeting here for Friday to address the regional embassy security picture, evaluate needs, draft a budget, write a report. Holly's input will be important. Critical, you might say."

"When exactly do you expect her back?"

"Sometime Thursday."

"Libyan Airlines?"

"I imagine."

"Thanks."

"You're welcome."

He turned to leave and stopped. "Oh, and one other thing. Please don't tell her I'm here. I want to surprise her."

"Sure thing."

CHAPTER SEVEN

Anyone who isn't confused doesn't really understand the situation.

—Edward R. Murrow

THE GUESTHOUSE was roughly six blocks away, a relatively modest three-bedroom behind a concrete wall topped with broken glass and barbed wire. The oval pool in the backyard was covered with a blue tarp.

He found most of his team loading in supplies and cleaning the kitchen. Mancini had his head in the fridge, a plastic bucket at his feet, the floor around him covered with old food containers, muttering to himself. Seeing Crocker, he stopped. "Hey, boss," he said. "You alright? Heard you had a difficult night."

"I'm running on fumes. How's the place?"

"Not half bad," Mancini answered, "but the people staying here before us left a goddamn mess."

From the closet Akil said, "You should have called us."

"When?"

"Last night."

"No time. Everything happened so fast."

"Davis told us. Heard you kicked some butt."

Mention of the SEAL's name jarred Crocker's memory. "How is he?"

"Davis? Got his bell rung good. Minor concussion. Damage to one of his eardrums. Doctor says he'll be fine."

"Where is he?"

"In the back bedroom jerking off."

Ritchie walked in carrying a box of groceries. "Hey, boss. Welcome back. Cal needs to talk to you when you get a chance."

"What's wrong with Cal?"

"Mommy issues."

"What?"

"I can never quite make out what he's saying. He mumbled something under his breath about his mother."

Crocker found Cal sitting in the living room next to a bag filled with weapons. The components of an MP5 lay on loose newspaper on the floor—the carrier, bolt head rollers, blast bore, and chamber. As Crocker watched, Cal spread some Tetra Gun Action Blaster on the chamber and scrubbed it with a wire brush.

Without looking up he said, "Big mash-up last night, huh, boss?"

"Turned out that way, yeah."

"Sorry I missed the fireworks."

The SEAL sniper, who was never very communicative, looked lost in his own thoughts as he wiped down the bore, barrel, and trigger pack.

Crocker said, "Ritchie said you want to speak to me. You okay?"

Cal raised his head and looked toward the window,

which was covered with dusty yellow curtains. Crocker noticed puffiness around his eyes.

Cal spoke in a whisper. "I think so."

"That scorpion bite still bothering you? Sometimes the effects of the venom can linger for weeks."

"It's not that."

"What, then?"

"My mom."

"Your mother?"

"Weird, huh? I dreamt about her the other night. Today I find out she's in a hospice, dying."

Crocker was so tired he wasn't sure he'd heard right. "Your mother's dying, and you just found out?"

"Yeah. Stage three lung cancer."

Crocker knew there was almost zero chance of recovering from that. "Cal, I'm so sorry."

"Doctor says she only has a few days left."

Crocker flashed back to his own mom, suffering from cancer and hooked to a respirator. "You speak to her?" he asked.

"Weird how things change. She's always been the most energetic woman, running businesses, doing all kinds of things, always in a hurry. Never stopped, until now."

Crocker had left his mom one afternoon when she wanted him to stay. She died the next day.

"Where's your mother now?" he asked, feeling the guilt wanting to punish him again.

"San Mateo."

"You've got to visit her, Cal. You'll regret it if you don't."

Cal looked down at the tile floor and nodded. "I guess I will. Soon as this mission is over."

"We're likely to be here a week at least. That might be too late. I don't think you should risk it."

"Yeah."

Cal put a drop of oil on the locking piece, then reassembled the bolt head and carrier. The emotional side of him that was never much in evidence seemed completely shut down.

"Cal?" Crocker asked.

"Yeah."

"Soon as I get my hands on a laptop that's working, I'll e-mail our CO. Tell him you're taking emergency medical leave effective immediately. You should get ready to leave first thing in the morning. When you're done in San Mateo, report back to Virginia Beach."

Cal pointed at the weapons on the floor. "I'll check and clean the rest of them tonight before I go."

"We can do that, Cal."

"Not as good as I can."

"Okay, Cal. Then pack your gear."

"Yes, sir."

An important part of Crocker's job was to look out for the emotional welfare of his men. As highly trained and disciplined as they were, they were human beings, not machines. They needed to be able to focus and think clearly.

He had learned from personal experience that family roots run deeper than some people realize. Early in his career Crocker had missed both his sisters' weddings and his uncle's funeral because he was working 24/7 with ST-6. He deeply regretted that now.

As Cal checked the reassembled mechanism, Crocker saw him stop to wipe a tear from the corner of his eye. He placed a hand on Cal's shoulder, then left him in peace.

Minutes later Crocker found Davis in the back bedroom, sitting on the edge of a double bed, flipping through the channels with the TV remote. The left side of his head and his left ear were covered with a white bandage.

"Akil said that you were back here beating off."

Davis said, "Thirty-some channels, and all but one of them is in Arabic. The only one in English is BBC World News."

"No *Criminal Minds* or *CSI*, huh?"

"No, nothing."

"We'll survive."

"I'd rather read anyway."

"How's your head?"

"Hurts, but it seems to be working."

Crocker held up the fingers of his right hand. "How many digits?"

"Seventeen."

"You're fine. Any mention of the Sheraton bombing on the news?"

"Some still pictures. Nothing about casualties."

"That's because the war is over, so reporters are busy elsewhere. What'd the doc say about your head?"

"I should expect headaches the next couple of days. Probably lost a shitload of brain cells. Otherwise, I'm fine."

"Maybe you should take some emergency medical leave, spend some time with your family." Davis and his wife had an infant son and another baby due in six months.

He asked, "What's going on with Cal?"

"He's leaving in the morning to spend some time with his mom."

"Then you need me."

Sometimes team spirit and loyalty got in the way. "Think about it," Crocker said.

"As long as I've got plenty of eight-hundred-milligram Motrin, I'll be fine."

They ate at a long table in the kitchen. Mancini had whipped up a big bowl of pasta with tomatoes, capers, peppers, and canned tuna. Pretty damn good, under the circumstances. They were talking, eating, and listening to Raj Music on the radio when they heard someone banging on the gate.

It was John Lasher, carrying several shopping bags that contained DVDs, paperbacks for Davis, peanut butter, crackers, bars of chocolate, boxes of energy bars, and bottles of Italian wine. The back of his SUV was loaded with hazmat suits, digital Geiger counters, a bolt cutter, a couple of acetylene torches, maps and charts.

As Crocker helped him carry the gear in, Lasher turned to him and asked, "How do you know Farag Shakir?"

Because his mind was clouded with exhaustion, it took him a moment to remember. "Farag? Yeah, Farag. He's the brave kid who fought beside me at the Sheraton last night."

"He asked me to thank you for helping save his cousin's life."

"I didn't know the injured boy was his cousin. How is he?"

"Hanging on, apparently."

"Tough kid, that Farag. What's his background?"

"He's from one of the tribes west of here, near the Tunisian border, called Zintani. Ended up in Tripoli during the war for one reason or another. He wants to be helpful, so we've used him for a couple of things, mainly for backup security. That's why he was at the Sheraton last night."

After they finished eating, Lasher spread out a map of Libya on the table with several locations circled in red. He explained that he was a former marine major and UN weapons inspector in Iraq, then said, "Remington wants us to do this quickly and low profile, so we'll focus on the three most important sites."

"I was in Iraq, too," Crocker said. "March 2003, right after it fell. Minutes after I landed, I ran into the chief of CIA Operations at the airport. He said, 'Crocker, if you came here looking for WMDs, you're not gonna find any.' "

Lasher: "I worked for Scott Ritter when we did the UN inspections. We knew that months before the invasion."

Crocker had learned not to try to second-guess the president or his foreign policy team, but he wasn't afraid to call out a mistake if he saw one. "Fucked up, huh?"

"A major international black eye, yeah. But at least we took down Saddam."

"Sure did."

Lasher pointed to one of the red circles, only a short distance west of Tripoli. "We might as well start with the closest one, Busetta, which was Gaddafi's former naval base. I'm not sure what's left of it now."

"What are we looking for?"

"Mustard gas, stocks of VX gas, missile engines, ingredients for the production of missile fuel, shells, chemical bombs."

Crocker knew that VX was a very dangerous nerve agent developed by the British, a compound of organic phosphorus and sulfur that can penetrate the skin and disrupt the transmission of nerve impulses, causing paralysis and death.

"And you think these weapons exist?" he asked.

"NATO claims to have inspected the sites."

"But you don't trust them?"

"We know that Gaddafi vowed to dismantle his WMD program after the Iraq War. But instead of destroying anything, he spent the next eight years playing cat and mouse with the international community. According to our intel, at the time of his death his regime was in possession of at least 9.5 metric tons of mustard gas and 100 metric tons of VX."

"Code name Scorpion."

"Yeah, Scorpion. Designed to strike when no one's looking."

"How much of that mustard gas and VX has NATO recovered?"

"Almost none."

"Then it looks like we've got a real job to do."

"Sure does."

Crocker spent that night dreaming about his mother. He saw her barefoot in the kitchen, making pancakes. Then he hid from her as she called him to come with her to church.

He woke before dawn, breakfasted on yogurt, cereal, and oranges. Ran ten miles, did some calisthenics, then showered and watched the kids next door pedal their bicycles up and down the street. Two brothers ages six and eight, named Bouba and Mohi. The younger one, Bouba, was having trouble reaching the pedals, so Crocker adjusted the seat as their father smoked a cigarette and watched silently from the front gate.

"Great kids," Crocker said.

The father smiled and nodded.

Just before eight Lasher arrived with a short older man with thinning gray hair and a tight smile. "This is Dr. Jabril," Lasher said. "He used to run Colonel Gaddafi's chemical weapons program, before he was dismissed in 2002 and thrown in jail."

"Nice to meet you."

"Dr. Jabril has been living in exile in southern France. He agreed to return to Libya and help us."

That meant that the CIA had probably paid him a shitload of money.

Jabril said, "I hope I can make a small contribution to the future of my country. It looks like it needs all the help it can get."

After saying good-bye to Cal, they all drove in a black Chevy Suburban to the Corniche and hung a left. The city was slowly coming to life under low-lying gray clouds. Vendors, most of them male, were setting out their goods—bags of fresh oranges, dates, and tangerines, pistachio nuts, spices, tribal rugs, cartons of cigarettes, counterfeit CDs and DVDs. Traffic was light, bikes, motorcycles, a few cars and trucks driving at their customary ninety miles an hour.

What's the hurry? Crocker wondered as he tried to orient himself to the layout of the city.

After a few miles following the coast, they approached the Sheraton on their right. Crocker's stomach tightened. The thick burning smell—a combination of electrical wire, other building materials, and death—made him nauseous. It reminded him of the spilled guts and blood, his buddy Al Cowens.

"That's it. Right, boss?" Akil asked from the backseat.

"Yeah." Covering his nose.

The streets leading to the hotel were blocked and manned by NATO and NTC soldiers wearing red berets. Two unmarked helicopters swooped overhead.

"Nice of them to secure it now," Davis remarked.

"You got that right."

People tended to respond to specific types of threats after the fact, which was a problem if the terrorists stayed a step ahead. Crocker thought they should be pursuing the men who had attacked the hotel. The fact that they weren't made him angry.

After forty-five minutes of bouncing down the potholed highway, they reached the Busetta naval base. Lasher and Jabril got out and spoke in Arabic to armed men guarding the gate.

When the conversation had gone on for more than five minutes, Crocker turned to Akil and asked, "Can you understand what's going on?"

"They showed them a letter from Abdurrahim El-Keib, who is the prime minister of the National Transitional Council. But I don't think the guards can read."

Crocker: "Get out and tell them that if they don't let us in, we'll arrest them."

"And what happens if they resist? We're unarmed."

"We'll kick their asses anyway."

Akil: "Chill, boss. It's hardly worth the risk."

He was right. Even though Akil sometimes acted like an immature asshole, Crocker appreciated the fact that he wasn't afraid to tell his boss when he thought he was out of line.

After a few more minutes of arguing, the guards stepped aside and waved them in.

The place was a wreck. Bombed-out hangars and warehouses, scorched pieces of sheet-metal roof flapping in the breeze. They passed burnt-out trucks and jeeps.

Jabril said, "I heard that Belgian and Spanish warplanes attacked this place in early March of last year, after Gaddafi had already moved most of his ships out to sea. He tried to disguise them."

"What did he have in terms of a navy?"

"Several Koni-class missile frigates he bought from the Soviets, some minesweepers, six Foxtrot-class submarines built in the nineteen sixties."

"Why? What was the threat?"

"They were mainly defensive weapons. The colonel was deeply paranoid."

"You knew him well?"

Jabril shook his head. "Not well. I met with him several times and listened to his vision for Africa and our country. He did most of the talking. He was convinced of his own brilliance. Nobody around him was allowed to disagree."

Mancini came back from inspecting the burned-out vehicles and said, "They're all Soviet era, Russian made. Mostly T-72 and T-54 tanks, BTR-60 eight-wheeled armored personnel carriers, a couple Strela-2 and Strela-10 surface-to-air missile systems."

In another warehouselike structure that was mostly destroyed but hadn't been burned, they found a huge pile of torpedo shells in one corner and barrels in another. While Mancini and Davis were pulling on their hazmat suits, Crocker was hit by a powerful stench.

"What the hell's that?"

Lasher pointed to a bombed-out four-story concrete structure a hundred yards down the coast.

"It's probably coming from that camp over there."

"What kind of camp is it?"

"A refugee camp, I think."

A couple of mangy-looking dogs wandered past. Mancini reported that the barrels contained acetone and other chemicals used to clean machinery.

"Anything that could be used to make a chemical weapon?"

"Negative, boss."

Several gunshots went off from the direction of the refugee camp. Crocker turned and watched birds taking flight.

About a hundred feet from where he was standing, near the edge of the concrete driveway, Jabril and Lasher knelt down and were inspecting the ground.

Crocker went over to join them and asked, "What do you see?"

"Nothing."

"Then what are you looking for?"

"There used to be an underground storage chamber around here," Jabril answered, pushing back strands of gray hair. "A German company helped us build it back in the nineties."

Mancini and Akil retrieved an underground locating

device, a shovel, and other tools from the back of the SUV. The locating device was a handheld gadget about the size of a toaster. Within minutes it started buzzing.

Akil removed his shirt and started digging. Under three feet of sand he struck a concrete door.

"That's it," Jabril said.

Akil cut through the lock with an acetylene torch.

A dozen concrete steps led down to a room that stank of mildew and rotting garlic. Mancini, holding a flashlight and wearing a white plastic hazmat suit and hood, went down first. He scurried back seconds later and removed his hood.

"What's the matter?" Crocker asked.

"There are snakes down there. Lots of 'em. Give me the shovel. Davis, you hold the light."

They'd brought only two suits, so Crocker descended nine steps and crouched down to look. It was a long, narrow room, approximately ten feet wide and sixty feet long. The side of the room to Crocker's left was filled with racks of artillery shells and torpedoes, and the floor was covered with snakes.

The chamber looked as if it hadn't been touched in years.

After they'd scared away the snakes by waving their arms and stomping on the floor, they managed to remove one of the artillery shells, which tested positive for sulfur chloride—a main ingredient of mustard gas.

Jabril said, "This whole area needs to be sealed off immediately. This material could be terribly dangerous if it falls into the wrong hands."

"The mustard gas?"

"Even if it has decomposed, the substances it creates can be extremely toxic."

Lasher used his satellite phone to notify NATO command, which said it was dispatching a team to secure the base.

"Tell them to get here fast."

They stood in the afternoon sun and waited. Akil, whose mind always seemed fixated on women, asked Jabril if it was true that Gaddafi had surrounded himself with an entourage of sexy female bodyguards.

"He called them his Amazons and had sex with all of them."

"How many of them were there?" Akil asked.

"Four or five hundred."

Akil smiled. "Nice."

"A group of them traveled with him everywhere, dressed in tight-fitting camouflage uniforms and high heels, nail polish, mascara. He also had a staff of Ukrainian nurses who stayed by his side all the time. His favorite was a girl named Galyna, a beautiful blonde, like a Playboy Playmate."

Akil said, "I'd love to meet her."

"She's an old woman now."

"What do you mean by old?"

"Fifty."

Ritchie said, "As long as she's still breathing, Akil doesn't care."

Jabril told them a story of traveling with the Libyan leader to Paris. Since Gaddafi didn't trust elevators and didn't like staying in hotels, he had ended up pitching his Bedouin tent on a farm outside the city.

Coincidentally, the soldiers who arrived to secure the

base were French. There were a dozen of them, with German shepherds. They were businesslike and unfriendly. As they unloaded sandbags and rolls of razor wire from the back of a truck, Akil said, "I think we interrupted their nap."

The French captain, who spoke English, got in his face. "I think you should show a little more respect."

"Sorry, monsieur, I meant no offense."

"He's a wiseass," Crocker offered, aware that NATO soldiers might be especially sensitive after the heat they had taken over the Sheraton attack. "He can't help himself."

The French captain grinned and, leaning toward Crocker, asked, "How much longer before this country turns into Iraq?"

It was a question that Crocker had been quietly asking himself for the past two days, and it was underscored by more gunshots and screams from the refugee camp.

"Brutal savages," the French captain said with a sneer.

On the way back to the SUV, Crocker nodded in the direction of the camp and said to Lasher, "I think we should take a look."

Sunshine gleamed off his Oakleys as Lasher shook his head. "Bad idea. Besides, we're not allowed in there without permission."

Lasher's skin had turned bright red in the afternoon sun.

"Says who?"

"The NATO commander."

"It sounds like they're shooting people. We'd better find out what's going on before it gets ugly."

Remembering how NATO had been caught off guard

at the start of the genocide in Rwanda, Crocker ordered the driver to proceed a couple of hundred yards farther east to the camp gate. Several dozen women were crowded in the shade of the concrete arches, waiting to get inside. Most were carrying food and clothing; some were accompanied by young children.

When they saw Crocker and his men getting out of the vehicle, they surrounded them and started pleading. Jabril, Lasher, and the driver elected to stay inside.

"What do they want?" Crocker asked Akil.

"They're hoping for news about husbands and sons they believe are inside the camp."

"It only houses men?"

"Apparently."

"And it's a refugee camp?"

"That's what they call it."

"Strange, don't you think?"

"Very."

A trio of buzzards circled overhead.

The dozen guards at the gate wore a motley collection of military and civilian clothes and ranged in age from teenagers to men in their forties. Some of the younger ones were cocky and menacing, shouting at the women and waving automatic weapons.

Another gunshot went off inside, and the women screamed together.

Crocker turned to Akil and said, "Tell the guards we're UN inspectors and we have permission to enter."

Initially the guards didn't want to let them in, but Akil threatened to call the prime minister and have them arrested.

"No problem... no problem," said an eager young man

with a big set of brilliant white teeth and a red baseball cap worn backward, stepping forward with what looked like a Russian submachine gun—a PP-91 KEDR. "We want no trouble. We are *Thwar.*"

"*Thwar* is the local word for militia," Akil explained.

"Who left them in charge of this camp?"

Akil asked the young man in Arabic, then translated for Crocker. "He says they're in charge of policing the whole area."

"What about the national police?"

"All bad men here," the young man said in broken English as he led them down a hallway that stank of human waste. Dirty water dripped from the ceiling.

The five unarmed Americans entered a large concrete room. The windows had been shot out, which created a big open space that overlooked the sea. But the breeze blowing in was foul with the smell of excrement and rot.

"Look," Ritchie said, pointing down to a multitude of red, blue, green, and yellow plastic tarps. They had been used to create makeshift tents on the land below that led to the beach.

The rectangular space was surrounded by a high fence topped with barbed wire.

It was a dramatic juxtaposition—the calm turquoise water of the Mediterranean and the human degradation.

"What's that saying, hell in a very small place?" Akil asked. "I think we've found it."

"Revolting."

Mancini: "Reminds me of a scene from the movie *Saw.*"

Crocker said, "Follow me."

There seemed to be a stark contrast in skin color between the lighter men running the camp and the darker ones living there.

Crocker turned to the smiling young militiaman who strode next to him and asked, "Approximately how many people are housed here?"

He held up two fingers.

"Two hundred?"

"Two thousand."

"All men?"

"Bad men."

A table with one leg missing stood on a wooden platform on the left side of the room. Three men sat behind it wearing sunglasses, one of whom was enormously fat, with a brown shirt and dark goatee. They seemed to be presiding.

Beyond the table rose an aluminum fence, and behind it stood several dozen refugees watching with grim faces.

"What's going on here?" Crocker asked.

"These men…mostly criminals. Killers. Gaddafi soldiers."

"I thought this was a refugee camp."

The young man shrugged.

"Who gave you authority to run this camp?"

No answer.

About twenty gaunt prisoners sat on the floor in front of the table with their hands and ankles bound by TUFF-TIES. All had pieces of bright green cloth clenched in their teeth. Some had soiled themselves. Some were bleeding, others had festering wounds.

"Some of these men need medical attention," Crocker said. "Has the Red Cross been in here?"

Their escort shrugged.

"Do the men get a hearing? Is there a judicial process?"

The young escort frowned as if to say *I don't understand.*

A guard jabbed one of the prisoners in the chest with the barrel of his AK-47 and shouted.

Earlier in his life, before he'd gone to BUD/S and become a SEAL, Crocker had served briefly as a prison guard at the Adult Correctional Institute in Rhode Island. He had witnessed degradation, but nothing on this scale.

"What's he saying?" Crocker asked.

Akil: "He said this man is a former soldier who was captured in Misrata."

The prisoners watching from behind the fence moaned and shifted anxiously. When the prisoner who was being accused got a chance to speak, his voice was barely audible.

Akil whispered, "He says he's a cigarette vendor who was forced to join the army at the end of the war."

Their escort said, "Don't believe him. They all liars."

"How can you be sure?"

He pointed to his nose. "We know."

As Crocker and his team watched, the three men behind the table whispered to one another. The fat one in the middle extended his arm and pointed his thumb to the floor.

The guard raised the AK-47 and clubbed the prisoner in the head. Blood and teeth shot out of his mouth.

"Hey!" Crocker shouted. "Stop that immediately!"

Another guard pulled the prisoner up by the back of his collar and dragged him to the right side of the room, where a stripped metal frame had been attached to the wall. The concrete floor around the frame was spotted with blood.

Crocker turned to the militiaman and said, "Tell them to stop! You know what stop means?"

"Yes." The young militiaman shouted, *"Doapiful!"*

Everyone in the room turned toward the Americans. The big man at the table stood and starting screaming.

Crocker said, "Tell these men that this isn't the correct way to treat prisoners!"

"What?" the young militiaman asked, surprised.

"Tell them to stop, immediately. And drop their weapons, before I put them all under arrest!"

The young militiaman relayed this. The men behind the table laughed as if it were a big joke. One of them said something to the guard with the AK-47, who started to chain the prisoner to the frame. Another guard stepped forward with a five-foot length of metal pipe.

As the soldier drew back the pipe, Crocker grabbed the PP-91 KEDR from their escort and pointed it at the men sitting behind the table.

"Stop!" he shouted. "I mean it. I'm not fucking around!"

He shot a volley of bullets over their heads, into the ceiling. Guards and prisoners ducked and covered their heads.

"Tell your men to drop their weapons!"

Several of the guards complied. Others dropped to the floor. One of the men behind the table raised his weapon. Crocker turned and shot him in the hand, causing the rifle to fall to the floor.

The SEALs quickly retrieved the discarded weapons

and established a fire circle. Within seconds they had gained the upper hand.

Guards and prisoners looked at one another, nervous and confused.

Davis shouted, "Boss! Now what?"

"Anyone who points a gun at you or makes an aggressive move, shoot."

"Check."

"Follow my lead."

Crocker was making it up as he went along. He took aim at the men behind the table. The fat man smiled and held up his arms.

"You think this is funny, you big piece of shit?"

Crocker was about to pull the trigger when the big man shouted something and the last two guards lowered their AKs, which Ritchie and Mancini quickly wrestled away. A murmur of excitement rose from the prisoners behind the fence.

Akil whispered, "Careful, boss, or we'll incite a riot."

Crocker grabbed their escort by the shoulder and said, "You tell these men that what they're doing is illegal. There's something called the Geneva Conventions."

"Geneva . . . what?"

"It states that all captured soldiers have to be treated with respect. If any of them are accused of crimes, they have the right to stand trial. But not like this!"

The militiaman translated. The men behind the table spoke all at once.

Crocker cut them off. "*STOP!* Tell them to listen. If they don't do as I say, if they harm another prisoner, I'll call in NATO troops. There's a battalion of them right next door. All I have to do is give the signal and they'll come in here weapons blazing, arrest all of you, and throw you in the same compound with the prisoners. You understand me?"

The leaders behind the table seemed to comprehend this time.

"No more beatings. No more abuse!"

"Yes. Yes."

Akil whispered, "Maybe we should get out now, while we still have the upper hand."

Crocker: "Alright. Slowly move toward the exit."

As they did, the prisoners behind the fence started to shout.

Crocker said, "What the fuck are they screaming about now?"

Akil: "They say that there are more rooms downstairs where they torture the prisoners."

"I want to see them."

"Bad idea, boss."

"Then tell these assholes that all this shit has to stop immediately. There are NATO troops next door. More inspectors will be here tomorrow. They need to clean this place up, now, before they're all arrested!"

After Akil delivered the message, the fat man started shouting at the top of his lungs.

"He says that this is their country and they'll do what they want."

"Tell him I'm placing him and his two colleagues under arrest!"

"He wants you to leave."

"Tell them to keep their hands on their heads and their mouths shut!"

When the young man who escorted them tried to grab

his PP-91 back from Crocker, Crocker clocked him in the face. The man went down, blood spurting from his lip. Another guard made a quick move for a pistol in his belt. Mancini fired the AK he was holding and hit the guard in the leg.

Crocker released a long salvo from the PP-91 that flew over the guards' heads. All the soldiers and prisoners dropped to the floor, except for the three men behind the table, who stood with their hands on their heads.

Davis: "Boss, this is getting ugly."

Akil: "Real fucking nasty."

Ritchie: "Just the way I like it."

Crocker fired again. As the smoke cleared, he said, "Grab those three bastards. We're taking them with us. They're under arrest."

Ritchie and Davis moved quickly and seized the three men roughly.

Akil: "Now what?"

"Back out slowly. Shoot anyone who raises their head."

They exited in formation, with the three prisoners in the middle, past the startled guards at the gate, who lowered their weapons. As they scrambled into the SUV, Mancini shouted, "Start the engine, fast!"

The driver complied, spun the Suburban in a half circle, and flew down the road.

Jabril: "We heard shooting."

Akil: "That was fucking insane."

Lasher pointed to the three prisoners Davis and Mancini were tying up. "Who are they?"

Crocker: "The men handing out the punishment. I arrested them for war crimes."

Lasher: "On what authority?"

Crocker: "My authority."

Ritchie: "Is anyone really in charge of this shithole country?"

Akil: "Boss, you did the right thing."

Crocker turned to Lasher and said, "Tell Remington that they're torturing and executing people over there."

Lasher: "I warned you not to go in."

Crocker: "Call Remington!"

Lasher: "You're a madman."

Ritchie: "Fuck you, Lasher."

Crocker: "Alright, everyone calm down."

They rode back in silence, grumbling to themselves, a dozen thoughts swirling in Crocker's head. He decided he wanted to complete their mission and get out of Libya as soon as possible. The place was starting to remind him of Somalia in the early nineties, when lawlessness prevailed as warlords running teenage gangs vied for power. He'd been in Mogadishu back in October 1993 when nineteen U.S. Special Forces soldiers lost their lives. The bloody rescue was re-created in the movie *Black Hawk Down.*

He'd also served in Iraq after the fall of Saddam and seen American soldiers and civilians caught in the middle of the Sunni-Shiite violence there. A good friend of his had been overwhelmed by a gang of Iraqis, stripped naked, hung from a bridge, tortured, and killed.

Peacekeeping missions could be ugly and difficult. He much preferred missions that targeted a specific enemy.

But who was the enemy here? Nobody seemed to know.

After dropping off the prisoners at NATO headquarters

and his men at the guesthouse, Crocker continued with Lasher to the embassy. Both men were upset.

There, Crocker met with Jaime Remington and the U.S. ambassador in the ambassador's office and described what he and his men had found at both the naval base and the refugee camp next door.

Ambassador Andrew Saltzman was an older man with a headful of thick white hair. He looked like a Wall Street banker—soft around the middle, self-confident, meticulously groomed and dressed. The office was cool and dark, with dark blue curtains covering the windows. Crocker stared down at the Great Seal of the United States—an eagle clutching a scroll in its mouth—and waited for the ambassador's response.

He took his time, grunting and pulling at his bottom lip. When he answered, he seemed equally upset by what the SEALs had seen at the refugee camp and by the discovery of the aging chemical weapons. Then he asked, "What provoked you to enter the camp in the first place?"

"We were at the naval base, sir. We heard gunfire and people screaming. I decided we should take a look."

"Understandable. Commendable, too."

"After receiving some resistance, we ended up arresting the three men who were ordering the torture and executions."

"Where are they now?"

"They're behind bars at NATO headquarters."

"Good work. I'm going to call the NATO commanders tonight. First I want to make sure those prisoners are turned over to the NTC and made an example of. Then I'm going to demand that NATO inspect every single one of these so-called refugee camps. If Amnesty International ever gets wind of what's going on, we're in serious hot water."

"Yes, sir."

"Thanks again."

Crocker started to get up. But since the ambassador sounded sympathetic, he decided to ask him a question. "Sir, I mean no disrespect to anyone, but I'm unclear about who the enemy is here."

"The enemy is anyone who is trying to destabilize the NTC."

"Thank you, sir." He got up.

Hardly a satisfactory answer. Weren't the militiamen running the so-called refugee camp members of the NTC? But he didn't say anything. He figured it would take him and his men another six days max to inspect the remaining weapons sites before they could return to Virginia. Until then they'd move carefully and keep a low profile.

Despite the fact that his stomach was growling, he stopped in to see Leo Debray before he left. Debray was sitting in his office with his assistant, Kat. As soon as they saw Crocker, their expressions grew graver.

"What's wrong?" Crocker asked. "You don't look glad to see me."

Debray rose from his chair and draped an arm across Crocker's shoulder. At six feet five he towered over him.

"Not at all. I spoke to your wife about an hour ago. Seems like the plane they were flying on experienced some mechanical problems. So they're spending the night in Sirte."

"Where's that?"

"About three hundred miles east of here. Site of big oil

fields, great beaches. They're planning to catch another flight in the morning."

"She'll be in Tripoli tomorrow, then."

"That's correct."

A doubt popped into Crocker's head. He asked, "Is that normal? I mean, are local flights routinely canceled?"

"Since the war, airplane service has been extremely erratic."

"Thanks."

CHAPTER EIGHT

Learn from yesterday, live for today, hope for tomorrow.

—Albert Einstein

THE NEXT morning Crocker rose early, drove to the beach, and ran ten miles in the sand. Reminded him of BUD/S and of being back home in eastern Virginia. He passed men standing in the surf fishing, a family walking their dog, women covered from head to toe collecting shells. Despite what Volman had said about Libyans being the friendliest people in the world, the ones he saw seemed frightened and on edge.

Maybe on Saturday he'd take Holly to the Roman ruins at Leptis Magna, two hours east. According to Mancini it was a UNESCO World Heritage Site and remained one of the best-preserved Roman cities in the world, with a triumphal arch in honor of Emperor Septimius Severus, a theater built in the second century BC, a forum, baths, a basilica, and more. The city had been founded by the Phoenicians and became a prosperous Roman commercial center until it was sacked by a Berber tribe in AD 523.

They could pack a picnic lunch and spend the day exploring the ruins by themselves. Maybe stop for a swim afterward. Make love on the beach.

Back at the guesthouse he sat with his men in the living room listening to a briefing by Jaime Remington and an officer from the BND (Bundesnachrichtendienst, the German equivalent of the CIA)—a tall, fit woman named Sandra Lundquist. She reminded him of a taller, slimmer, slightly older Scarlett Johansson, which explained why Ritchie and Akil were staring at her like she was lunch.

Crocker listened as Lundquist spoke in a dry, almost monotone voice, a stark contrast to her ripe sexuality. He knew they would be leaving in an hour to inspect a chemical plant near the border with Niger, 450 miles south. She explained that the BND had already inspected the facility, which was a few kilometers north of the town of Toummo. Built in the 1980s with the help of a dozen German, Italian, Soviet, and French companies—including Pen Tsao, Ihsan Barbouti, and Imhausen-Chemie—the plant almost immediately raised international suspicion. The Libyan government claimed it was being used to manufacture medicine and other consumer products, but soon it was discovered that the German company Imhausen-Chemie had been shipping chemical weapons equipment to Libya, using Hong Kong as a cover.

On August 3, 1987, SPOT satellite pictures confirmed that the plant, then known as Pharma 150, had been completed. Considered the largest chemical weapons facility in the Third World, at full capacity it could produce one hundred metric tons of sarin nerve gas a year. The Libyans had also constructed a metal fabrication plant nearby to produce bombs and artillery shells designed specifically to deliver chemical agents.

"Didn't the Reagan administration threaten to bomb Pharma 150 in the late eighties if it wasn't shut down?" Mancini asked.

"You're correct," Sandra said. "But before they had a chance to, the Libyan government claimed that a fire set by the United States had destroyed the plant. However, satellite imagery indicated only minor damage."

"So the fire was a hoax."

"That was the conclusion of your CIA, yes. Again the Reagan administration threatened to destroy it. In late 1990, Colonel Muammar Gaddafi announced that he was shutting the plant down, but not before it had produced an estimated hundred tons of mustard blister agent and sarin nerve gas."

"Sneaky bastard."

"The site was reopened in 1995 as a pharmaceutical plant, jointly run with Egypt's El Nasr Pharmaceutical Chemicals Company, designed to produce medicines, detergents, and cleansers," Sandra continued. "But we concluded that it was still capable of making chemical weapons."

Ritchie: "Why am I not surprised?"

"In 2004, Libya signed the Chemical Weapons Convention. But leaked classified cables from Gaddafi's government proved that they were not in compliance and still possessed 9.5 metric tons of mustard gas, an unknown quantity of phosgene gas, and sarin nerve agent, most of which was stored at Pharma 150."

Ritchie: "We should have leveled it back in the eighties."

Crocker asked, "What's the status of the facility now?"

"An Italian company called SIPSA Engineering has been pressuring the interim government to sign a contract for destruction of all chemical agents at Pharma 150. So far the contract hasn't been signed," Lundquist answered.

"So what's our mission?" Crocker asked.

Remington leaned forward and answered, "One, make sure the chemical weapons stored there are secure. Two, inspect the nearby metal fabrication plant. We know that it hasn't been open for years, but as far as I know, no one has eyeballed that particular plant in years, either."

Lundquist said, "I've been there as recently as two months ago. There's nothing to see at the metal fabrication plant. Ruins, a shed that some locals use to store grain, not much."

Remington: "Dr. Jabril won't be going with you, but he drew up a map of the fabrication plant. He says he helped run it back in the nineties."

"Where's Lasher?" Crocker asked.

"He and the doctor are out interviewing some former Gaddafi scientists."

"And the city is safe?" Crocker asked.

"Toummo? It's hardly a city. Barely qualifies as a village. It's a desert border town. NATO has a base there to guard the uranium mines nearby. There've been some recent skirmishes with local tribesmen, raids across the border, but the Polish commander, Major Ostrowski, is firmly in charge. He'll be your host."

As Akil, Mancini, Davis, and Ritchie loaded their gear into the Suburban for the trip to the airport, Remington pulled Crocker into the kitchen.

"Keep close to Ms. Lundquist," Remington said.

"That won't be a problem. But...why?"

"She was attacked in the old quarter a couple of nights ago. A group of young men tried to force her into a car. She fought them off but is still a bit shaken."

The Royal Canadian Air Force CC-130 took off with a roar that afternoon with Crocker and Mancini in the first row of seats; Davis, Akil, and Ritchie occupying the middle row; and Sandra Lundquist stretched out in the back row by herself. The space behind her was filled with jugs of water, propane tanks, and other supplies for the NATO camp. When she wasn't talking on her cell phone she was typing on her laptop, frustrating Akil and Ritchie's attempts to engage her in conversation. So they started ribbing Davis about getting his wife pregnant twice in less than a year.

Ritchie asked, "You ever hear about pulling out?"

Akil: "He can't. He's too quick."

Ritchie: "You've got to learn to prolong it, enjoy it. Right, Manny?"

Mancini: "What do you two know about heterosexual love?"

Then they tried to get her attention by telling off-color jokes.

"Hey, you hear the one about the woman at home who hears a knock on her front door? She answers and sees a man standing there who asks: 'Do you have a vagina?' She slams the door in disgust. The next morning she hears another knock on the door. It's the same man who asks, 'Do you have a vagina?' She slams the door again. That night when her husband gets home, she tells him what happened the last two days. Her husband tells his wife in a loving and concerned voice, 'Honey, I'm staying home from work tomorrow, in case this idiot shows up again.' The next morning, sure enough, there's a knock on the door. The husband whispers to the wife, 'I'll hide behind the door. If he asks you the same question, answer yes.' She opens the door and sure enough, the same man is standing there. He asks again, 'Do you have a vagina?' She answers yes. The man replies, 'Good. Then would you mind telling your husband to leave my wife's alone and start using yours?' "

The men all laughed, Mancini so hard he started to choke.

Akil asked, "You like that one, Sandra?"

"Not bad."

"You're hard to please."

Mancini: "How about this? There was this older guy who wanted to make his younger wife pregnant. So he went to the doctor to have a sperm count done. The doc tells him to take a specimen cup home, fill it up, and bring it back the next day. The next day the old guy comes back. The specimen cup's empty and the lid's still on it. The doctor asks, 'What was the problem?' The old guy says, 'Well, I tried with my right hand... nothing. So I tried with my left. That didn't work, either. Then my wife took over. She tried with her right, then her left, then her mouth. Each time... nothing. Then my wife's friend tried. Right hand, left hand, mouth. Still nothing.' Hearing this, the doctor said, 'Wait a minute. Your wife's friend tried, too?' 'That's right,' the old man answered. 'None of us could get the lid off the specimen cup.' "

Sandra laughed this time and said, "I like that one better."

Akil leaned over the seat and asked, "What about you, Sandra? You know any good jokes?"

Crocker was about to change the subject, but the German seemed game.

She shut her laptop and said, "Three guys go to a ski lodge, and there aren't enough rooms, so they have to share a bed. In the middle of the night the guy sleeping on the right wakes up and says, 'I just had this wild, very vivid dream about getting a hand job.' The guy on the left says, 'That's funny. I had the same dream.' The guy in the middle says, 'Not me. I dreamt I was skiing.' "

They laughed, then Ritchie said, "The guy in the middle was Davis!"

Davis: "Grow up, Ritchie."

"Never. Fuck you."

Crocker: "Okay, guys. Settle down. We're almost there."

After a little more than four hours in the air, the CC-130 started to descend. All Crocker could see out the side windows was a thin ribbon of highway surrounded by desert. When the plane passed a few hundred feet over a collection of what looked like shacks on either side of the highway, Sandra said, "That's it. That's Toummo."

Akil: "You've got to be kidding."

"Looks like the end of the earth, yes?"

As soon as the plane touched down on a landing strip alongside the NATO base, Polish soldiers arrived in trucks and started unloading the supplies. Crocker and the others exited out the side door and were greeted by a big man with enormous arms and a broad chest wearing an olive-green tank top and camouflage shorts.

He said in English, "I'm Major Ostrowski. Welcome to

our base. Officially, it's known as Base Toummo, but we call it Base Piasek Burza. Or you might prefer the English translation, Base Sandstorm."

The camp housed two dozen soldiers and was roughly two hundred feet square, surrounded by a ten-foot-high wall of sand, gravel, rock, Conex containers, and sheets of metal. Inside were tents, mud buildings, lookout towers, picnic tables, electric generators, an oven, showers, a latrine, a pen filled with goats, and a barbecue pit.

The major showed them to their quarters—cell-like rooms in a mud-walled structure with a corrugated metal roof. Tiny windows allowed very little air to circulate, so even though the sun had set, the quarters continued to be stifling.

Two men were assigned to a room, except for Crocker and Sandra, who each got their own.

Crocker said, "You can give mine to someone else. I'd rather sleep outside."

"Not a good idea," the major answered, scratching the bristle of light brown hair on his square sunburned head. "For the past seven nights the tribesmen have been shelling us. Terrible aim, but maybe they get lucky."

The major seemed to view the recent fighting as no big deal.

"Are these Tuareg tribesmen you're talking about?" Crocker asked, knowing that they populated the area.

"Tuareg. Yes."

"What do they want?"

"Control of the open-pit uranium mines, what else? That way they can sell the ore to Iran and China."

"And the mines are close by?"

"About seventy kilometers northwest of us, past the town and deeper into Libyan territory."

"That far?" Crocker asked.

"The terrain makes it hard to get to them if you don't take the road. In my opinion, the camp's too close. The dust is going to make all be radioactive by the time we leave. Already my penis glows in the dark."

That night, after dining on roast goat and couscous, and watching the movie *Iron Man* dubbed in Polish, they retired to their quarters. Soon after Crocker lay down he heard the first mortar land and shake the ground. Shards of shrapnel rained onto the metal roof. Then the NATO troops returned fire with machine guns and artillery of their own.

Enemy shells continued to land intermittently through the night and into the morning breakfast of yogurt, goat cheese, figs, and tea. As Crocker and his team ate, Polish soldiers shouted instructions to one another as they prepared their weapons and put on body armor.

Akil: "Imagine being assigned to this place."

Ritchie: "I've been in worse."

Akil: "When?"

Ritchie: "November 2004, Fallujah, Iraq. The whole damn city turned against us. We were getting attacked from all sides."

Sandra looked miserable. She said the percussion of the mortar shells hurt her head.

After breakfast a sweaty, heavily armed Ostrowski led them to a Polish AMZ Dzik armored truck parked in the courtyard. He leaned toward Crocker and said, "Today we're going to have some fun with these asshole tribesmen."

The major introduced them to a Polish corporal who said he knew the way to the chemical plant. But a half hour later, as they sped north on the highway through the dusty, sun-baked town of Toummo, Sandra told him she thought he'd missed the turnoff.

The driver turned the vehicle around and veered left on a dirt road that led them past a little school, primitive houses, a pen filled with camels and goats, and up a gradual incline where the road seemed to end.

"Keep going," Sandra instructed.

When they reached an eighty-foot mound of rock, dirt, and sand, Sandra told the driver to steer around it. On the other side they met a ten-foot wall of rock and sand.

Sandra said, "Stop here. This is where we get out."

Akil: "You sure?"

There was nothing but sand everywhere they looked. She walked ahead, all business, her tight black shorts accentuating her long legs and feminine curves.

Ritchie leaned toward Crocker and whispered, "What do you think?"

Crocker shrugged, "She seems to know where she's going."

"That's not what I meant."

They watched her climb the ten-foot wall of dirt, then turn back and wave at them to join her.

Upon reaching the top, Crocker looked down and saw a large compound that had been dug into the earth. The whole plant was surrounded by walls of sandbags. It contained at least a dozen buildings, distillation and cooling tanks, and a concrete road that ran the length of the site. The road and roofs of the buildings had been painted with desert camouflage so they would be hard to see from above. Reminded him of a scene from the movie *Andromeda Strain*: perfectly preserved buildings, but no people.

"Clever, isn't it?" Sandra asked, her blond hair whipping in the wind.

"Very clever," Crocker answered.

According to the thermometer on his watch, the temperature had soared to over 110 degrees Fahrenheit. Hot gusts of wind kicked up angry twirls of dust.

Ritchie spotted a snake resting in the shade of the fence and picked it up with the barrel of his MP5.

"Don't mess around," Davis, who hated snakes, warned. Years earlier Ritchie had thrown a dead rattlesnake into Davis's sleeping bag and freaked him out.

"It's a sand viper," Mancini said, examining the marking around its head. "Highly venomous."

Ritchie waved it in front of Davis's face, then tossed it over his shoulder.

When they rattled the chain on the gate, a stooped man with one eye emerged from a shed with an old M1 Garand rifle slung over his shoulder. He explained to Akil that he was a member of the NTC militia.

"Tell him we have permission from the prime minister to inspect the site."

Akil spoke Arabic to the man, who nodded respectfully.

"He says a team from Germany arrived here months ago and locked away all the chemicals."

"I know," Sandra responded. "I was with them. Tell him we want to look around, make sure nothing has been touched."

As the guard removed a key from under his tunic, the

sky started to darken. Crocker looked at his watch. It was only 1 p.m. local time. "Looks like a storm's approaching. Grab the goggles from the truck. Make sure everyone has a scarf."

Akil ran off and came back as a big red cloud of sand and dust started to build around them.

Crocker said, "Keep your nose, mouth, and eyes covered. Everyone stick together."

The one-eyed guard led them down the main road past modern buildings and equipment that had been partially covered with sand. At the end of the drive stood a sand-colored water tower. Past that was a storage shed filled with red, green, and orange barrels.

"You know what's in them?" Crocker asked.

"Machine oil and other harmless chemicals," Sandra answered. She was wearing stylish yellow goggles.

The guard turned and beckoned them with a finger. Just then a gust of sand hit the shed, almost lifting off its roof. It pounded the water tower. More gusts followed.

Akil shouted, "He's leading us to an underground chamber."

"Where?"

"Follow me!"

They walked in a cluster, pushing through the wind, to a concrete ramp with a set of steps beside it. At the bottom was a metal door that was bolted shut and locked. Pasted on it were warnings in Arabic, French, and English.

Sandra: "This is the same one we inspected two months ago."

"Who has the keys?" Crocker asked.

"NATO command," Sandra shouted over the wind.

"We're waiting for the toxic materials to be removed and disposed of."

"Who's responsible for that?"

"The NTC."

"Alright," Crocker said turning to Akil. "Show the guard the map Dr. Jabril drew of the metal fabrication plant. Tell him we want to take a look at that, too."

The man studied the map as fine dust swirling around them made it hard to breathe. Sandra appeared to be suffering. Ritchie wrapped his kaffiyeh around her head.

Crocker said, "Hand her a bottle of water. Make sure she wets the scarf and ties it over her nose and mouth." Then he turned to Akil and shouted over the roar, "What did the guard say?"

"He says part of the facility is destroyed. What's left of it is on the other side of the hill."

"How far?"

"Five minutes at the most."

"Let's wait down here."

After twenty minutes the wind started to abate. Crocker said, "Sandra, why don't you stay here with Ritchie? We're gonna go look at the metal plant, then come back."

He turned to Akil, who looked disappointed, and said, "Let's go."

It was like midnight, with dust and sand swirling everywhere. Crocker, Mancini, Davis, and Akil tried to keep up with the guard, but he was fast, scrambling up the embankment and hanging a right, then circling a mound of sand whose top they couldn't see.

"Where'd he go?" Davis asked.

Akil: "Beats me."

Crocker located him near a forty-foot-long rectangular building, waving his scarf. Through the clouds of dust it appeared that windows were broken and the roof had partially caved in.

The guard smiled with broken teeth, then led them around the other side of the building to another stairway and ramp that descended into the ground. The door to this chamber was blocked by sand, so they had to clear it by hand. Then Mancini went to work on the rusted lock with his electric saw.

Inside they found napalm bombs and white phosphorus shells that Akil was able to identify by the warnings painted on them in Arabic. The SEALs had no way of telling how long they'd been there, or if they were still live.

They did a quick inventory, then wrapped the chain around the door and fixed it with a new Sargent and Greenleaf hardened-boron-alloy lock, which was almost impossible to pick, saw, or cut with a torch.

Crocker turned to Davis and said, "Run back to the truck and use the sat-phone to call Remington. Tell him what we found."

"Yes, sir."

They left the site as the storm started to pick up again, negotiating what they could see of the road until they found the highway.

Feeling a sense of accomplishment, the five men and one woman told stories and joked as the Polish driver struggled to keep the vehicle on the road through the wind and sand. Most of the stories had to do with their various scrapes with the law. Crocker's were the most outrageous—numerous arrests for fighting, drunk driving, and resisting arrest as a wild teenager growing up in northern Massachusetts.

Sandra's one legal infraction was less serious but far more provocative—a misdemeanor charge for nude sunbathing. All of them quickly imagined it, including Crocker, who said, "That cop was an idiot."

"Yeah," Ritchie said, "he should have left an ideal situation alone."

By the time they arrived back at the NATO base the wind had let up and the sky had turned a strange shade of purple. When the truck turned into the compound, Crocker saw Major Ostrowski and his soldiers unloading a group of five prisoners from the back of two SPG Kalina armored personnel carriers.

"We used the storm to surprise them," the major crowed. "While they keep shelling the base, me and my men circled around and attacked them from behind. Killed about a dozen and captured these guys."

Crocker noticed that one of the tribesmen was badly wounded in the chest. He and Akil carried him into the compound, where they applied blowout patches. But the kid had lost so much blood that all they could do was try to comfort him as he spent his last minutes clutching the large silver amulet that hung around his neck and praying.

Afterward they joined the major, who loomed over the prisoners sitting on the ground looking hungry, thirsty, and scared. Ostrowski ordered his men to bring water and bread. Then he turned to Akil and said, "Tell the prisoners I'll let them eat and drink, and will treat them well, if they answer a few of my questions. Otherwise I'll drop them in the middle of the desert to be eaten by buzzards."

The tribesmen whispered among themselves. Then one

skinny kid spoke in a high, shrill voice. He told Akil that he and his fellow tribesmen were all under the age of twenty, and were simply trying to recover land and property that had previously belonged to their families. They had no beef with NATO, he said, and were not the men responsible for shelling the base.

"Bullshit," the major said. "I suppose their property includes the uranium mines, yes? Who do they consider the enemy?"

"The NTC and the Arab radicals who overthrew Gaddafi."

"Who supplies them with guns and ammunition?"

"The Iranians," the man said to Akil, who translated his words into English.

"See?" Ostrowski said, turning to Crocker. "What did I tell you?"

Crocker: "Ask him if there are any Iranians over the border in Niger."

The young man nodded and held up the fingers on one hand.

Ostrowski: "Ask the little man if he knows the name of the Iranian in charge."

Akil said, "He doesn't know the man's full name. They call him Colonel D."

Crocker stepped closer to the prisoner. "Is Colonel D a short man with a badly scarred face and hooded eyes?"

After Akil translated, the young tribesmen nodded.

"Colonel D is the alias of Farhed Alizadeh of the Qods Force," Crocker stated.

Akil: "Isn't he the guy you saw when we raided the *Contessa*? The one who escaped?"

"That's him."

* * *

They flew out on the same RCAF CC-130 early the next morning, accompanied by the four surviving prisoners and two Polish guards. Back in Tripoli, Sandra said she was returning to Germany in two days and hoped not to return to Libya anytime soon.

"We'll always have Toummo," Akil said, paraphrasing a line from *Casablanca.*

Sandra shook her head and smiled.

Crocker had a lot on his mind, including the news about Farhed Alizadeh, which he wanted to report to Remington. But Holly came first.

As soon as he and his men returned to the guesthouse, he called the embassy. Knocking out the rhythm to "Lonely Boy," the Black Keys song playing in the living room, he waited for Leo Debray to get on the line.

"So tell me, Leo," Crocker asked, "where is she staying?"

"Holly?"

"Who else?"

"Holly's not here yet," Debray answered in an official tone of voice.

"Why? What happened?"

"Nothing happened, really. She and Brian never arrived."

Crocker sensed something wrong. "What do you mean, they never arrived? I thought they were supposed to land here this morning. Was the flight delayed again?"

"I don't know."

He felt his blood pressure rocket up. "What do you mean, you don't know?"

"I mean the flight did land earlier today, and they weren't on it. Why, we don't know. We've tried to contact them but don't know where they are. We haven't heard from them since last night."

He felt like he'd been kicked in the balls. Trying to breathe normally, he said, "You're telling me my wife is missing?"

"I'm sorry to report that's more or less correct."

He wanted to say that things like this weren't supposed to happen to American officials traveling overseas. Instead he looked out the window and asked, "Holly doesn't have a cell phone with her?"

"She has one but isn't answering. We've left numerous messages but so far have received no calls back."

"What about Brian?"

"Same thing."

"And the last place you heard from them was Sirte?"

"That's correct. Last night, like I told you."

"You don't have any people there who can check on them?"

"Not in Sirte."

"How come?"

"Because the city was almost completely destroyed during the war."

CHAPTER NINE

Act like a man of thought. Think like a man of action.

—Thomas Mann

THE SKY was pitch black by the time the NATO helicopter landed at the airport in Sirte, which was some 280 miles southeast of Tripoli. The town of seventy-five thousand was the birthplace of Muammar Gaddafi and the place where he had been captured and killed on October 20 of the preceding year. The airport and terminal still showed signs of the recent fighting: damaged and pockmarked buildings, the rusting carcass of a tank with slogans painted on it in white, pickup trucks with mounted antiaircraft guns and .50-caliber guns in back, their barrels pointed at the sky but covered with tarps.

Leo Debray had called ahead and arranged for a NATO rep to meet Crocker in the terminal. Since it was a personal matter, he had decided not to bring any members of his team.

Crocker found the rep standing in the entrance under

a flickering fluorescent light in his olive-green uniform, a Canadian major with a gleaming shaved head. Behind him local men were sweeping the floor and collecting trash. The airport was closed for the night.

Major Cummings said, "Your wife and Mr. Shaw were booked to fly on a Libyan Airlines flight at nine this morning. Service at this airport has been spotty because several members of the control tower staff disappeared during the recent fighting. The upshot is, the flight didn't take off until eleven. Your wife and Mr. Shaw weren't on it. It was the only flight that left this airport bound for Tripoli today."

"So they couldn't have caught a later flight?"

"No. That was the only one."

"Did they call and change their reservation?"

"Apparently not."

"You checked?"

"Yes, sir. And I checked the passenger list for the flight that left at eleven. Your wife and Mr. Shaw's names aren't on it."

"How accurate are those lists?"

"I wouldn't bet the farm on them."

"What about a military flight or a private plane?"

"Chances are they would have left from this airport, and there's no record of any flight bound for Tripoli this afternoon."

The fact remained that Holly hadn't been heard from. Calls to her cell phone went unanswered. Nobody had seen or heard from her since yesterday.

Crocker ran through other possibilities as he followed the Canadian up a narrow flight of stairs to the second floor. The odds that they had decided to drive to Tripoli were remote. One, the road was dangerous and passed through numerous checkpoints. Two, Holly and Brian didn't have a car, which meant they would have had to hire one.

Still, he held out hope. Holly was resourceful and generally lucky. She knew how to handle herself.

The airport manager was a little man, coffee-skinned with a wispy gray beard and hair. A framed photograph of President Barack Obama hung behind his desk. It turned out he had spent a year at Baylor University and spoke decent English. "The last time anyone saw your wife was yesterday afternoon," he said. "She missed her flight today. That's all I can tell you, I'm afraid."

Crocker asked, "Do you have any idea where she stayed last night?"

The airport manager rubbed his head. "Nobody comes here anymore, so the hotels are all closed. You're sure they stayed the night?"

"Yes. That's what they told the embassy."

The manager nodded and left.

Through the open window Crocker heard a woman's wailing voice. He couldn't understand the words she was singing but was moved by the sadness behind them.

Was it possible that Holly had decided to stay another night? Why?

He hated the thought, but a hookup wasn't out of the question. Holly was an attractive woman, Brian a good-looking younger man who had recently left his wife. Crocker hadn't seen Holly for almost a month. He hadn't spoken to her in weeks.

The station manager returned with a smile. Holding up a finger, he said, "I have the answer. How? Because I found the man who drove your wife and her friend to the house where they're staying. This man is downstairs now, in front of the terminal."

Outside, bullet holes and craters from rocket attacks marked every building. Many of the streetlights were damaged; burnt-out hulks of cars lined the street.

To their right, three men sat on the curb sipping coffee out of glass cups. One of them, an older man with badly bowed legs, rose and approached cautiously. He pointed to a black-and-white Datsun cab and nodded. Crocker and the Canadian opened the back door and got in.

It felt like a fever dream—the destruction everywhere, the savagery he'd witnessed here and throughout the Middle East, the empty streets, stars sparkling in the sky above, fresh air blowing in from the sea, the moon a crescent resembling an off-kilter smile.

The driver hummed to himself as he drove. Displayed on the dashboard was a laminated photograph of his family framed in black cloth, with a bouquet of dried flowers clipped to the top.

The city seemed abandoned. Crocker looked for lights in the houses they passed, like signs of hope.

After about ten miles the driver stopped at a one-story house set back from the beach. It sat on an incline and was topped by a white wall that almost reached the roof. Because of the angle, Crocker was able to see lights on inside.

"Give me a minute," he said, turning to the Canadian major. "I'll be right back."

"Call me if you need me."

No buzzer at the front door, so he tried knocking.

Once, twice, a third time so hard the door shook.

No answer. The front wall was too high to climb, so he pushed past some low shrubs and descended along the side. The property ended at the beach, where gentle waves washed across the sand. A second door sat in the middle of the back wall. No bell or buzzer there, either, so he hoisted himself up, put his foot on the knob, and climbed over, past palm trees that rattled overhead. The lights were on in the oval pool. Someone had left a white towel and an old issue of *Us* magazine by one of the lounge chairs.

It struck Crocker as a strange place for two professional colleagues to spend the night. Seemed more fitting for a romantic vacation.

Doubts started to stalk him. As he peered through the patio window he tried to remember precisely when he had spoken to Holly last and what they had discussed. There wasn't much to see—modern living room furniture, a vase filled with peacock feathers, a fireplace that opened to both sides of the house.

The patio door wasn't locked, so he slid it open and stepped in.

Saw a light and heard murmuring voices from inside.

This was starting to remind him of a movie scene where the husband returns home unexpectedly to find another man sleeping with his wife.

Holly would never do that.

Right?

He followed the light and voices up two steps and stopped. His heart seemed to be beating in his throat.

He tried to prepare himself. Took a deep breath.

What if I find them together? What will I do then?

He blocked out these thoughts and concentrated instead on the sounds: a rumble of waves crashing in the background, the low murmur of voices from the room. Bracing himself, he entered. The light came from a lamp on the far side of the bed. The sheets and coverlet had been pulled aside but the bed was empty. The murmuring sound was coming from a television on the opposite wall. He looked for signs of Holly and saw an open lipstick on the dresser alongside the white-handled brush she always carried in her purse, a pair of her running shoes on the floor.

She's still here!

Where?

Turning, he crossed along the front of the house through a long kitchen and dining area to a hallway on the far end. The bathroom door was open, the toilet inside running.

One door at the end of the hall; another behind him. He opened the one ahead and entered, let his eyes adjust to the darkness. The place was a mess—clothes, men's shoes, and papers strewn across the floor, the sheets pulled off a bed, a chair turned over. The dresser drawers emptied.

Crocker pulled aside the curtains so the moonlight streamed in and quickly confirmed that there was no one in the room.

His heart beating wildly, he spun and doubled back to the front of the house. Alarms were going off in his head.

A faint bluish light spilled out the bottom of the door. He clenched his fists and entered.

The first thing he noticed was the light from the desk lamp filling the small rectangular room with strange shadows. Next, his eyes focused on a single bed. In the folds of the covers Crocker saw a shiny object he identified as a six-inch kitchen knife.

Then he noticed a pool of blood on the floor near the desk. Stepping past the bed, he saw a man's body lying facedown. The back of his head had been blasted off, indicating an exit wound.

Instinctively, Crocker felt for an artery on his neck to confirm that he was dead. No pulse.

Lifting the body under the shoulders, he turned it over carefully.

It didn't resemble Brian Shaw or anyone else he recognized. Poor fellow looked to be a local—dark skin, hair, and eyes, a couple of days' growth of beard.

Crocker set the body back down, relieved and unsettled—relieved that his worst fears hadn't been confirmed, unsettled because he realized that something equally terrible had happened. A man had been killed, and Holly and Brian were missing.

He wanted to run and find her but had no idea where to go.

He also felt violated.

Nobody touches my wife and gets away with it. No one!

The *whoop-whoop-whoop* of the helicopter blades still echoed in his head as he sat in a comfortable leather chair in Ambassador Saltzman's office. Air-conditioned air tickled his nose. He wanted to sneeze but caught himself. The ambassador sat behind his desk speaking into a cordless phone.

Crocker had remained in Sirte the previous night with a group of Canadian soldiers who worked the scene. Canucks, they called themselves. Good guys who loved the North African weather but missed their girlfriends back home. All the female residents of the city were hiding, they reported as they gathered evidence from the house, searched the area, and set up local roadblocks, all in a frenzy.

They'd come up with practically nothing. The deceased man in the house turned out to be the caretaker, a Libyan engineering student named Ali ak-Riyyad, twenty-one years old. The owners had fled to Morocco before the war and hadn't returned. When friends and family members weren't using the place, they rented it to visitors.

Holly and Brian Shaw had learned about the house from the man who ran the information desk at the airport. They had driven there in a cab two afternoons ago. Judging from the condition of Ali's body, the attack had taken place in the early morning hours of the following day, approximately eighteen hours before Crocker arrived.

Shoe marks and handprints indicated that the attackers had climbed over the front wall and entered the house through an open kitchen window. They had exited out the front door. Someone had been injured, because drops of blood were spotted leading outside.

Now, sunlight streamed in through a crack in the curtains of the ambassador's office. A quick glance at his watch showed Crocker it was almost one in the afternoon.

"Please, general, this is a priority. You must do everything in your power," Saltzman said into the phone, "and act quickly. The last thing we want is for this to reach the press."

The last sentence jarred Crocker's attention. *Who gives a shit about the press?*

He looked up. Remington sat across from him, next to a framed photograph of the ambassador standing next to the Clintons. He was writing something on a yellow pad as the ambassador spoke.

"No. Absolutely not," the ambassador continued. "We haven't heard anything here. I'll let you know as soon as we do. Remember, speed is of the utmost importance. Yes. Yes. Thanks."

He hung up, undid the top button of his white oxford shirt, and called, "Nancy, find Leo Debray and tell him I want to see him."

Crocker was picturing Holly—the way her long brown hair framed her face, the warmth in her brown eyes, the fullness of her lips. She was strong, but delicate inside.

Amazing woman... Grace under pressure... A beautiful, compassionate soul...

He jerked his head up when he heard his name. "Crocker? Warrant Officer Crocker?"

"Yes, sir."

"This is a terrible situation. I wish I knew you and your wife better."

Strange thing to say.

"Why?"

"Why?" The ambassador pulled up a chair, sat directly in front of him, and adjusted his suspenders. "Sometimes people in authority are put in a godawful position. So please excuse me for asking, is there any chance that your wife and Mr. Shaw ran off together?"

It was like a slap in the face. "Why do you ask?"

"Not that I've heard anything. No. I'm referring to a

spur-of-the-moment decision. Maybe they realized they had some time off and chose to explore the country together."

"Where would they go?"

"I don't know. Misrata? Benghazi? One of the towns along the coast?"

Crocker's throat had turned so dry that he found it difficult to speak. "Why, sir? Has someone said something?"

"No. No. Not at all. I don't want you to think..."

"Think... what?"

"The fact is that we've seen very little residual violence in that area. It's been more or less completely calm."

Crocker felt his fists clenching. He wanted to shout something but held back. He took a breath and said, "Sir, the house was attacked. There's no doubt about that. The caretaker was killed. My wife and Mr. Shaw left behind a good number of their personal belongings."

"But not their suitcases, correct? Did you find their suitcases?"

This line of questioning was pissing him off. "No, I didn't, but—"

"It makes one wonder..."

"What, sir? I found my wife's favorite hairbrush. She takes it with her everywhere. Her grandmother gave it to her. There's no way in..."

Remington crossed his long legs. He was clearly uncomfortable.

The ambassador rubbed his chin. "I see."

"See what, sir?"

"I'm sure there's an explanation."

Crocker said, "The obvious one is that they've been kidnapped."

Remington jumped in. "Let's not rush to conclusions. Transportation and communication in this country are both problematic. It's something we deal with on a daily basis."

"This is clearly more than a transportation problem."

"Jumping to conclusions doesn't help."

He wanted to shout "Fuck you!" But before he could, the ambassador spoke.

He said, "Crocker, I can assure you that we'll do everything in our power. Everything. We're currently deploying all our in-country assets, which are considerable. We've got on-the-ground assets; we've got drones we can deploy in the air. We'll find your wife. I promise."

"Yes, we will," Remington echoed.

"You can count on us, dammit. I'll stake my career on that."

It's exactly what Crocker wanted to hear. Gazing down at the coat of arms in the rug, he said, "I appreciate that, sir."

"What good are we, if we can't look after our own?"

"I agree, sir."

"Try and get some sleep. You must be exhausted."

True, he hadn't slept. But it seemed like a ridiculous idea. Crocker muttered, "I'll try, sir," and rose to his feet. His head hung like a huge weight on his shoulders. He wanted to do something to help recover his wife but didn't know what.

The ambassador said, "I have one request before you leave."

"What's that, sir?"

"Under no circumstances are you to talk to the press."

The press. The press? Why would I talk to the press? He didn't trust what they reported and did everything he could to avoid them. Besides, the presence of SEAL Team Six operators in Libya was supposed to be top secret.

Doesn't Saltzman know that?

Someone drove him to the guesthouse in a black sedan. An Amy Winehouse song was playing on the stereo. He opened his eyes as the tire wheels crunched on the gravel drive. Birds were singing. Two green parrots with red beaks chased each other past the windshield and into a nearby tree.

He thought he might be dreaming, but then saw the grim, determined faces of Ritchie, Mancini, Akil, and Davis emerging from the house to greet him. They'd heard the news and crowded around him, expressing their sympathy.

Akil: "We'll get her back."

Mancini: "Holly's a tough lady. She'll be fine."

Davis: "Just tell us what to do, boss. I'm in."

Akil: "We all are."

Ritchie: "Whatever it takes."

He knew that if he could count on anyone at a time like this, it was his men. "Thanks, guys. Where's Cal?"

"He went home. Remember?"

Feeling a hundred years old, he sat at the kitchen table and drank a cup of bitter coffee. Mancini stood before him with his hand over the receiver of a satellite phone. "It's the CO. You want to talk to him?"

"Who?"

"Our CO back at headquarters in Virginia. I'll tell him you'll call back."

"No."

"You sure?"

"Yeah. Hand me the phone."

He recognized Alan Sutter's smooth voice, the distinctive Kentucky accent. Remembered that he had bought land in his native state and planned to retire there and raise horses. Racehorses.

Their CO was saying all the right things—about loyalty, sticking together, praying for Holly, doing anything that could possibly be done.

"Thank you, sir. I appreciate that."

"We're family, Crocker. Holly's one of us."

"I know." Emotion built in his chest.

His CO paused. He was a no-nonsense guy. Sentimentality didn't figure into his decisions.

He said, "Crocker, this is a difficult situation for all of us. I pray that the whole thing's a misunderstanding and Holly shows up untouched."

"Me, too, sir."

"But here's the hard reality. No point pussyfooting around."

He sensed what was coming and steeled himself.

"You and your men are there to complete an important mission."

"Understood, sir."

"Mancini told me that you're under way but still have a few more sites to inspect."

"One or two more, sir. That's correct."

"Under the circumstances, I should recall you, relieve you of your duties there."

"Sir—"

His CO raised his voice. "Let me finish!"

"Sorry, sir."

"But I can't."

"Can't what, sir?"

"Order you back. I know you want to be there close to your wife. I would, too. So I leave that decision up to you."

Crocker started to get choked up. "Thank you, sir. That means a lot to me."

Sutter said, "Here's the situation. I want you to turn over the inspections to Warrant Officer Mancini. I know that you also lost Calvin, so I'm sending two other men."

"Sir, that won't be necessary."

"I think it is."

"I disagree, sir."

"Why?"

"First, I have sufficient men with me to complete the inspections. Secondly, I'm perfectly capable of continuing to lead them myself."

The CO paused, then said, "That doesn't sound realistic."

"Trust me, it is, sir."

"Seriously, Crocker. You mean to tell me you think you can ignore the situation with your wife and continue?"

"A mission is a mission, sir."

"Dammit, Crocker. Don't do anything stupid. Don't get in the way."

"I won't, sir. The ambassador has assured me that he has people out there looking for Holly. Frankly, I don't know the country well enough to know where to start."

Sutter: "I should probably have my head examined."

"You make perfect sense to me, sir."

"If I hear about any interference from you, you're out of there."

"I understand."

"Alright, Crocker. My prayers are with you and your wife. Godspeed."

CHAPTER TEN

Because we focused on the snake, we missed the scorpion.

—Egyptian proverb

THE TWO Ambiens Davis gave him knocked him out. In the morning he couldn't remember anything except the Lord's Prayer, which he repeated over and over in his head.

Our Father who art in heaven,
hallowed be thy name.
Thy kingdom come.
Thy will be done
on earth as it is in heaven.
Give us this day our daily bread,
and forgive us our trespasses,
as we forgive those who trespass against us,
and lead us not into temptation,
but deliver us from evil.
Amen.

Crocker had never been much of a believer in prayer or organized religion, but this morning he got down on his knees beside the bed and said out loud: "God, please look after Holly and deliver her from whatever evil might await her. Don't let anyone harm her. She's a good woman, filled with love and light, and worthy of your mercy and compassion. Amen."

He was still repeating the Lord's Prayer to himself like a mantra when they arrived at the airport. As he stood with his cell phone waiting for Remington to come on the line, Akil, wearing a tight black T-shirt, said, "Doug Volman stopped by last night."

"Who?"

"Volman. You know, that goofy guy from the State Department."

"What did he want?"

"He said he wanted to talk to you."

"What about?"

"Wouldn't say."

Remington picked up, sounding hoarse and tired, as though he'd been speaking all night. "What's up?"

Crocker said, "I want to let you know that we're assembled at the airport, about to leave for the military base in Sebha."

Remington provided background, explaining that Sebha was nearly five hundred miles almost directly south of Tripoli, a transportation hub in the middle of the Sahara that Gaddafi had transformed into an agricultural oasis thanks to the Great Man Made River, a network of 1,750 miles of pipes that transported fresh water from wells to cities throughout Libya. It was the largest irrigation project on earth, described by Gaddafi as the eighth wonder of the world.

"Interesting. In all the confusion about my wife, I forgot to tell you about our trip to Toummo, particularly our discovery that Iranians are stirring up trouble along the border with Niger."

"We knew that already."

"What about the fact that Farhed Alizadeh is down there directing things?"

"It's got our attention."

"What do you think Alizadeh's presence there means?"

"It means that the Iranians want uranium, which we already knew."

"I'm not an expert," Crocker said, "but it seems significant."

"Are Lasher and Dr. Jabril there yet?" Remington asked, changing the subject.

Crocker saw a black sedan crossing the tarmac. "I think they've just arrived."

"Good. Oh, and, regarding Holly, we're following up on a lead now. I've had my men out working since we met with the ambassador. I'll let you know as soon as I hear something."

"Thank you. I appreciate all that you're doing and wish you good luck."

He wanted to trust Remington, the ambassador, and the people who worked for them. Wanted to believe that they had a network of dependable sources throughout the country that would find Holly and Brian Shaw and quickly bring them back unharmed. But he had doubts, most of which related to the Sheraton bombing. He chased them away by running through Colonel Boyd's OODA loop in his head, which he had committed to memory as a young SEAL and repeated to himself every time he launched a mission.

1. <u>O</u>bservation—the highest priority. Find the threat before it finds you.
2. <u>O</u>rientation—take in the situation and surroundings. Anticipate steps that will be difficult for your enemy to predict.
3. <u>D</u>ecision—trust your subconscious mind to weigh all the variables and present your conscious mind with the option that will offer your highest chance of success.
4. <u>A</u>ction—act and don't worry about your chances of survival. If you're wounded, you'll receive medical care once the threat is neutralized.

Their gear sat waiting on the same RCAF CC-130 Hercules they had flown to Toummo—weapons, Geiger counters, hazmat suits, shovels, saws, breaching material, acetylene torches, new locks.

Jabril strapped himself into the seat next to him and said, "My friends and I are worried about the future of our country."

"I would be, too, if I were a Libyan."

They were only a few minutes aloft and were already passing over endless tracts of desert.

Jabril, who was in a talkative mood, started sharing his impressions of Gaddafi. How he used to sit around a fire in the backyard of his compound and talk all night—about his dreams for Libya, his theories of human evolution, and the relations between men and women.

He spent most of his time outdoors, despite the fact that he'd built a palace decorated with a white baby grand piano, indoor pools, a golden mermaid sofa, and closets stocked with his eccentric wardrobe, ranging from uniforms covered in gold braid to African tribal gowns.

He considered swine flu a biological weapon, and had even designed and built his own car, called the Rocket, which he called the world's safest automobile. Why had he built it? To better protect his people, many of whom were killed and injured on Libyan roads every year.

Crocker nodded and listened politely. If nothing else, Jabril was helping him keep his mind off his own problems.

"Have you ever heard the name Sheik Zubair?" the scientist asked.

"I don't believe so."

"Gaddafi believed that William Shakespeare was really a poet from Basra, Iraq. He claimed to have studied Shakespeare and discovered a strong resemblance in his work to the teaching of the Zenith sect of Islam."

"That sounds pretty out there."

"I agree. But aren't all men shades of gray? Even Gaddafi did some positive things."

"For example?"

"He gave everyone in Libya free electricity, free health care, and free education. All loans were interest free. Gasoline cost fourteen cents a gallon. The country was debt free."

"Then why was he overthrown?"

"My friends claim it was more like a coup d'etat from abroad," Jabril answered.

"A coup?"

The elfin-faced scientist nodded. "My friends are sophisticated men. Businessmen, professors. They opposed

Gaddafi, but claim that anti-Gaddafi sentiment was never very strong."

Crocker wasn't particularly interested in Libyan politics and had no way of judging if what Jabril was saying was true. Still, he nodded and listened politely.

"A coup d'etat from abroad to get two things, oil and gold," Jabril continued.

Oil sounded reasonable, but... "Gold?"

"Gold, yes." Jabril grinned and leaned closer. "Gaddafi owned one hundred and fifty tons of gold that he kept in banks in Tripoli. He was also talking about introducing an African currency called the gold dinar, which would have rivaled the dollar and euro, and shifted the economic balance."

"Shifted it which way?"

"Oil would no longer have been traded exclusively in dollars."

"And your friends believe that's why Gaddafi was overthrown?"

The Libyan raised a crooked index finger. "Consider this. In the year 2000, Saddam Hussein announced that Iraqi oil would be traded in euros instead of dollars. Sanctions and war followed, and he was ousted. The same thing happened to Gaddafi."

Crocker wasn't a big believer in conspiracy theories. He'd heard them all—the Illuminati were secretly running the world, or the Rothschild banks, the oil cartels, the drug cartels, Opus Dei.

After two more hours of listening to the doctor reminisce about his childhood in Libya and his wife and children, they touched down in Sebha. As he exited the aircraft and felt the midday heat bearing down on him,

Crocker noticed several MiG-25s parked beside the runway. "They used to be a mainstay of Gaddafi's air force," said Lasher. "Now they belong to the NTC. Trouble is, they don't have anyone to fly them, because all the pilots left the country."

They piled into a van for the short ride to the military base, past a domed mosque and a large hill of sand with a castle on top that Jabril said had been built by the Italians in the 1930s, when Libya was still a colony.

Sebha appeared to be a sleepy, windswept town. The streets were paved and modern, most of the buildings white one- or two-story dwellings.

Akil pointed out the green pro-Gaddafi flags flying from a number of houses and vehicles. "What's that about?"

"Curious," Lasher answered. "I noticed them, too."

The base looked abandoned, except for two elderly men in olive-green uniforms who guarded the gate. It was surrounded by a ten-foot-high chain-link fence topped with barbed wire and consisted of several barracks, a shed with two disabled tanks inside, a shooting range, and a water tower that looked like it hadn't been used in years.

Several skinny, mangy dogs slept in the shade created by a broken-down transport truck. "Soviet make," Mancini reported. "A KrAZ, I believe they called it. Remember, boss, Afghanistan in 2000?"

"Didn't we drive one of these through the Panjshir Valley?"

"Correct."

It had been a CIA-led mission to assassinate Bin Laden that was aborted by President Clinton. They were stationed in the Panjshir, working with the

Afghan Northern Alliance, particularly its leader, the charismatic Ahmad Shah Massoud. He and his small force of Tajik tribesmen had held off the Soviets for ten years. Back in late 2000 they were resisting the Taliban and al-Qaeda and seeking American help, but Washington was more interested in the come stains on Monica Lewinsky's dress.

Massoud was assassinated by al-Qaeda on September 9, 2001—two days before the World Trade Center attack. The memory still produced a pain at the pit of Crocker's stomach. Sometimes political leaders and policymakers in Washington didn't understand, because they were too far removed from the realities on the ground.

The van bounced up and down as Jabril directed the driver down a road mostly obscured with sand. It wound around a several-hundred-foot-high mountain of dirt and loose rock to a second fence and a gate posted with warning signs in Arabic.

After Ritchie cut through the lock with a battery-operated saw, they entered and drove past a fifty-foot mound of dirt and boulders to an opening between two even higher mounds of barren sand and rock.

This was another unlikely place to find anything, especially the modern refinery-type plant that occupied the three-hundred-by-hundred-yard space. White metal, glass, and aluminum all sparkled in the sun like a mirage.

"Where'd this come from?" Ritchie mumbled as they stepped out of the parked vehicle. "Mars?"

They walked under the cloudless pale blue sky as Jabril pointed out the plant's features—the long production shed that had once housed his office, the storage and distillation tanks, drying facilities, and cylinder filling station. Unlike the plant at Toummo, this one hadn't been inspected in recent years.

"This is where we manufactured mustard gas and sarin in the nineties," the Libyan scientist said.

"How much?" Crocker asked.

"Roughly two hundred tons until I defected in 2003."

"Two hundred tons? That's a hell of a lot."

Jabril explained that the plant had been built in the nineties with the help of a German company and Japanese engineers.

"Where are the chemical weapons now?" Crocker asked.

Jabril said, "You're about to find out." He stopped to adjust his sunglasses and mop the sweat off his brow. Then he continued toward the opposite two-hundred-foot mountain of dirt and rock. The sun was impossibly hot.

Following twenty feet behind with Lasher and Akil, Crocker didn't notice the indentation in the mountain until Jabril disappeared.

"Where'd you go?" he called.

"I'm over here," the doctor shouted, his voice echoing through the mounds of sand.

When they joined him, he pointed to a pile of boulders positioned against the side of the mountain. "There's an entrance somewhere behind there," he said.

"Are you sure?"

"Yes. Unless the whole chamber was destroyed."

It took almost an hour for Crocker, Davis, Akil, Ritchie, and Mancini to clear away the rocks. Behind them stood a metal door tall and wide enough to accommodate a truck and painted to blend in with the terrain.

"Clever, yes?" Jabril asked.

"Very clever," Crocker answered. The hard work had made him sweat through his clothes.

"This must have cost a shitload to build," Akil said.

"Hundreds of millions," Lasher offered.

"What for?"

"To produce chemical weapons."

"I know that already," Akil answered. "My question is, What did Gaddafi want them for?"

"Back in the nineties, he had a vision of creating a united Africa. He called it the African Union and saw himself as its godfather. Planned to lead a united continent that would rival the United States or the Soviet Union in military and economic strength."

"The man had ambition."

"So did Hitler," Mancini added.

The door had an internal lock that Mancini managed to pick—which was convenient, because the next option would have been to use explosives, and they didn't know what was housed inside.

It took three men to push the door open. The awful screeching sound reverberated up Crocker's spine. Hundreds of little black birds took flight and circled overhead.

Crocker, Lasher, Jabril, and Mancini were selected to wear the hazmat suits.

Unlike the Class C suits they had worn at Busetta that used gas masks to filter the outside air, these suits were Class A, which meant that they were vaporproof right down to their special seam-sealing zippers, two-ply chemical-resistant nitrile gloves, and supplied-air respirator with escape cylinder. Each man breathed from an oxygen tank strapped inside his suit.

The hiss of Crocker's breath through the respirator and

the crinkly roar produced by every movement of the thick plastic material drowned out all other sound. The suit was so bulky that Crocker couldn't see his feet. And it was hot.

Holding a high-powered flashlight, Jabril led them inside one of two high tunnels that had been carved into the mountain. At one end was a twenty-by-twenty-foot chamber stacked to the ceiling with narrow five-foot-long aluminum cylinders.

"Mustard gas," he said through the two-way radio built into his suit.

"Which ones?" Crocker asked.

The scientist pointed a purple glove to his right.

"And that's sarin over here," he said pointing to the cylinders to his left.

"That's a whole lot of destructive power."

"Serious stuff."

"The sarin degrades quickly. But the mustard gas might still be lethal."

"Even ten years later?"

"It's possible."

"I feel like I'm about to faint," Lasher shouted through the radio. Mancini helped him out of the tunnel. The others followed.

Outside, Lasher removed his hood to reveal a head and face covered with sweat. After chugging a bottle of water, he said, "We've got to secure this place immediately. If the wrong people get their hands on this, the NTC could be fucked."

"They're fucked already," Ritchie mumbled.

Davis: "The sat-phone's in the vehicle."

Lasher held up a hand. "Wait..."

Once he caught his breath, he explained that the United States had known about the chemical weapons stored here for years, but the Department of Defense had refused to allocate the $100 million it would cost to clean up the site and dispose of them.

"Why?" Ritchie asked.

"Politics. DOD wanted Congress to pass a special provision. The House held hearings back in 2007, but never allocated the funding."

Akil: "I hope someone's willing to spend the money now."

Ritchie: "Either that or we bury the whole fucking thing under the mountain. I can rig up a bomb with the extra can of gasoline attached to the back of the van."

Crocker: "Not yet."

When they'd rehydrated and cooled down as best they could, Crocker and Mancini accompanied Jabril for one last look around the tunnel. Sand gophers and lizards scurried about in the dark. When Mancini switched on the handheld digital Geiger counter, it went berserk, whining and flashing.

"Hey, boss!"

"Is it working correctly?"

Jabril said through the radio, "Let me see that machine."

The device squealed even louder when he approached the chamber at the far end. In the cone of light Crocker saw a dozen green canisters—each one the width and half the length of a coffin—propped against the rear wall.

Jabril handed the flashlight and Geiger counter to Mancini and started to unfasten the metal clasps along the side of one of them.

"Is that safe?" Crocker asked.

"Probably not."

The scientist pulled back the lid and pointed to where he wanted Mancini to shine the light. Embedded inside the canister were four dozen glass ampoules filled with white and silver crystals.

"What's that?" Crocker asked.

"I believe it's uranium hexafluoride," Jabril said.

"UF6?"

"Yes."

Crocker knew that UF6 was a compound needed to enrich uranium. It was hard to make and carefully monitored by the International Atomic Energy Agency (IAEA).

He tried to locate Mancini's eyes through the plastic mask but it was completely fogged up.

"You okay in there?" Crocker asked.

"Yeah. You need UF6 to make a nuclear weapon," Mancini shouted into his radio.

"I know. I know. Lower the fucking volume."

"Sorry. What do we do now?"

Crocker said, "Let's seal it back up and carry it out of here."

"Why?"

"Just do it. I'll explain outside."

The two SEALs lugged the canister under their arms, set it down near the entrance, then went back to help Jabril, who seemed to be struggling. Once outside they helped him take off his hood and saw that the scientist's face was deep red.

"It's my heart."

"Sit down, breathe deeply," Crocker said, unbuttoning

the top of the Libyan's shirt and checking his pulse. "I'll get you some water."

Meanwhile, Mancini joined the other men, who were sitting in the shade, and explained what they had found. At the mention of uranium hexafluoride Lasher jumped to his feet. "Jesus Christ! You found UF6? You're kidding. Where?"

"The ampoules are in the canister we carried out. Right there."

Lasher ran over to it and examined the labels and writing on the outside.

Mancini warned, "It's leaking radioactivity, so don't get too close."

Lasher said, "It was shipped to Tajoura in 2010. In 2010!"

Davis: "What's Tajoura?"

"It's a nuclear research facility about ten miles east of Tripoli. Houses a research lab and a ten-megawatt reactor built by the Soviets. But it was shut down in 2004, after Gaddafi told the world he was abandoning his plan to build a nuclear weapon. Back in March of that year the IAEA oversaw the removal of weapons-grade enriched uranium from Tajoura, which was then shipped to the Russian Federation."

"Incredible," Mancini muttered, shaking his head.

"Why is it here?" Crocker asked.

Lasher: "Good question."

"What's it mean?" Davis asked.

"It's a smoking gun," Lasher offered. "The proof that Scorpion is real—a lethal weapon buried in the desert sand."

"A smoking gun in what sense?"

"The presence of UF6 proves that Gaddafi was still trying to build a nuclear weapon after the invasion of Iraq and the whole furor over WMDs. Back in 2004 he was afraid he was going to be invaded next. Made a speech before the UN, telling the whole world that he was going to play nice from now on."

"What do we do with it now?" Crocker asked.

Lasher: "Was that the only green canister?"

Mancini: "There were about a dozen more like it."

"You check those, too?"

"No."

Lasher: "Doesn't matter. We'll take this one back as evidence. NATO will have to figure out how to deal with the rest."

Jabril was feeling better. He said, "It's too dangerous to handle."

Lasher: "I brought a lead sheet in the truck. We'll wrap it in the lead sheet and take it with us."

Crocker: "Sounds like a plan."

They'd parked the van at the second gate—the one that connected the military base to the chemical plant. Lasher and Ritchie volunteered to walk back and get it.

While the others waited, Crocker and Davis went to explore the far side of the hill. There they found a vent hidden behind a boulder, but nothing else.

Davis said, "Sometimes I wonder what kind of world we brought our kids into."

"It was a hell of a lot easier to defend yourself when men fought with rocks and slingshots," Crocker answered.

"You read about all this apocalyptic end-of-time stuff and it makes you wonder."

"Sure does."

They sat in the shade talking about how advances in technology, designed to make the world safer, seemed to be having the opposite effect. Crocker heard a car horn honk three times.

"There's the van," he said getting to his feet.

He had taken half a dozen steps around the hill when he heard angry voices speaking Arabic, and stopped.

"What's wrong?" Davis asked.

"Listen," Crocker whispered back, pointing to the other side of the hill, then holding a finger to his lips.

Davis looked perplexed.

Very carefully, Crocker craned his head around the edge of the hill to look. In the distance he saw the van driving away, accompanied by two white pickups armed with .50-caliber machine guns. In the foreground, approximately two hundred feet from where he was standing, a dozen men wearing black and brown kaffiyehs pointed automatic weapons at Mancini and Jabril, who were seated on the ground with their hands tied behind their backs.

As Crocker watched, the armed men led Mancini and Jabril to two more white pickup trucks, pushed them into the back, then piled in themselves and drove off, leaving behind a cloud of dust. The canister was gone.

"Who the hell are they?" Davis asked.

"I didn't see any patches or insignia. Did you?"

"No, but there was a green flag painted on the door of the truck."

"Fuck."

The two SEALs ran along the back of the three hills and arrived at the fence surrounding the military base.

Seeing parked pickups on the other side, they hid behind some rocks and waited almost an hour, until the sky started to turn dark, so they could enter the base with a diminished risk of being discovered.

“What do we do now?” Davis asked.

“First we climb the fence. Then we try to find our guys.”

CHAPTER ELEVEN

Pain is weakness leaving the body.

—Tom Sobal

CLIMBING THE chain-link fence was the easy part, the only danger being the razor wire on top. Once Crocker and Davis got over that, they scrambled down the other side, crouched on the lid of a dumpster, then eased themselves down to the ground. They were completely unarmed and had no comms.

A wild animal howled in the distance. Otherwise, the landscape around them was eerily still. Abandoned tanks and vehicles in front of them, the shooting range to their left. Most of the camp, including the barracks, storage shed, and water tower, stood to their right. Beyond that rose the front gate.

"You wait here near the dumpster," Crocker said. "I'll go surveil the base."

"Careful, boss."

"Let's hope our guys are still here."

"What do we do if they're not?"

"We'll figure that out later."

His excitement grew as he moved alone in the dark, hiding behind the wheels of an abandoned transport truck, checking to see if the coast was clear. He felt like he was a kid back in the town he'd grown up in, playing with stolen cars. Canvas flapped in the breeze that arrived as the sky turned black. A window on one of the storage sheds banged open and closed.

The four white pickups were parked thirty feet in front of him, the barrels of their .50-cals pointed at the stars.

Seeing no one near the vehicles, he ran toward them in a crouch, then heard someone cough and spit to his right. He ducked behind a barrel that reeked of urine, his heart pounding.

There was an armed man at two o'clock. Another farther to Crocker's right, smoking a cigarette. They stood at the entrance to one of the barracks, talking in low voices, cradling AK-47s, recognizable by their long, curved magazines. A chill ran up his spine as he remembered the dozens of them that had been fired at him in places like Pakistan, Somalia, Afghanistan, and Iran.

Here I go again.

He waited for the soldier to toss his cigarette butt to the ground and enter the barracks with his colleague behind him. Then Crocker continued to the trucks, hoping to find a weapon of some kind. When he looked into the cab of the nearest Toyota, he saw a man sleeping on the front seat clutching what looked to be a brand-new Soviet-design PPSh-41 submachine gun.

Crocker thought for a second of wrestling it away but decided the noise might attract attention. He needed to assess the layout of the base first.

So he made a wide arc to the water tower, pausing to hide behind its legs, then continued to the far end of the two-hundred-foot-long concrete barracks. This part of the structure was badly in need of repair. Windows were missing on both floors, and so were many of the tiles on the roof. Dozens of bats darted in and out.

No sign of the van or the men. Desperation started to creep under his skin.

Someone screamed near the other end of the barracks, causing his hair to stand on end.

He saw a light on the second floor, then heard the man screaming again. This time it sounded like Jabril.

He ran along the front of the barracks and abruptly stopped when he saw two soldiers sitting out front. One of them tossed a rock toward the trucks. Crocker held his breath, turned on his toes, and hurried back.

This time he circled around the back of the barracks, which seemed deserted. What appeared to have been an exercise yard was now littered with garbage and pieces of rusting metal. The long building had been constructed in three forty-foot-wide sections, each with its own entrance in front and back. Each section had its own metal fire escape that ran the length of the six second-story windows and led to a ladder in the middle.

He hurried past barrels, broken bicycle parts, and rats scurrying through the trash to the ladder at the first section. Dim lights shone from the windows above. He heard someone talking in a loud voice.

The bottom of the ladder was beyond Crocker's reach, so he jumped, held on to the bottom rung, and pulled himself up. As the ladder extended, it made a screeching metal sound.

The man who was speaking stopped. But no way was Crocker turning back, now that he'd come this far. He climbed to the second floor, lay facedown on the metal slats, and waited, feeling his chest rising, adrenaline rushing through his body.

One minute passed, then another, then three. No sound from inside. He looked along the length of the barracks.

Seeing no soldiers, he pulled himself up onto his knees and walked in a crouch to the window with the light. Eased his head up so that his eyes barely reached the bottom of the window. Saw shadows against the wall and ceiling, but his view was blocked by the backs of several men in mismatched camouflage.

The same male voice he had heard before was scolding someone. Crocker heard the sound of something hitting flesh, then a muffled yelp.

When one of the men blocking the window stepped aside, he saw the terrified eyes of Ritchie, Lasher, and Mancini, who were squatting along the opposite wall. Their mouths were covered with tape and their hands were tied behind their backs.

A light of some sort beamed from the back of the room. Everyone's attention seemed to be directed to the front. When the man standing with his back to Crocker shifted, he saw that they were all looking at Jabril.

He'd been tied naked to a chair so that his arms were behind him and his genitals exposed. A soldier stepped into view and hit the doctor across the face with a stick. His head snapped back, splashing blood across the wall and floor.

Crocker had to restrain himself from busting through

the window right then. He was shocked, offended, and knew he had to move fast—before Jabril was beaten to death, or his men executed or moved somewhere else.

A peal of automatic-weapons fire went off in the distance. Crocker ducked below the window. He heard the squealing cry of an animal, followed by more gunshots, men shouting.

Hearing steps approaching along the back of the building, he hurried to the ladder and slid down, his hands wet with sweat. The steps were coming fast. On reaching the ground he turned to face the sound. An animal lunged at him, claws first. It was big, quick, and black—a dog? a hyena? He pivoted left and ducked so that it sailed past his shoulder and hit the ground, losing its footing and skidding on its side. It gathered its feet under it and turned, reared onto its back legs, and bared its teeth as if it was about to charge.

Crocker grabbed a chunk of concrete off the ground and faced it.

I dare you! I fucking dare you! his eyes blazed.

Hearing something behind it, the animal turned to look, and tore off.

Crocker took a deep breath, then hurried to the end of the barracks and circled back, retracing his steps. He found Davis hiding behind the dumpster, holding a four-foot length of lead pipe.

"I heard shots," Davis whispered. "I thought they got you!"

"I'm fine," he said, his chest heaving.

"Then what the fuck was that?"

"Hyenas, I think."

"They must have crawled through the fence."

"Maybe," Crocker whispered, catching his breath. "I saw our guys. I know where they're holding them."

"Who? Where?"

"Ritchie, Mancini, Lasher, Jabril."

"What about Akil?"

"I didn't see him."

"Where are they?"

Crocker pointed. "Second floor of the barracks. But I didn't see the van."

"I did. It's behind that shed."

"Which shed?"

Davis pointed to his left. "That one over there. But the doors are locked."

"Shit."

Davis unwrapped a rag he held in his hand. "Look what I found."

In the light of the half moon Crocker saw a rusted jigsaw blade, a plastic lighter, a section of metal wire, an empty bottle, and several large rocks.

"The lighter works?"

"Yeah."

Crocker's mind was processing fast. "You see any more bottles?"

Davis pointed to the dumpster. "I think there are more inside."

"Grab a few extras."

"Now?"

Crocker nodded as he formulated a plan.

Davis hoisted himself up into the dumpster, handed Crocker two soda bottles, and climbed out.

"Good."

"What now?"

"They don't know we exist. We've got one chance to surprise them. Show me the van."

"Now?"

"Go!"

They ran in a crouch, Davis first, Crocker right behind him. Around the back of the warehouse, past a broken-down tank painted with graffiti to where the van was parked under sheets of tin rattling in the breeze.

The canister of UF6 lay in back, but their weapons and gear were missing. And, as Davis had said, the doors were locked. So was the lid to the gas tank.

Crocker grabbed the container of extra fuel strapped to the rear door.

"Help me get this down," he whispered.

They undid the latch, set the container down, untwisted the cap.

Crocker said, "Now set down the bottles."

He lifted the container, filled the bottles with gasoline, then ripped the rag Davis was carrying and stuffed the pieces into the necks of the bottles as fuses.

Davis grinned at the three Molotov cocktails. "Nice."

"Now," Crocker whispered, "we need a gun."

"Unlikely we'll find one lying around."

"Follow me," he said.

Again they made a wide arc past three trashed transport trucks and the edge of the shooting range to avoid the barracks and the other soldiers.

Crocker stopped behind a concrete structure with a flagpole in the center that stood thirty feet from the four white pickups. On the other side of the trucks was the middle entrance to the barracks.

They huddled together, clutching the bottles. Crocker whispered, "See that Toyota facing us?"

Davis nodded.

"There's a soldier sleeping on the front seat. I'll circle around the other side. When you hear me jump the bastard and smash him with this rock, you come up from this side and grab his weapon."

"What about the bottles?"

"Leave 'em here."

"You sure?"

"Yeah. Let's go."

Crocker ran like a Mohawk—on his toes, as close as possible to the ground. Reaching the front of the Toyota, he ducked below the grille and slowly slithered around the bumper to the passenger side. But when he peeked in the window, the soldier was gone.

Fuck!

Standing halfway up, he signaled to Davis to go back and was about to leave when he heard someone mumbling behind him. He froze, took a deep breath, and pivoted slowly. Looking past his shoulder into the trapezoidal space created by the parked trucks, he saw a soldier with his back to him, kneeling on a blanket, praying. An old submachine gun with a perforated barrel lay beside him.

Without a moment's hesitation he crossed the four feet between them on his toes, reached over the soldier's head with both hands, and covered his mouth. He pushed the soldier's head down and then, pressing his knees against his shoulders, pulled the man's head back with all his might until he heard vertebrae snap. Instant death.

"Go with God," he whispered as the soldier's body

twitched one last time and relaxed. Crocker set him down gently, then grabbed the submachine gun.

He ran back to Davis, who asked, “What happened?”

“No time to explain.”

“Where’d you find the weapon?”

“This is what we’re going to do. You’re going to give me two minutes to run around back and climb up the fire escape.”

“Two minutes.”

“We’ll both count off our watches. When you reach two minutes, you’re going to light two of the Molotov cocktails and throw them at the pickups in front of us. Set those babies on fire.”

“Got it.”

“Then you’re going to follow my route, but stop at the front side of the barracks, over there. Wait at the corner. If you hear firing on the second floor of the farthest section, that’s me.”

“You’re taking the weapon with you?”

“That’s correct.”

“It looks ancient. What is it?”

“I believe it’s a PPSh-41. The Soviets manufactured millions of these suckers during World War Two.”

“Will it fire?”

“I hope so.”

“Boss—”

“Listen! If you get an opportunity to surprise a soldier and grab a weapon, do it. Then enter through the front door of the section on our right. You’ll find me on the second floor. When you get close, shout ‘Delta Bravo’ so I know it’s you.”

“And if I’m not able to get a weapon?”

"Wait at the corner of the building, like I told you before. You'll still have one more cocktail. Use it at your discretion."

"Roger."

"Improvise, but figure that there are at least a dozen enemy."

"I'll keep that in mind."

"One other thing."

"What's that?"

"I'm gonna need that saw blade."

Davis reached into his back pocket and handed it over. "Good luck."

"Two minutes. Start your timer…"

"It's engaged."

"See ya in a few."

He was running.

Looking up, Crocker saw a shooting star flash across the sky. His mother had told him they were good luck. He hoped so.

Glancing at the timer of his watch, he saw that fifty seconds had passed. At sixty, he was rounding the end of the barracks. At seventy-nine, he reached for the ladder. Ninety, he was on the metal fire escape. At a hundred and five, he knelt under the second-floor window.

Light spilled out. Looking down at the PPSh-41 and its drum magazine, he took a deep breath. Inside, the same man was still shouting questions. His voice sounded angrier this time.

At 119 seconds, Crocker took the weapon off safety, checked to be sure that a round was chambered, put it on full auto, and got ready to throw himself through the window.

He heard an explosion. Soldiers shouted in Arabic from the front of the building. A gun discharged.

He waited ten more seconds, praying that Davis was safe, then threw himself through the window back first. Hitting the floor, he somersaulted and started looking for targets. Two soldiers near the back wall were reaching for their weapons. He squeezed the trigger and ripped them with one long stream of bullets. Tore one soldier's leg in half at the knee. Caught the other in the groin. The PPSh-41 made a loud clanging sound and felt like it was going to come apart in his hands.

The bearded guy who had been doing all the shouting threw his stick at Crocker and reached for the pistol in his holster, but before he could remove it, Crocker peppered him with bullets from his chest to his head—a modified Mozambique, in SEAL lingo.

The little man stumbled back, hit the far wall next to where Ritchie was seated, and slumped to the floor. Crocker blasted another couple of rounds into his head just to be sure.

Ritchie started squirming and tried to talk through the tape plastered across his mouth. He wanted to be cut free. Crocker turned to his right to exchange the ancient PPSh-41 for one of the more modern AKs the soldiers had been carrying. But just as he started to pivot, two more soldiers came rushing into the room. Seeing Crocker with the Soviet submachine gun pointed at them, one of them jumped behind the door. The other raised his AK.

Crocker squeezed off three bullets before the Soviet submachine gun jammed. The bullets tore into the soldier's right arm. But instead of giving up, the young man with a thick black beard tried to shift the AK-47 to his left. It was a valiant effort that ended when Crocker, wielding the submachine gun like a club, took his right knee out, then finished him off with a blow to the head.

Crocker heard more automatic-weapons fire down the hallway and below.

He grabbed one of the AKs and pulled the tape off Ritchie's mouth.

"Motherfucker!" Ritchie shouted. "You took off half my lip."

"You don't need it anyway. Hold still."

He removed the rusted saw blade from his pocket and used it to cut through the tape around Ritchie's ankles and wrists. Then he handed him the blade.

"Cut the others free. I'll watch the door."

"Ten-four."

The room was a mess of blood and smoke. A bleeding, bruised, naked Jabril lay in the fetal position in a corner. His eyes were closed, but Crocker noticed the skin near his sternum was rising and falling. John Lasher sat slumped in a chair, long red slash marks over his chest and face. He too looked unconscious. Crocker would attend to them later. He had to deal with the enemy first.

It sounded like all-out war downstairs. Made him feel proud of Davis.

When he stuck his head out to look, bullets tore into the concrete wall, spitting dust into his mouth and eyes.

He dropped to the floor and fired back. The AK felt smooth and light in his hands, producing half the noise and recoil of the PPSh-41. But the hallway was dark, and he couldn't see anything except a dark object coming toward him that landed with a thud on the floor and rolled.

"Grenade!" he shouted, jumping inside and hiding behind the wall.

The concussion was so strong he thought his head was going to burst open. So powerful, in fact, that it picked up the four fallen soldiers and threw them against the wall facing the window he'd jumped through only minutes earlier. The room was foul with entrails and smoke.

Ritchie and Mancini staggered to their feet, armed themselves, and were ready to exact revenge.

"Where's Akil?" Crocker asked.

"He wasn't with us," Mancini answered, wiping gore off his face with the back of his hand.

"What happened to him?"

Ritchie: "Don't know."

"You two okay?"

"More or less."

Ritchie: "Fucking savages hadn't gone to work on us yet."

"Lucky."

"Sodomized the doctor with the stick."

"Jesus!"

"What now?" Mancini asked.

Crocker said, "Manny, you and Ritchie stay here. Defend the room. Kill as many of those fuckers as you can."

"Where you going?"

"I'm going to circle around front and hit the bastards from behind."

"Nice."

Crocker started toward the window and stopped to retrieve an automatic pistol from the dead leader's blood-and-guts-covered holster.

He was about to grab the frame of the window when

he heard someone shout. He looked back to see Mancini using a hand to break his fall.

"You okay?"

Mancini had a vague, confused look on his face. "The explosion fucked my head up a little."

Crocker turned back to check him. Since Mancini wasn't bleeding from his nose or ears, he figured it was a mild case of shock. He said forcefully, "We're depending on you, Manny. We need you to focus."

"I will."

Another, much milder explosion shook the building as Crocker climbed out the window. The concussion made him stumble.

Fuck!

He ran to the ladder and slid down. The back side of the building appeared deserted. All the action seemed to be going on out front. He heard something stir in the field to his right and readied the AK.

Something moved near a shattered wooden crate. Another hyena? A soldier?

He made out the form of a tall man holding a piece of wood or metal. The outline reminded him of someone.

"Akil?" he whispered.

"Boss?"

Akil dropped whatever he was brandishing and approached, holding his right wrist. He whispered, "I managed to get away, but I fucked up my hand again."

Crocker handed him the pistol. "Here. Hold this with your left. Follow me."

He proceeded quickly to the end of the barracks and peered around the corner. Saw orange flames as high as the roof of the barracks coming from two of the Toyota trucks. They lit up the whole front of the camp.

"What's going on?" Akil whispered.

Crocker held a finger to his mouth. Soldiers were trying to save the other two trucks. He took aim with the AK and fired. As he did, someone started shooting at them from behind the barracks.

Akil pushed him. "Boss, get down!"

Bullets slammed into the ground around them and whizzed overhead.

Crocker said: "Use the pistol and try to take out the driver. I'll deal with the bastards behind us."

But the building cast a dark shadow, making it hard to see. He squinted into the ribbon of black. Saw someone move, followed by a shoulder-fired rocket discharge. He shouted, "Hit the ground!" as he dove belly-first to the cement.

The rocket screamed overhead and exploded against the side of a disabled tank. Hot metal spun through the air, smacking the side of the building and ricocheting.

Akil stopped firing.

Crocker whispered, "You get hit? What's wrong?"

"I ran out of ammo. You got an extra mag?"

A moment after he answered no, soldiers opened up behind them with automatic weapons. In front of them and around the corner of the building, the driver of one of the Toyotas gunned its engine and spun it in a half circle so that its .50-caliber machine gun faced them from less than forty feet away. A soldier in the truck's bed aimed it and started firing—*pop! pop! pop!*

It tore chunks of concrete from the side and corner of the building, making it almost impossible for Crocker to return fire.

Akil, urgently: "Boss, we'd better circle back!"

"How?"

The soldiers behind them inched closer. Their only protection was a two-foot-high concrete wall that extended from the end of the building; their only options were facing the soldiers in back or making a wild dash for the disabled tank. But the Toyota backed toward them with its .50-cal firing, cutting off that possibility.

Crocker returned fire at the soldiers in back and was about to make a desperate run toward them when his ammo ran out. Now they were really fucked.

"What now?" Akil shouted, prone on the ground.

Crocker shrugged and flashed on an image of Holly getting out of the shower.

They had nothing to defend themselves with. The enemy was closing in on both sides. Bullets were tearing into the concrete from front and back.

He said, "Let's make a run for the tank!"

Akil nodded, resignation in his eyes. "Why not?"

Crocker took one last glance at the Toyota, which had backed to within twenty-five feet of them, and saw something flicker beyond it and to his right. A small flame moved forward. He made out Davis, running. The gunner in back tried to maneuver the .50-cal so he could train it at him.

Holy shit!

When Davis got within fifteen feet of the Toyota, he threw the Molotov cocktail, twisted, and fell to the ground.

The gunner exploded in flames and screamed.

Crocker to Akil: "Let's run! Now!"

He flew past the burning truck and was looking for

Davis when someone hit him and tackled him from behind. Next thing he knew he was grappling with a soldier in the dirt, smelling his putrid breath, grabbing for his neck.

He heard Akil shouting, "Boss, I recovered some weapons! Boss, where the fuck did you go?"

He was about to yell back when something exploded in the back of the truck, blowing dirt and debris into his mouth and eyes. This allowed his attacker to spin on top of him, grab the knife from his belt, and aim it at Crocker's throat.

He saw the hatred in the man's eyes, then started choking. As his mind flashed back to Holly, a bolt of energy surged through his body. He reached up, grabbed the arm holding the knife, and twisted his torso sharply right. As soon as the soldier spilled off, Crocker spun and kicked him in the face, then grabbed the knife and thrust the blade into his heart.

Breathless, blood dripping from his hands, he found Akil and Davis standing behind the burning trucks.

"You saved our asses," he mumbled as the latter handed him an AK with a green flag painted on its wooden stock and extra mags. "Thanks."

"I'm returning the favor."

He wasn't sure what Davis was referring to. He was trying to clear his head, assess the situation—the soldiers with the rocket launcher in back of the building; Lasher and Jabril badly injured; Ritchie and Mancini defending them in the room on the second floor.

Still work to do.

"What now, boss? Wanna set something else on fire?" Akil asked, grinning.

"Let's take out the fuckers in back first."

"Works for me," Davis offered.

Akil: "Can't buy entertainment like this."

"You guys engage them from behind the tank. I'll circle around the other side."

"Now?"

"No, tomorrow!"

He took off at a gallop. Forty seconds later he reached the other side of the building, peeked around, and waited for his eyes to adjust to the dark.

Three-quarters of the way down, approximately a hundred feet away, he saw two dark figures hugging the side of the building. One of them knelt and fired an RPG into the side of the tank.

Davis and Akil returned fire.

During the ferocious exchange, Crocker snuck up behind them. When he got within thirty feet, one of the soldiers turned, and Crocker squeezed a volley of bullets into the man's chest. Watched him fall back and stumble into the second man, who dropped the RPG and reached for his rifle. Crocker cut him down, too. He imagined the bones in his legs shattering. Heard the man mouth a last plea for help.

He watched the two of them bleed out. Then he whistled to his men, gathered the RPG, three unfired rockets, a Russian PKM machine gun, and a pistol, and distributed them to Davis and Akil, who had arrived still out of breath.

"More toys to play with," Akil wisecracked.

Sucking wind, Crocker said, "Now let's attack the barracks from the front."

"No fucking rest?" Akil asked.

Davis: "Hell, no!"

"You feeling better?" Crocker asked Akil.

"Aces, boss. I'm juiced on adrenaline. The hand is numb."

"Let's hit the rest of those fuckers. Hard!"

They stepped around some debris in front and entered through the door—Akil with the RPG-2, Davis cradling the heavy PKM, Crocker leading the way with the AK with the green flag painted on it and a 9-millimeter pistol—all of them covered with sweat, dirt, and blood.

They took the steps two at a time to the second floor. From the second-story landing they saw three of the enemy halfway down the hall, trying to fight their way into the room holding the other four men.

Akil loaded a rocket into the RPG and lifted it onto his shoulder. Crocker held up his arm and shook his head no.

He waited for Davis to set up the PKM on the floor and open fire. A tremendous noise filled the narrow hall. Bullets flew and ricocheted off the concrete floor and walls, sending up sparks and dust. Davis kept up the barrage for a full forty seconds, until Crocker held up his hand and crunched it into a fist.

The three SEALs waited for a response from the enemy soldiers. None came. When the dust and smoke cleared, they found them all dead, perforated with bullet holes.

Crocker to Davis: "Nice work."

CHAPTER TWELVE

They got to live before they can afford to die.

—John Steinbeck

THE SUN was just starting to rise by the time they limped back to the Sebha airport. Thankfully, the CC-130 was still waiting, along with its Canadian pilot and copilot, who looked at the bloodied, exhausted men and asked, "What the hell happened to you fellows?"

"Get us the fuck out of here," Crocker answered. "I'll tell you when we're in the air."

Ritchie and Akil stood guard as the others loaded Jabril, Lasher, and the aluminum canister containing the UF6 wrapped in the lead sheet. Crocker didn't care that it was probably leaking radiation. He said to the pilot, "Radio ahead. Tell them we're bringing back two badly injured men who are in need of emergency medical care."

"Got it."

He buckled in and breathed a sigh of relief as the plane tore into the early morning sky.

"Fuck that hellhole," Ritchie muttered, setting down

the AK and looking down at the city roofs that had turned gold in the sunlight.

Davis crossed himself and said a quick prayer of thanks.

Mancini asked, "Don't think you'll be going back, huh? We can rent a couple of camels. Explore the desert."

"Un-fucking-likely."

Mancini: "Come on, Ritchie, it's a fun place. Great scenery. Spirited locals."

Ritchie: "Hey. Who were those assholes? Where the hell were the NTC and NATO?"

"Good question," Crocker said. "I was under the impression that the city was safe."

"Safe, my ass."

Mancini had collapsed into an aircraft seat and started snoring. Akil sat back and closed his eyes.

"Unlikely I'm going to sleep in the next day or two," Davis offered. "My body's so pumped."

Ritchie: "I'm staying wide awake 'til we leave this fucking country."

"Then you guys can help me," Crocker said, getting up and moving to the medical cots bolted to the side of the fuselage where Lasher and Jabril were strapped.

"What do you need, boss?"

"If one of you can find the emergency medical kit on this crate, I'd like the other to remind the pilot to radio ahead for two ambulances and a couple of doctors."

Ritchie: "Done."

First he attended to Jabril, who was out cold and seemed to be suffering from stage-two hypovolemic shock as a result of the blood loss from his various wounds. His skin was cold and clammy, his pulse extremely rapid, which meant that his heart was working overtime to pump the little blood remaining in his body.

Crocker raised the doctor's legs to facilitate blood flow to vital organs and the brain, and checked to make sure that all his external wounds had stopped bleeding. What he couldn't do anything about now was any internal bleeding that might have been caused by the stick the savages had thrust up the doctor's rectum. All he could do was tuck several blankets around him, drag over the tank he found nearby, strap a mask around Jabril's head, and administer oxygen.

Turning to Davis, he said, "Keep an eye on him. Watch for vomiting. Make sure his breathing remains unobstructed. Anything changes, shout. I'll be back to check his vital signs."

"Okay, boss."

John Lasher was also unconscious. His shock appeared to be neurogenic, caused by a severe blow to his head or spinal column. Judging from the state of his body, it looked like he'd received both. His pulse was less than forty beats a minute, and he'd been asleep for almost twenty minutes. Crocker tried to gently wake him by calling his name.

After several tries he responded, "Where am I?" Then closed his eyes. A few minutes later he opened them and asked the same question.

Crocker answered, "We're on a plane flying back to Tripoli."

Lasher blinked, looked up at Crocker, and said, "You wait here. I'll go back and get the truck."

They landed in the capital city at around noon. Only one

ambulance was waiting, and instead of a doctor, NATO had sent a couple of young Moroccan nurses. Crocker struggled hard to keep his cool. He wanted to vent all the anger and frustration he was carrying.

Phone calls were made; another ambulance was sent. An hour later Jabril and Lasher were being treated at Tripoli Central Hospital.

Crocker and his team returned to the guesthouse, where he showered, changed his clothes, ate a bowl of yogurt, then turned around and drove to the U.S. embassy.

Remington sat huddled with some of his station officers when Crocker entered, red-eyed and haggard. The SEAL team leader was so mentally and physically exhausted he wasn't sure that what he was seeing was real or a dream. So he sat down, poured himself a glass of water, drank it, and willed himself to focus.

Remington rubbed his close-cropped salt-and-pepper hair and said, "Jesus, Crocker. What the hell happened in Sebha? We've been hearing all kinds of rumors all morning."

"We were attacked."

"By whom?"

"About a dozen men with green flags painted on their vehicles and on the butts of their weapons."

Remington said, "We got a report that Lasher and Dr. Jabril are in the hospital. Is that correct?"

"Yes, it is. We had just recovered a canister of what Dr. Jabril said was UF6 from a hidden chamber behind the camp when a dozen armed locals kidnapped Lasher, Jabril, and two of my men. One of them escaped and hid. The other two of us managed to get the captured men back, but it was bloody, exhausting, and difficult. Lasher and Jabril were beaten and tortured. They're in bad shape."

"UF6?" Remington exclaimed.

"That's correct."

"Where is it now?"

"The canister we brought back is under NATO guard at the airport here. The rest is still hidden in a tunnel behind the base."

Perplexed, worried looks were exchanged around the table.

"Where was the local constabulary?" one of the officers asked.

"I have no idea," Crocker answered. "When we drove through the city, we saw green flags flying from buildings and vehicles but didn't realize that the transition government had completely lost control."

Remington leaned back in his chair and moaned. "This is bad."

"Very bad. We barely escaped alive."

"Did these men identify themselves?"

"No, they did not."

"And you engaged them in combat?"

"Yes, we did. At least a dozen armed men. As far as I could tell, we killed them all."

Crocker was waiting for the CIA officer to get mad or lose his temper. Instead he maintained a state of weary consternation. His fellow officers looked completely overwhelmed.

Remington said, "Let me make sure I've got this right. You brought one canister of UF6 back with you, which is at the airport. The rest you left in a tunnel behind the base at Sebha."

"That's correct."

"How many canisters are there in all?"

"Twelve."

Remington looked at the other officers and said, "We're going to have to figure out how to secure them."

"Yes, sir."

"And Lasher confirmed that it is indeed UF6?" Remington asked.

"Dr. Jabril did. He opened one of the canisters and examined the glass ampoules inside."

"Where is Dr. Jabril now?"

"I believe the name of the facility is Tripoli Central Hospital. He and Lasher are being treated by a Belgian doctor."

"How serious are their injuries?"

"Critical. Both men went into shock. I was told they're going to be medevaced to Germany as soon as their conditions stabilize."

Remington rose, leaned both hands on the table, and shook his head. "This is awful. Horrendous."

Crocker asked, "Any news about my wife and Brian?"

Remington shook his head as though he didn't want to be bothered. "No. Not yet."

Crocker groaned. "Shit."

The acting CIA station chief looked up at him and said, "Before you leave, the ambassador wants to see you."

Feeling numb, Crocker followed him down several halls and past the ambassador's secretary, who said, "Go in."

They found the ambassador leaning toward a mirror,

adjusting the knot in his tie. CNN International was playing in the background.

"Gentlemen, gentlemen. Sit down. I want to hear what happened..."

Crocker's brain wanted to shut down, and the muscles in his legs were shaking. But he forced himself to relate everything in detail again. The ambassador didn't seem as upset as Crocker had expected him to be.

He said, "Transitions are messy. After forty years of a military dictator, no one expected this to be easy. I'm sorry for your trouble, Crocker. I commend you and your men. Trust me when I tell you that we'll deal with this and put it behind us."

Saltzman took his hand and squeezed his shoulder. "Thank your men for me. Get some rest."

Crocker stood, but his feet didn't want to carry him out.

He felt awkward, disoriented, unsure that what he'd just experienced was real. The ambassador's low-key reaction seemed at odds with the importance of his team's discovery.

A red-haired secretary entered and whispered something to the ambassador, who was combing his hair.

Remington put an arm around Crocker's shoulders and asked, "Are you alright?"

As he looked at Remington, his whole body started to tremble, and he realized that neither man had mentioned Holly, even though she'd been missing for more than two days.

"Sir, you haven't mentioned my wife."

Remington tried to pull him out the door, whispering, "Not now."

Holding his ground, Crocker said, louder this time, "Mr. Ambassador, is there any news? Any new developments I should know about?"

Saltzman looked at Remington, who cleared his throat and said, "Yes, your wife. Of course. We've been working on that 24/7 and believe she's safe."

"Where, sir? Where is she?"

"We're tracking down some leads on that, which I can't divulge."

"You know who's holding her?"

"We have some ideas, yes."

"And you believe she's being well treated?"

"Yes we do, Crocker."

He felt overcome with emotion, as though he was going to cry. He bit down hard and said, "Please do everything you can to get her back safely."

"We will, Crocker," Remington said.

Ambassador Saltzman: "We're doing all we can."

He wanted to scream "All isn't enough!" but used every ounce of his willpower to restrain himself.

"Okay," he muttered, turning on his toes. He walked back to the Suburban feeling he was about to explode.

He dreamt he was underwater. The tank on his back had run out of oxygen, and he was trying to fight his way to the surface, but the hulls of several large ships blocked his access.

Holly whispered urgently in his ear, "Tom. Tom. Help me! I'm up here!"

His lungs burning, he tried to squeeze between two ships and got stuck.

"Tom! Tom, quick!"

Kicking, pushing, and squirming with all his might.

"Holly! Holly, I'm coming!"

He woke up in the guesthouse bedroom gasping for air, his entire body covered with sweat.

Akil lay gently snoring on a cot under an open window. The light was fading outside. In the distance he heard the call for evening prayers being blasted from loudspeakers.

The door opened with a creak. He turned and looked for his weapon.

"Boss," Davis whispered, "you awake?"

"Yeah. What's going on?"

"Doug Volman's here to see you."

"Volman? What does he want?"

"He's here to talk to you. Says it's important."

What Crocker really wanted to do was go back to sleep, but he forced himself awake. "Alright."

Crocker found Volman standing in the living room wearing a yellow-black-and-white Hawaiian shirt and black pants. He was sipping a can of Coca-Cola and looked more like a college kid on vacation than a State Department officer.

He said, "I heard you guys had a rough time down south."

"Yes, we did. What's up?"

Volman scowled. His watery eyes protruded and his skin was splotchy. He said, "I shouldn't be telling you this, but sometimes personal feelings trump career ambition, if you know what I mean."

It hurt Crocker even to think. "Please explain what you're talking about."

"I'm talking about being a human being first. You know, Do unto others as you would have them do unto you."

Crocker was familiar with the Golden Rule. "I don't mean to be rude, but I still don't understand."

Volman removed a crushed carton of Camels from his pants pocket. His hands shook as he started to separate one from the pack. "Okay if I smoke?"

Crocker walked across the room on bare feet, leaned on the sofa behind Volman, and cranked open the window. Beyond the wall that separated the two residences, he heard the neighbor's kids laughing. "Go ahead."

Volman fumbled with the lighter, then dropped the lit cigarette on the floor. "Sorry." He bent down to scoop up the ashes.

"Don't worry about that. What's this about?"

Sitting down on the faded wine-colored sofa, Volman blew the cigarette smoke over his shoulder. "Your wife and Brian Shaw."

Crocker pulled up a chair and sat across from him. "What about them?"

Volman looked down at the cigarette he was holding and asked, "You spoke to Remington earlier today, right?"

"Yes, I did."

Volman leaned forward and whispered. "Did he mention anything about a ransom offer?"

"No, he didn't."

Volman nodded. "I didn't think so."

"The kidnappers issued a ransom note? Who are they? What did the note say?"

"I could be fired for telling you this. Dismissed from the service."

"I won't tell anyone." Crocker's whole body started to tingle. He was wide awake now.

"You're going to have to force them to be more proactive."

"Force who?"

Volman inhaled smoke from the cigarette and shook his head. "The ransom offer came from a group that calls itself Martyrs of the Revolution."

"Who are they?"

Volman exhaled and shrugged. "Nobody's ever heard of them before."

"What do they want?"

"I don't know the details. I heard one rumor that says they want the release of prisoners, another that they want ten million dollars in gold."

"Gold?"

"Yes, gold. Apparently the logistics are daunting. I've heard it involves a bank vault in Benghazi and a plane to fly it to the Sudan. Once the gold arrives safely there, the hostages will be released unharmed."

It sounded fantastic, almost implausible.

"You sure about this?" Crocker asked.

"According to the rumor, the kidnappers claim that it's Gaddafi gold seized illegally by the French. Apparently it's still in French custody. But the French say they're guarding it for the interim government."

Crocker's head started spinning—gold, a group of kidnappers nobody had ever heard of. He asked, "Who are these Martyrs?"

"I don't know," Volman answered.

"Who does?"

"If anyone does, it's Ambassador Saltzman. You need to push him. That's why I'm here. If I were you, I'd talk to him immediately."

Crocker: "You know where he is now?"

"Yes. My car's outside."

Crocker pulled on a pair of khaki pants, a blue polo shirt, a pair of black Nike sneakers. Combed his hair back. He found Davis on the computer, talking to his wife and infant son on Skype, and asked, "Any news about Jabril and Lasher?"

"They left an hour ago for Germany."

"Good. Where's everyone else?"

"Ritchie's next door watching *Cars 2* with the neighbor's sons. Akil and Mancini drove into town to look for dinner."

"I'm going to see the ambassador. I'll be back."

"Wait a minute. You need help?"

"I'm fine. Hold down the fort."

He joined Volman, who was outside the gate, standing next to a new powder-blue Mustang convertible. The night air was cooler than he'd expected.

"Is this your car?" Crocker asked, climbing into the passenger seat.

"My mother gave it to me as a birthday present. She's Hungarian"—as though that explained why he was driving something so conspicuous.

Volman drove like a wild man, way too fast and barely maintaining control, almost slamming into the back of a truck that had stalled on the road. As he swerved around it he started to shout over the engine noise about their destination, Janzour, a few kilometers west of Tripoli. How it was home to an equestrian academy, olive, lemon, orange, and fig orchards, and a Punic tomb discovered in the nineteen fifties.

Crocker wasn't paying attention. He was wrestling with the incredible tension he was feeling and trying to imagine what he could do to save his wife.

"The Punics were Phoenician settlers who were based in Carthage, which was in Tunisia, to our west," Volman continued. "They were traders who were eventually wiped out by the Romans before the birth of Christ."

Sirens wailed behind them, only adding to Crocker's anxiety.

"You should visit it sometime—a beautifully preserved burial room decorated with frescoes of women, antelopes, and lions."

Crocker realized they were leaving the city. He said, "Hey, Volman, where the hell are we going?"

"I told you. Palm City, in Janzour."

The speedometer had drifted past ninety. The air carried a whiff of salt from the ocean, combined with a citrusy scent.

"Why?"

"Because that's where the French ambassador lives, and Saltzman is attending a party at his house."

As they sped along the coast, Volman talked about how developers from Malta, the UK, and Italy had selected this area in the late nineties for the development of luxury expat communities. The newest and most elegant of these was Palm City, a secure enclave of over four hundred units with its own private beach, tennis courts, and swimming pools, right on the coast.

Crocker, meanwhile, was focused on names and faces flashing in his head—Brian Shaw, Farhed Alizadeh, Major Ostrowski, Dr. Jabril. As he sat wondering if there was some way they fit together into an explanation of what was going on and what had happened to Holly, he became aware of the car stopping in front of a guard station.

Volman reached into his pocket and said, "I forgot something."

"What's that?"

He handed Crocker a folded envelope. Inside was a letter from Dr. Jabril. It read:

> Dear Mr. Crocker:
>
> I am leaving Libya today with Mr. Lasher, before the work we were doing is finished. First, I apologize for that. Then, I want to thank you and your brave men for saving my life. Finally, I ask you to please complete the job we started. It is very important that you visit the nuclear facility at Tajoura, because this was the destination of the UF6. Talk to the man who runs the facility. His name is Dr. Salehi. Also, inspect the facility to determine what the UF6 was used for. It is critical that you do this.
>
> Thank you again and God bless you,
>
> Dr. Amadou Jabril

Crocker stuffed the letter in his pocket as they pulled into the driveway of a sand-colored townhouse.

"This is my place," Volman announced.

"Saltzman is here?"

"No."

"What the fuck..."

"Like I said, he's at a dinner party at the French ambassador's house, which is also in Palm City. You can walk there from here. I'll show you the way. Calm down."

"I can't."

"I've got to change. Help yourself to something from the kitchen or the bar."

"You know anything else about the ransom offer?"

"No. I'll be right back."

It was a modern place, decorated in bland tones of beige and brown. Pleasant and comfortable, but Crocker didn't want to be there.

He reminded himself that Volman was trying to be helpful. A sad song by one of Holly's favorite composers, Antônio Carlos Jobim, played on the stereo. Everywhere he went he seemed to find reminders of his wife.

He wanted to move, do something. But what?

The French ambassador's residence was a five-minute walk away, in one of the compound's luxury villas. Volman explained that many of the residents, predominantly foreigners, had fled during the war. Those who hadn't already departed had left abruptly in late November of the previous year, when militiamen from the Misurata Brigade tried to take over the compound. They engaged in a firefight with some of the compound guards and eventually ran off when soldiers from the Tripoli Brigade were dispatched by the NTC.

"None of the residents were hurt," Volman said, "but four soldiers were killed."

"What do you know about the Tajoura nuclear facility?" Crocker asked.

"I know that it's close to here, and I believe it's no longer in operation."

"Can you get me some background info about it? History, capacity—you know, stuff like that."

"Sure. When do you need it?"

"First thing in the morning, if possible. More important, find out anything you can about the kidnappers, the ransom."

"I will. There it is," Volman said, pointing at a sand-colored house surrounded by tall palms. "I'll wait for you at my place."

"Thanks a lot."

Crocker was stopped by a phalanx of French soldiers and plainclothes security personnel who checked his passport before escorting him into a round vestibule festooned with blue-white-and-red French flags. Edith Piaf was singing "La Marseillaise" over the sound system. Many of the hundred or so people crowding the large central room were singing along. The mood was more festive than anything Crocker had expected.

"What's the occasion?" he asked a young man holding a small American flag.

"V-E Day, of course."

Crocker felt underdressed, out of place. Young women wearing World War Two–era French military uniforms circulated with trays of champagne. One of them stopped in front of Crocker and asked, "*Vous êtes américain?*"

"Yeah, I'm American, and proud of it."

She looked more North African than French—Algerian, most likely. Winking, she said, "You are the heroes tonight. *Vive les Etats-Unis!*" and left.

Crocker surveyed the crowd. Under other circumstances he would have been more than ready to join in the celebration. But the frustration and anxiety he felt tonight were completely at odds with the frivolity around him. In fact, the party seemed perverse, given the violence he'd experienced in Sebha and the situation with Holly and Brian. Spotting the U.S. ambassador, who was dressed in an elegant blue shirt and silver-gray slacks and was talking to a tall man in a vintage French military uniform, he pushed his way through the crowd.

"Sir!"

Saltzman smiled warmly when he saw him and extended a hand. "Tom Crocker. It's good to see you again. I want you to meet Ambassador Moreau."

Crocker: "It's an honor, sir."

"Mr. Crocker is the leader of a group of American engineers who are doing a study of the city's electrical grid."

Moreau: "My pleasure. We're celebrating one of those critical historical moments, you know. The whole map of Europe could have been different. We could all have been speaking German if you, our American friends, had not decided to join the war in Europe."

"Our fathers did, yes," Crocker answered. In fact, his father had quit high school the day after the attack on Pearl Harbor and joined the navy. He was the most honest person Crocker had ever known.

Moreau: "Maybe the situation in Europe was not too different from what the Libyans are facing now."

Crocker wasn't sure about that.

The French ambassador put his arm around him and whispered, "Enjoy yourself, Mr. Crocker."

"I will, sir. Thank you."

Smiling confidently, Moreau slipped into the crowd, leaving Crocker alone and feeling like a visitor from another planet. A radio-controlled model of a B-19 buzzed overhead.

He spotted Saltzman, who was now huddled with a pretty young brunette, and made a beeline for him. Whispering into the ambassador's ear, he asked, "Can I talk to you a minute? It's important."

"Now, Crocker?"

"Yes. In private, sir."

They walked out onto a terrace overlooking the moonlit sea. A couple to Crocker's right giggled and kissed, then left holding hands. Another reminder of Holly.

"Mr. Ambassador, I heard there's been a ransom offer," Crocker said.

"Oh, that. Yes," Saltzman said with a groan, looking as if he wanted an excuse to escape.

"What do you make of it, sir?"

"What do I make of the kidnappers' ransom demand?"

"Yes."

"This is very difficult, Crocker. I like you and respect you. I can only imagine the agony you're in."

"You can't, sir. Believe me."

"Alright. You're a man who likes the unvarnished truth, so here it is: The ransom note is almost irrelevant."

Crocker felt staggered. "Irrelevant? Why?"

"Because, one, it tells us very little about the kidnappers except that they're opportunistic. And two, we can't make a deal."

"Why not, sir?"

"I'm surprised you don't know this. It's United States

policy never to negotiate an exchange of money or prisoners with terrorists or kidnappers."

Crocker leaned on the rail and clenched his teeth. "You're fucking kidding me! I thought the policy was amended in 2002."

"It was modified briefly but has reverted back. When I first heard about Holly and Brian's disappearance, I contacted the State Department legal office to get a clarification. Officials there read me the policy. Quote: The United States Government will make no concessions to terrorists holding official or private U.S. citizens hostage. It will not pay ransom, release prisoners, change its policies, or agree to other acts that might encourage additional terrorism."

"That's bullshit, sir! After all Holly and I have done to serve our country!"

"Easy, Crocker."

"Sir—"

"At the same time, I'm at liberty to use every appropriate resource to gain the safe return of American citizens held hostage by terrorists."

"What does that mean?"

The ambassador stepped closer. "It means we're doing everything in our power to get Holly and Brian back. It means we're using all our assets and leaning hard on the NTC. It means we've got teams out looking for them now, risking their lives, gathering intelligence, leads."

"Are you, sir?"

"I said I was. The only thing I'm not allowed to do is negotiate or make any concessions to terrorists."

Crocker swallowed hard. "Okay."

"The same policy applies to me, Crocker, in the event

I'm kidnapped. It's a risk all of us take when we choose to represent our country overseas. It's in the best interests of our country."

Crocker wasn't sure about that, but he knew there was no point debating the policy now.

"Trust us, Crocker. We'll get them back."

CHAPTER THIRTEEN

No crowd ever waited at the gates of patience.

—Arab proverb

IF THE ambassador and Remington knew where Holly and Brian were being held, they weren't telling Crocker. So he and his men spent the entire night searching the city on their own, stopping at roadblocks manned by local militiamen and showing them her photo, questioning the few men they saw on the streets. They even drove out to the refugee camp next to the Busetta naval base and spoke to the French soldiers stationed there, who in turn questioned some prisoners and local guards. Nobody seemed to know anything about the kidnappers or where Holly and Brian might be. Crocker also called the Canadians in Sirte, who were continuing their search of that city but hadn't come across any clues, either.

He returned to the guesthouse at dawn, angry and exhausted. He paced the living room floor and screamed in the shower. Put in more calls to Remington, Volman, and Debray.

Then he got down on his knees and prayed for a suggestion, a lead, anything.

His body and head literally burned with frustration. The word "trust" kept bouncing around in his brain like a taunt. Crocker knew that when it came down to it, when the shit hit the fan, justice and patriotism fell away and the only people he could really trust were his wife and his men.

He was sitting down with a cup of coffee when Remington called. The CIA officer said, "The good news is that I just heard that Dr. Jabril and John Lasher are recovering nicely in Germany. The unfortunate part is that they're not returning to Libya anytime soon."

"Any news about Holly and Brian?"

"We're working on that. Trust me."

At the word "trust" he winced.

"Crocker," Remington continued, "I'd like you to write up a report of what you've found so far, especially as it relates to Sebha. Include a detailed map of where we can find the UF6."

It was almost impossible to concentrate. "Now, sir?"

"Today or tomorrow. Then we can wrap this up."

He remembered the letter from Jabril that he still had in his pocket. "What about the trail of the UF6?"

"Once I receive your report, I'll forward it to headquarters and make sure they send out a team to Sebha to move it to a safe location."

Crocker said, "Aren't you interested in why the Libyans were in possession of the UF6 in the first place, and why it was hidden in a tunnel in Sebha?"

"Most likely it was being used for their energy program."

"Maybe not. And what about the presence of the Iranians right across the Niger border?"

"I don't see what one thing has to do with the other."

"The presence of UF6 indicates that Gaddafi was enriching uranium, which is exactly what Farhed Alizadeh has been trying to get his hands on."

"That's a stretch. Besides, we have no evidence that Gaddafi succeeded in enriching uranium to the level needed to build a bomb. Even when he was trying to assemble one he didn't succeed, because it's not so simple. And in the unlikely event that he succeeded, who is the threat now? The pro-Gaddafi opposition? I highly doubt that they would ever consider destroying their own country."

Even though Crocker wanted to focus on his wife, he knew the UF6 was important and that Remington's line of reasoning was unsound. "What about al-Qaeda?" he asked.

"They don't have a strong presence here. Besides, we keep them closely monitored."

"What if my team and I take a look around the Tajoura Nuclear Research Center?"

"That's not necessary. The center is inspected routinely by the IAEA."

Crocker said, "Is this about not wanting to question the authority or the effectiveness of the NTC?"

Remington said bluntly, "I'll expect the report on my desk tomorrow. Thanks."

Crocker hung up with Jabril's message burning in his head.

Akil asked, "What did he want, boss?"

"Pack the truck. You and Mancini and I are going out

again. Tell Ritchie and Davis I want them to stay here by the phone in case there's any news."

"Yes, sir."

They spent several hours driving the coast road east in the direction of Sirte and stopped at NATO headquarters, where Crocker was kept waiting half an hour only to be told that all NATO units in the country had been alerted to report any information relating to Holly and Brian Shaw's location.

Then they drove south to NTC headquarters. No news there, either. Just a promise from the colonel in charge that he would alert the U.S. embassy the minute he had news.

Finally, they entered some of the poorer neighborhoods on the edge of the desert packed with ramshackle mud structures and tents. They showed Holly's photo to women cooking and mending clothes, men drinking tea and attending to camels. All they got back were shrugs and suspicious looks. No clues.

"Now where, boss?" Mancini asked.

Crocker's frustration level was almost unbearable. He looked at the map and saw that they were only a short distance from the Tajoura Nuclear Research Center. He said, "Let's call the house one more time, then take a quick look at the nuclear center."

"Why?"

"Duty. Dr. Jabril's letter. A vague hunch."

Mancini: "Didn't you ask Remington, and he told you not to?"

"He said it wasn't necessary. I think he's wrong, and it's too important to ignore. Let's go."

Crocker picked up the information packet Volman had given him and handed it to Akil, who read it out loud. The Tajoura Nuclear Research Center consisted of a ten-megawatt pool-type reactor, a neutron generator complex, and radiochemical laboratories containing gas centrifuges for the production of isotopes for use in agriculture, medicine, biology, and industry. The center also included a research laboratory, machine shop, and computer center.

The main reactor had been built by the Soviets in 1979. At one time the center was staffed by as many as 750 Libyan scientists and technicians. Now the only thing in operation was a German-built reverse-osmosis desalination plant that produced over ten thousand gallons of potable water a day.

As the black Suburban turned into a wooded area that led to the main gate, Akil read from a series of IAEA reports. The agency had been established in 1957 to promote the peaceful use of atomic energy and to inhibit its use for any military purpose, including nuclear weapons. According to one of the documents, Libya had begun receiving nuclear-weapons-related aid from Dr. A. Q. Khan, chief architect of the Pakistani nuclear weapons program and proliferator of nuclear technologies to Iran and North Korea, starting in 1997. Khan had supplied Libya with twenty assembled L-1 centrifuges and two tons of UF6—enough to build a single nuclear weapon.

In early 2002, U.S. intelligence officials discovered that Khan had also provided the Libyans with the blueprint for making a fission-type weapon that the Chinese had tested in the late 1960s. This document set forth the design parameters and engineering specifications for constructing an implosion weapon weighing over a thousand pounds that could be delivered by an aircraft or missile.

After the September 11, 2001, terrorist attacks on New York and Washington, which Gaddafi denounced, he sought to make peace with the United States and offered to dismantle all of his WMD programs. According to CIA analysis, several factors contributed to Gaddafi's decision. First, thirty years of UN economic sanctions had significantly limited oil exports and hurt the Libyan economy. Second, Libya's nuclear program had progressed slowly and was extremely expensive. Third, the elimination of WMDs was a prerequisite to normalizing relations with the West. Fourth, Gaddafi wanted to avoid the fate that Saddam Hussein had suffered in Iraq. Finally, CIA operatives had seized a shipment of centrifuge-related equipment bound for Libya in October 2003, which may have persuaded Gaddafi that he would have great difficulty procuring materials needed for the manufacture of WMDs in the future.

In March 2004, IAEA officials assisted Libyan authorities in the removal of weapons-grade highly enriched uranium that had been stored at the Tajoura center. About thirteen kilograms of fissile uranium-235 was airlifted from Tripoli to Dimitrovgrad in the Russian Federation, where it was later blended down into low-enriched uranium (LEU). (Roughly that amount of uranium-235 was required to make one atomic weapon.) The fuel removal project had been funded by the U.S. Department of Energy and had cost approximately $700,000.

Since then the Tajoura Nuclear Research Center had been used strictly for developing a nuclear power infrastructure for electricity production, seawater desalination, and the creation of medical isotopes. In September 2008 IAEA director general Mohamed ElBaradei announced that because of Libya's cooperation, the Tajoura center would be subject only to routine inspections. The last one had taken place in December 2009, and Libya was found to be in full compliance.

"What do you think, boss?"

Crocker didn't answer. He had heard only about half of what Akil had read, but it was enough to make their discovery of UF6 in Sebha even more troubling. He remembered that John Lasher had called it "a smoking gun."

The SEALs were stopped at the Tajoura center's gate by a guard in an olive uniform who directed them to the main research facility, a three-story concrete-and-glass structure. The big red, green, white, and yellow abstract mural decorating the front featured palm trees on one end and minarets and missiles on the other.

"An interesting juxtaposition," Mancini said as they climbed the steps to the lobby.

There they were greeted by an attractive young woman in a long dress and black headscarf. "Welcome," she said in unaccented English. "My name is Assa. Director General Dr. Salehi will see you in his office."

Upstairs, Dr. Saleem Salehi greeted them warmly. He was a slight man of medium height, with dyed black thinning hair and a mustache. On the walls behind him Crocker saw a large map of Libya and framed photos of landscapes and of Albert Einstein holding a white cat. On his large desk lay an open brochure for the new Audi A8 sedan, a car that Crocker knew cost in the vicinity of $80,000.

After the Americans had taken seats on a sofa and stuffed chairs in one corner, the director general's secretary served coffee, tea, and cookies on a large silver tray.

Salehi said, "I started my higher education at Penn State. That's when Coach Joe Paterno was still a god. I knew nothing about American football. I grew up in a town outside of Tripoli, playing what you call soccer. I remember the first football game I attended. It was fantastic—the marching band, the cheerleaders, all the pageantry. I was enthralled."

Crocker pointed to Mancini, seated to his right. "My colleague, Mr. Mancini, played college football."

"I'm impressed," the director general said. "It's a very violent game. I think it takes great courage and skill."

"You've got to be a little crazy. I'm more of a climber, paddler, and cyclist myself," Crocker added.

Salehi said, "One of the things Libyans admire about Americans is their energy. You know—the physical fitness, the striving to be the best. Libyans love sports as well. But Colonel Gaddafi did not allow any sports stars to gain prominence because he feared they would draw the national spotlight away from him."

"An egomaniac," Akil muttered.

"Did you know that soccer stars could only be identified in newspapers and on TV by their numbers?"

It was hard for Crocker to sit there and be polite. He said, "I never knew that."

"So many things are changing now."

"For the better?" Akil asked.

"In the long run for the better. Yes."

He was a charming man, but Crocker detected some sort of hidden resentment around his mouth and in his eyes.

Crocker asked, "How long have you been the director general?"

"Here at Tajoura, three years," Salehi answered. "I was recently asked to stay on by the interim government, but since the center is more or less closed, there is very little for me to do."

"Oh."

"I'm almost never paid, which is also a problem."

Mancini: "I thought the NTC had plenty of money from oil revenues."

Salehi shrugged. "I don't know the reason. They're very disorganized. Sometimes I don't even know who to ask."

"Are you planning to stay?" Crocker asked.

He pointed to several photographs on his desk. "It's a question I ask myself every day. My wife and daughter went to Malta during the fighting. They like it there and don't want to return."

After a few more minutes of small talk, Salehi led them downstairs for a tour of the center. They were joined by the chief engineer, a tall man with a huge nose who also spoke English. He led them past a big concrete-and-metal sculpture of a crescent with a sun in the middle. Beyond it rose a tall red-and-white ventilator stack.

Salehi explained that all the facility's structures were designed to withstand the specific seismic conditions of the region. The building housing the reactor complex and radiochemical lab were built to nine-point seismicity. These precautions almost completely eliminated the possibility of a core meltdown caused by an earthquake.

Crocker asked, "When was the last time you used your centrifuges to enrich uranium?"

Salehi raised one of his black eyebrows. "We have had no need to enrich uranium since 2003."

Crocker, who was exhausted and had no more patience, cut straight to the point. "I'm sorry, but that's not what I asked."

"Perhaps I didn't understand the question."

"I didn't ask if you needed to enrich uranium. I asked if you've done it since 2003."

"No, of course not," the director general answered curtly. He seemed offended.

Crocker didn't care. "But you continue to store low-enriched uranium fuel to run the reactor?"

"That's correct."

As difficult as it was for Crocker to focus, he understood that there was a big difference between reactor-grade uranium and weapons-grade uranium. But even low-enriched uranium could be used to fuel a dirty bomb. He was one of a handful of people who were aware that something like that had almost happened when Iraq's Tuwaitha Nuclear Research Center was looted in April 2003, following the fall of Saddam Hussein, and a quantity of low-enriched uranium was seized by al-Qaeda terrorists. Crocker had led a team into Iraq to recover the uranium in that highly dangerous environment. They succeeded, but Crocker still regretted that he had lost two men.

Even though Tajoura's security hadn't been compromised during the fighting in Libya, in his mind the situation here was even more troubling. Because while the IAEA had removed all existing weapons-grade uranium from Tajoura in 2004, it hadn't disassembled the facility's centrifuge plant. As ST-6's WMD officer, he knew the technology. One needed an elaborate centrifuge plant like that at Tajoura—which featured over ten thousand P2 gas centrifuges—to separate weapons-grade uranium (U-235) from the heavier metal. Uranium ore contained roughly 0.7 percent of U-235.

The process was complicated and time consuming. First, a cylindrical rotor housed in a glass casing was evacuated of all air to produce frictionless rotation. A motor was used to spin the rotor, creating centrifugal force. Heavier molecules separated to the bottom of the centrifuge, while the light molecules moved to the top. Output lines at the top of the centrifuge carried the lighter molecules to other centrifuges that kept refining them.

After separating the gaseous U-235 through many centrifuge steps, engineers then used another chemical reaction to turn the uranium gas back into a solid metal that could then be shaped for use as bombs.

As they continued to tour the facility, Crocker asked himself, *If they weren't enriching weapons-grade uranium, why were they storing UF6?*

It was a question that wasn't answered during their visit and that continued to bug him as they drove away.

"What'd you think?" Mancini asked from behind the wheel.

Crocker was trying to separate his anxiety about Holly from the questions he had about the center. He said, "Something about the whole thing leaves a bad taste in my mouth."

"I wonder why they let us tour the reactor complex but didn't show us the radiochemical lab, which is the probable location of the centrifuge plant."

"I've been asking myself the same thing." In fact,

Crocker had specifically asked to see it. He was told the lab was closed and unsafe to visit because of high levels of radiation.

Now what?

They called Ritchie and Davis again, but they had no news. Then he called Leo Debray at the embassy; he was out of the office. Crocker didn't feel like sitting around the guesthouse or driving around aimlessly. He also didn't see the point of going back to the embassy and trying to explain his suspicions about Tajoura to Remington. He preferred that Remington and his staff focus on locating—or better yet, rescuing—Holly and Brian.

Troubled about the UF6 and Salehi's evasions, and not knowing what to do next, he said, "Let's stop here and wait near the gate."

"Why?" Akil asked.

"I need to think."

They parked on the opposite corner under a clump of eucalyptus trees and sat in silence, Crocker in his private agony, with Jabril's warning echoing in his head. It was a horrible position to be in—wanting to be loyal and trust your superiors, while also being very aware of their limitations. Remington had lost his boss and seemed overwhelmed by his new position. Ambassador Saltzman—who appeared to be a kind, thoughtful man—was focused on building up the NTC so it could secure the country and lead the transition to some form of representative government.

A black Acura sedan emerged from the gate and turned left.

"That's him," Akil said.

"Who?" Crocker asked, still lost in thought.

"Salehi. He's in the backseat, behind the driver."

"Let's follow him."

Mancini made a U-turn and followed the Acura east, then south. They watched it turn into a compound surrounded by a high, burnt-sienna-colored concrete wall. A satellite dish leered from the terra-cotta roof like a big eye.

"Now what?" Akil asked, scratching his stubble-covered jaw and neck.

Crocker said, "We call the guesthouse again and see if there's news."

There wasn't any.

Mancini: "Boss, you want to explore another part of the city?"

All he had was an intuition and an urge to follow it. Even if it was hard to figure out how it related to Holly, it was better than wandering aimlessly. He said, "We'll wait a few more minutes, until it gets dark. Then Akil and I will go in, while you wait in the vehicle."

Mancini immediately protested. "You sure that's the best use of our time?"

"You stay on the radio and watch the gate."

Akil got out and eyeballed the area as Crocker sat listening to Mancini talk about the dangers of nuclear proliferation. More specifically, the possibility of terrorists like al-Qaeda getting their hands on some kind of nuclear device. Mancini thought it was more likely that they'd get hold of a biological or chemical weapon first.

"Why?" Crocker asked, trying to focus.

"One, because chemical and bio weigh a whole shitload less and are easier to transport. And two, because nuclear weapons are hard to make and even harder to store, because you need to separate the critical masses to prevent the bomb from detonating too early."

"I agree."

Akil returned with falafel sandwiches and cans of soda he had purchased from a nearby vendor.

Crocker said, "I told you to surveil the place, not buy dinner!"

"Ever hear of killing two birds with one stone?"

"Here's one," Crocker said, holding up the sandwich. "Where's the other?"

Akil smiled. "There's a big palm tree along the back wall that we can climb and use to get over the fence. No surveillance cameras, but at least two dogs."

"Yeah?"

"Big, mean-sounding motherfuckers."

"Your favorite kind."

"Not really."

Crocker was reminded of the two bull mastiffs in Bolivia who had bitten a friend's balls off during a mission. Sesame sauce dripped down his hand onto his wrist, then onto the faux leather seat, as he started to formulate a plan.

"Tasty, huh?" Akil asked handing him a napkin as thin as tissue paper.

"Next time, follow orders."

Akil: "It's really goat shit I scraped off the street."

"Whatever it is, it tastes good," Crocker said, as he picked a piece of chopped parsley out of his teeth. "Here's what we're gonna do..."

CHAPTER FOURTEEN

Never interrupt your enemy when he is making a mistake.

—Napoleon Bonaparte

THE SKY had turned a deep shade of blue by the time he and Akil circled around to the back of the compound. They waited until Mancini started pounding on the gate to attract the dogs to the front before they took turns scooting up a palm tree, leaning on it so it dipped over the fence, then jumping ten feet onto the lawn, making sure to bend their knees and somersault over their left shoulders as they landed.

It felt good to be doing something instead of slowly dying of frustration. Libyan music wafted out of a room near the garage, which was located in a two-story structure separate from the main house.

"That's Ahmed Fakroun," Akil whispered.

"Who?"

"Only the most popular Libyan singer of the last twenty years."

"Like anyone gives a shit. Focus."

"I'm focused."

"Quiet."

Crocker peered in the window and saw a man in white underwear lying on a bed watching TV, apparently mesmerized by the music video he was watching—peacocks, a waterfall, dancing girls in colorful outfits. He was in condition white, Crocker thought, which meant a total lack of awareness of the circumstances around him.

Crocker indicated to Akil to follow him to the left, to the rear of the main house. The back door was wide open, inviting entry.

Crocker was about to oblige when his cell phone lit up. He read the text from Mancini: "WTF. Dr. exited front of the h. Getting in a car."

Crocker quickly typed back, "Follow him w/ the Sub. Let me know where he's going."

The two SEALs entered the dark house, stood in a vestibule, and listened. Heard some birds chirping inside; sounded like parakeets. Saw a collection of worn men's sandals on the floor to their right, and big ceramic dog bowls filled with water and food. The air was cool and smelled of curry and exotic spices.

Crocker pointed down a dark hallway and entered first. He stopped at a little table with a tray that contained an empty teacup and a plate of cupcakes. They were small and decorated with what looked like candied rose petals.

Akil picked one up and smelled it.

"Persian love cakes," he whispered.

"So what?"

"Salehi is a Persian name."

That hadn't occurred to Crocker. During the time of Alexander the Great, the First Persian Empire extended east all the way to Afghanistan and west along North Africa to Morocco, which meant that Persian names were still found there.

Continuing down the hall, they arrived at a big stairway on the right, opposite a dining room with a crystal chandelier. In front of that was a living room with a portrait of a severe-looking older man on the wall.

Every room was dark and filled with shadows. The only light filtered down the stairway and through the curtain in front. The dogs had stopped barking, replaced by the birds chirping aggressively in the front room.

Crocker turned to Akil and signaled "Go back and close the back door. Lock it."

Akil nodded and left. When he returned, Crocker pointed to a door under the stairway. They carefully opened it and found it led into a library/office. The walls were lined with books, and a big wooden desk occupied one end of the room. On the carpeted floor were several dozen cardboard boxes, some half filled.

He's leaving, Crocker thought.

Akil watched the door while Crocker searched the desk drawers, looking for laptops, cell phones, passports, bank account ledgers. All he found were photos of Salehi's wife and daughter, medical records, a bottle of Johnnie Walker Red, an old .38 revolver, and letters written in Arabic.

Crocker pointed and gestured. They moved upstairs.

The TV in the master bedroom was on and tuned to Al Jazeera news, but the sound was off. Several DVD cases lay on the dresser, porn flicks with French titles. Akil held one up and smiled as if to say, "Maybe we should check these out."

Crocker shook his finger. *Focus!*

A half-filled suitcase lay open on the bed. On the night table, beside a copy of the Koran, Crocker found a receipt for a money transfer to Banque Pasche in Geneva, Switzerland. No amount, no account number, just a transit code and the name Salehi.

"Looks like he's been moving money," Crocker whispered, sharing his discovery.

"Or he just hit the lottery."

His cell phone lit up again. The text from Mancini read, "U'll never guess where Dr S went."

"A strip club?"

Akil whispered, "No strip clubs in Libya."

The answer from Mancini: "The Bab al Sahr H." This was the hotel the SEALs had stayed in when they first arrived. Crocker typed back, "WTF!"

"He went to 8th fl. Meeting some1."

This confirmed Crocker's hunch that Salehi was up to something. "Find out who."

"Who what?"

"Who he's meeting w/."

"Roger."

"Stay w/ him. We'll meet u."

Akil drew the dogs to the back of the house as Crocker exited out the front. Then Akil ran through the house, joined him on the street, and led him two blocks to a commercial boulevard where they flagged down a cab painted black and white, like a zebra.

The driver looked them over carefully before he let them in.

The Bab al Sahr appeared a whole lot better at night, but the sour smell in the lobby was the same—cherry-scented disinfectant mixed with nicotine and mildew. They found Mancini seated on a bench facing the elevators, leafing through an old issue of *Newsweek* with Sarah Palin on the cover.

"Where's Salehi?" Crocker asked.

Mancini set the magazine aside. "Still upstairs attending to his business."

Crocker abruptly shifted gears: "You talk to Davis recently?"

Mancini: "Texted him five minutes ago. Still no news."

Crocker returned to the business at hand. "Salehi went up alone?" he asked.

"That's correct."

Maybe he wasn't thinking clearly, but it was the only lead he had. "How long?"

"You mean how long has he been up there?" Mancini looked at his watch.

"Yeah."

"Sixteen and a half minutes."

Akil: "Ten to one he's meeting a woman."

Crocker: "Maybe not."

"If it's a babe, he could be up there all night."

Mancini: "The guy might have other motives. Try not to think with your dick."

Crocker: "I'm gonna go up and try to listen."

Akil: "Perv."

Mancini: "Room eight twenty-two."

Crocker: "You guys wait here."

Crocker rode up alone, trying to manage the flow of thoughts through his head—Holly, the suitcases and boxes, the receipt for the money transfer to Switzerland. Searching for a reasonable explanation for the last three, he got out on eight and saw a short man in a dark suit jacket exit a room down the hall.

He ducked into an intersecting corridor and caught a glimpse of the man passing as he walked to the elevator.

His face looked familiar. Very familiar. Short black hair and a close-cropped black beard, a big broken nose that veered sharply to one side. It was the cruel line of his mouth that struck him, and the fact that his black eyes were so deeply set.

Colonel Farhed Alizadeh of the Qods Force?

Then: *What the fuck is he doing here?*

As the elevator descended, Crocker was trying to figure out what to do next when he heard footsteps approaching. Seeing Salehi, he ducked farther down the corridor, found an emergency exit, and pushed through. In the stairway he tapped in Mancini's number and texted, "A Persian-look man will soon get off elev. Try not 2 let him see u, but keep an i on him. Follow him if he leaves."

Mancini texted back, "You want me to wait for u?"

"No worry about me. Don't lose him."

"10-4."

"I'm on my way down. Salehi is, 2."

Crocker ran down the stairs and found Mancini and Akil standing at the end of the check-in desk, looking at some faded tourist brochures.

"Where'd he go?" Crocker asked.

Mancini pointed his chin at the front window. "He's standing over there, smoking a cigarette."

Akil: "Looks like he's waiting for someone."

"Who is he?"

Crocker: "I'm not sure."

Akil: "Then what the hell are we doing?"

Crocker: "I'm not sure about that, either."

"Boss—"

"Ssh!"

The elevator door opened behind them. They turned to watch Salehi exit and walk briskly to the lounge.

Crocker whispered to Akil, "Go see where he's going."

Akil texted back a minute later, "He sat down at table alone and is looking at menu."

Crocker: "Stick with him. M and I are gonna tail the other guy."

"Why?"

"Just do it!"

"What do we do now, boss?" Mancini asked, bouncing on his toes, looking anxious.

"I'll keep an eye on the man at the window. You get the SUV, bring it around front."

"Okay."

"Exit out the side door to the patio, then through the gate to the parking lot so he can't see you. If my hunch is right, he's Farhed Alizadeh."

"Colonel D?"

"Yeah, the same individual who was trying to steal the high-speed triggers off the *Contessa.*"

"What's he doing here?"

"Good question. Go!"

An even better question: *Why was he meeting with Salehi?*

Crocker was left in the uncomfortable position of trying to satisfy conflicting tasks—looking inconspicuous so he wouldn't be discovered, and at the same time trying to confirm the man's identity. The latter was impossible, because the man faced away from him, looking out the window.

Meanwhile, Mancini drove the Suburban around front and parked it at the curb.

Crocker watched the dark-haired man put on a pair of sunglasses even though it was night, step outside, look around to see if anyone was watching, then climb into the backseat of a black Mercedes sedan with darkened windows. It took off at high speed.

Crocker waited a beat, then ran out and jumped into the Suburban.

"Follow him. Fast! Don't lose him!"

"Got it, boss."

They sped west along the coast, then turned left onto the causeway that ran south. Crocker's mind worked hard the whole time, calculating the Iranian's next probable move and how to counter it, calling on his training, experience, the little he understood about the current situation, and his intuition.

He asked Mancini, "Where do you think he's going?"

"My money says he's headed to the airport."

"I agree."

If the man really was Farhed Alizadeh, it sort of made sense. Horrible sense. Iran had been striving to build a nuclear weapon in order to make it the preeminent military power in the Middle East. But a combination of UN sanctions, international pressure, and IAEA inspections had so far thwarted their efforts to enrich uranium beyond the 20 percent needed to fuel a nuclear reactor for peaceful purposes. Enriching uranium beyond that was an extremely time-consuming and difficult process.

As they sped down the causeway, Crocker dialed Remington's number and caught the CIA station chief in a meeting with members of his staff.

"Crocker, my whole team is working around the clock. We're studying every little shred of evidence we've got. I understand your concern. I promise to call you the minute I know more."

Crocker said, "Sir, I'm on my way to the airport. I'm going to need your assistance. Looks like I might have to stop a flight and detain a foreign national."

"What does this have to do with Holly and Brian?"

"Nothing, as far as I know."

"Then what in God's name are you talking about?"

"I suggest you get out here a-s-a-p. I'm gonna need your help."

"Why, Crocker?"

"No time to explain, sir. It's highly important. Involves the possible exchange of nuclear material. You're going to have to trust me on this." Crocker enjoyed being the one to say that for a change.

"Where are you now?"

"Turning in to the international terminal. Gotta go."

The Mercedes burned rubber as it circled past the largely empty parking area, turned sharply right, and came to a screeching stop at a checkpoint reinforced with sandbags. One of the soldiers on duty waved it through. Between some one-story buildings Crocker caught a glimpse of the Mercedes as it sped down the tarmac.

"What now?" Mancini asked.

"I'll think of something."

"We can tell them we're IAEA inspectors."

Crocker pointed to the curb. "Park here. Make sure you bring your phone."

They climbed over a low fence to the tarmac and turned left. Past the low buildings, Crocker saw the main terminal ahead, a strangely shaped structure with high V-shaped arches in front.

He pulled Mancini behind a baggage cart as he watched the Mercedes stop. The Iranian got out and was greeted by another man who looked like a Libyan airport official. The two of them walked to the terminal as the Mercedes sped off past some parked passenger jets to a row of hangars.

"What now?" Mancini asked.

"You follow the Iranian. I want to see where the Mercedes is going."

"Okay."

In the several seconds it had taken to address Mancini, he'd lost sight of the car.

Must have turned in to one of the hangars.

That seemed the only reasonable explanation. He walked briskly past men cleaning and fueling various aircraft, trying to look as if he belonged there. There was a technique to not being noticed—act normal, keep as small as you can, avoid eye contact, look at the ground, be the gray man, no superfluous thoughts. He allowed himself one: *Thank God the security at this airport sucks.*

One more: *God, please lead me to Holly and Brian.*

Past the terminal, a gust of wind smacked his face. To his right, a United Emirates DC-10 was landing. He heard screeching rubber, the jet engines whining as they reversed. They were sounds he'd heard thousands of times, but tonight they seemed more vivid and important. Passing the first hangar, he squinted into the dark open space. Saw the hulk of a passenger jet. No cars. No people.

The next three hangars were empty except for miscellaneous airplane parts.

Where the fuck did it go?

A series of smaller hangars ahead. Some had what looked to be disabled planes in front of them. He was hurrying toward them when he heard a vehicle behind him and to his left. It sounded like a forklift in high gear.

Pausing, he heard scraping metal, men's voices.

Reversing course, he turned into the space between hangars 3 and 4. Behind them he saw a Boeing 727—white, no passenger windows, a small green-white-and-red Iranian flag painted on the tail.

What's this?

Seeing the parked Mercedes, he knelt beside the hangar and watched. The front cargo bay of the jet was wide open. The lights inside the fuselage were on. He heard the forklift again, then saw it swing into view carrying a large metal container that looked rust colored in the artificial light.

The forklift operator raised the container and fitted it into the cargo door. Men inside the aircraft pulled it farther inside.

Crocker waited until two more containers had been loaded, then texted Mancini his location and added: "Seen or heard from Rem?"

An answer rebounded quickly. "No."

Where the fuck is he? What's taking him so long?

Pushing aside his frustration, he willed himself to focus and tried to dispel doubts that what he was doing made sense.

LOW BATTERY flashed on his cell phone. He placed it in his back pocket.

Three men were walking toward the front of the jet.

Casually dressed, they were drinking coffee or tea from cardboard cups and speaking in Farsi.

The first man climbed the stairs to the cockpit, which soon lit up. The other two joined him.

The cargo bay was still open. Crocker inched closer along the side of the hangar to get a better view. Saw the forklift parked behind hangar 4. Two men wearing mustard-colored overalls stood beside it. They opened a door to the hangar and entered.

The tail engine of the 727 started up with a howl; then the two Pratt & Whitney side-mounted turbofan engines fired up together.

Crocker took a deep breath. *The coast is clear. It's now or never.*

He ran in a low crouch to the cargo door of the jet, grabbed hold of the metal lip, and pulled himself up. He flattened himself to the inside of the fuselage and waited, heard nothing but the engines. Light spilled from the cockpit door. Farther back, past his right shoulder, he saw six large metal shipping containers, three along each side of the fuselage. About twenty feet behind them stood a row of seats and beyond them, empty space.

With his back pressed against the side of the plane, he inched his way to the containers, hoping he might be able to learn what was inside them.

At the sound of footsteps he held his breath and ducked behind one of the containers, squeezing into the space between it and the fuselage wall and checking to make sure his phone was set on Vibrate.

Someone up front pulled the cargo bay door shut, and then the overhead lights came on.

He heard more footsteps, boots against metal. Caught

a glimpse of men in mustard-colored overalls approaching. They pushed on the container next to him, strapped it against the fuselage, and locked it onto a hook in the floor.

Crocker was trapped behind the adjacent one with no place to go. He heard one of the men say something. They pulled the container away, then slammed it hard, throwing Crocker back so that the side of his head slammed into the metal fuselage. He passed out.

A minute later he came to, lying on his side and jammed into the little space between the middle container and the fuselage wall. His left wrist was pinned. The pain was as terrible as the scream from the engine.

The plane moved quickly, took off, gained altitude, and banked sharply left, causing the container to shift and rip deeper into his skin.

What the fuck have I done?

He willed himself not to lose consciousness again, focusing on the dull roar of the engine, trying to block out the pain.

The big plane banked right, causing the container to shift a fraction of an inch, just enough that when he pulled with all his might, his wrist ripped free, leaving skin and blood behind. He was sure that bones had been broken but couldn't do anything about that. He could only wrap the wrist in a handkerchief to stem the bleeding.

Slowly and with difficulty he squeezed around the corner of the container and looked toward the back of the plane, where he saw two men in the row of seats. One was reading, the other had his head back and his eyes closed.

This is idiotic, he said to himself. *I'm trapped and I'm headed away from Holly. How am I going to help her now?*

His left wrist was a mess, the back of his head hurt, he had no weapons, and when he checked his cell phone he saw that it was out of juice.

What he didn't want was to land in Iran, be arrested, be subjected to some kind of public trial, then tortured and hanged.

So he squeezed to the front of the first container and planned his next move.

This was judgment day. Condition red.

Removing the web belt from his pants, he waited until both men in the row of seats had closed their eyes, then made his move, flattening himself against the front of the container to his right and sliding around it to the other side. He hugged the side of the fuselage and stepped sideways to the cockpit.

The door was ajar.

He saw the pilot slouched in his seat, headphones on, yawning. The copilot to his right had his stockinged feet on the console and was reading a magazine. The third man, the flight engineer, was seated inside the door with his eyes closed.

Crocker inhaled several times quickly, enriching his blood with oxygen. Then he bolted inside, grabbed the flight engineer's head in his right hand, and smashed it against the metal cockpit panel—one, two, three times.

All the frustration that had been bottled up inside him rushed out.

The copilot reached for something in the console beside his seat. Crocker let go of the flight engineer's head, reached over the seat, and wrapped his belt around the copilot's neck. Pulled him straight up out of the seat.

Watched him kick, flail his arms, try desperately to reach around and grab Crocker.

Meanwhile, the pilot was screaming in Farsi and swinging something that looked like a thermos with a strap around it that hit Crocker in the back of the head, stunning him for a second. He stepped out of the way and twisted the belt tighter around the copilot's neck until he felt his body spasm, then relax.

Crocker felt blood from a head wound dripping down his back. He saw the pilot reach over the copilot's body and grab a pistol—a black automatic—stuck in the seat. He cracked him hard on the side of his head with his left elbow, then grabbed the hand with the gun. As he tried to wrestle the pistol away a shot discharged, smashing into the instrument console and careening into the floor.

Fuck.

The sound numbed his ears and filled his nose with cordite. He was gaining control of the pistol when the pilot bit down on his hand. Crocker clocked him in the mouth with the side of the pistol five times, hard, until blood, teeth, and saliva spilled over his hand and wrist, and the pilot collapsed.

Now Crocker occupied a tight space between three bleeding bodies, adrenaline pounding through his veins, the nerves in his wrist, hand, and the back of his head sending distress signals to his brain.

He pushed himself past the pilot's body and took his seat, scanning the many instruments. Focused first on the engine panel in the middle, which indicated that all three engines were operating at 46,200 pounds of thrust; a machmeter, which measured the ratio of true airspeed to the speed of sound; then an altimeter, horizontal direction indicator, flight director, digital vertical speed indicator.

To his right he found the radio and audio selector panels, a VHF navigation and communications panel, an ADF panel with digital readout and rotary knob control. Overhead, a light panel divided into two sections—cockpit lighting and exterior lighting. Also overhead were subpanels for ignition, alternate flaps, cockpit/cabin/ground call systems, cockpit voice recorder, cargo fire detection/suppression system, wing-engine anti-ice, window heat, and pilot heat.

Crocker tried not to be overwhelmed. A Delta Airlines pilot had once told him that in a few years the only flight crew required on a large commercial jet would be a man and a dog—the man to feed the dog, and the dog to bite the man in case he tried to touch any of the controls.

He had friends who were ST-6 pilots and operated what they referred to jokingly as the top-secret Teeny Weeny Airlines. Several times they'd allowed him to take off and land Learjets and other small planes. Many years ago he'd also spent several afternoons training on a PPL flight simulator at an air force base near Las Vegas.

But this was many times more complicated—a big, 153-foot 727-200 at least twenty years old, which meant that it wasn't equipped with the very latest technology.

He knew enough to set the engine thrust to 85 percent and pitch the nose five degrees above horizontal to maintain current speed and altitude. The problem was that the Sperry SP-50 two-axis autopilot was engaged and programmed to direct the aircraft to Tehran. It was headed east at 479.8 mph, altitude 21,022 feet.

Crocker didn't know whether he should try to contact

ground control or try to turn the jet around. Concerned about alerting the Iranians, he chose the second option. He grabbed hold of the steering tiller in front of him and started to move it to the left.

Immediately an alarm went off and a red light started flashing, causing Crocker to panic. He realized that he had forgotten to shut off the autopilot first. Once that was accomplished, he said a quick prayer. With stars glimmering through the front and side cockpit windows, he slowly moved the tiller to fifteen degrees. His hand perspired as the plane bounced and started to dip and bank slowly left. It felt as if he was steering an enormous, inflated bus.

Once the jet had made the gradual turn, he set a course west-southwest, then breathed a sigh of relief.

They were headed back in the direction of Tripoli, with clear skies.

My good luck.

Moonlight glistened off the sea below. Blood from the pilot was sticky under his feet.

Feeling alone and slightly elated, Crocker figured that he might be able to locate the north coast of Africa, might even be able to find Tripoli. Then he realized he was getting way ahead of himself, because even if he did manage to navigate back to Tripoli, which was somewhat unlikely, how the hell would he land the big jet?

Since the aircraft was probably carrying a nuclear bomb or nuclear material, there was significant risk involved even in trying to land it.

Wouldn't it be better to crash it into the Mediterranean Sea?

That way he wouldn't expose tens of thousands—maybe hundreds of thousands or millions of people—to dangerous radiation. It was the safest, most sensible option. Even better, he thought, than trying to fly the plane out over the Atlantic Ocean.

Better to end it here. Get it over with, before he lost control of the plane or passed out from loss of blood.

He thought of Captain "Sully" Sullenberger landing US Airways Flight 1549 in the Hudson River. Remembered seeing him interviewed on *Letterman* after the incident, this humble, soft-spoken professional who had kept his head and made the right split-second decisions in a moment of crisis. But Flight 1549 had landed on a river, not an ocean, and Sullenberger was an experienced pilot, not a novice with little training.

Crocker's options were more limited.

The jet was currently 21,000 feet above the Mediterranean. Crocker lowered the flaps and pulled back on the throttles until the 727 slowly started to descend.

He'd led a full, exciting life. Now his wife was missing, and he was going to die. His only regret was that he couldn't save her. He prayed someone would. Then he wondered what would happen to his teenage daughter. Thinking of the two of them started to break him up inside. He flashed on images of his mother, father, sisters, brother, while his whole body started to tremble.

He shifted his attention to the altimeter, which had dropped below 20,000 feet. The jet hit a pocket of turbulence and jolted to the right.

He watched the numbers descend: 18,000, 17,000, 16,000. Thinking about Holly, he realized she was the person he would miss most. He prayed he'd meet her again, somewhere, and hoped there was a heaven, or something like it.

It seemed wrong that everything he'd seen and experienced would just end. He'd find out soon enough.

Now 14,000 feet.

Hearing the door creak behind him, he looked over his shoulder and saw two dark-haired men staring at the bodies on the floor. They looked at Crocker with hatred in their eyes, as if asking *Where the fuck did you come from, devil?*

The man standing directly behind him stepped forward and smacked him in the side of his head with a pistol.

Crocker felt a jolt of pain. Saw stars.

Facing forward and holding tightly to the steering tiller, he lowered the flaps further. Now 10,000 feet and falling. When he reached toward the center console to pull back on the throttles, the man bashed him in the head again. The second man grabbed Crocker around the neck.

The cockpit spun, and he lost consciousness.

He awoke seconds later to bloodcurdling screams. A man's body had fallen forward onto the center console, pinning Crocker's right arm.

The aircraft was gaining speed and altitude.

Crocker pushed the man off and noticed the blade of a Swiss Army pocketknife protruding from the back of his head. He eased back on the throttles again.

Turning, he saw Mancini struggling with the second of the two intruders. They looked like wrestling bears. The big SEAL had the smaller man in a headlock and was punching him repeatedly in the face. He heard bones breaking, the man cursing and gasping for breath. Saw him reach for a pistol that had fallen onto the flight engineer's seat.

Crocker rose, spun around, grabbed the man's wrist,

and snapped it back violently until it popped, just the way his defensive tactics instructor had taught him soon after he was selected for ST-6. The man arched his back and released a terrible wailing sound that ended when Mancini drove his head into the sharp edge of the cabin door. Then he let go and let the body slump to the floor.

Feeling the red gashes carved down his neck, Mancini said, "Ugly bastard scratched me like a girl."

Crocker, hugely relieved, said, "Manny, it's real good to see you. Your neck will heal."

"Sorry it took me so long." This comment delivered like it was no big deal. He plunked himself down in the copilot seat and took control of the second steering tiller as if he knew what he was doing. He started to level the jet off.

"You know how to fly something this big?" Crocker asked.

"Does a rabbit know how to fuck?" Mancini felt along the ridge of his front teeth and asked, "Jesus, boss, were you deliberately trying to crash this thing?"

"Yeah."

"Hey. That little fucker mess up my front tooth?"

Crocker waited for Mancini to push away the blood with his tongue, then reported, "There's a piece missing on top. Makes you look even meaner."

"You know I'm a nice guy. I just have zero tolerance for assholes, especially tyrants and fanatics."

"I'm real glad."

Crocker watched him check the gauges and reset the flight director. Wiping the sweat off his brow, he asked, "Where the hell were you?"

"Snuck onto the aircraft after you. Went up the back

stairway but got locked in the rear storage compartment where I was hiding. Luckily I had my Swiss Army knife with me. Couldn't tell if it was a lever lock or tumbler. After numerous tries, I picked it."

"Think there's a chance you can land this sucker?" Crocker asked.

"We wanna go back to Tripoli, right?"

"That would be good."

"You sure? I bet I can locate Ibiza. We can have a few days of R&R."

"I've got some unfinished business in the Libyan capital."

"Roger that. Love these old 727-200s. My next-door neighbor bought an entire cockpit instrument panel on eBay, and the two of us have been assembling it in his basement."

"What for?"

"Fun."

CHAPTER FIFTEEN

If you can keep your head when all about you
Are losing theirs and blaming it on you…

—Rudyard Kipling

TWENTY MINUTES later they touched down smoothly on runway 1B at Tripoli International Airport and were immediately surrounded by three pickups filled with NTC soldiers. Crocker refused to let them board the plane. He borrowed a cell phone from a Belgian soldier and called Jaime Remington, who showed up twenty minutes later with an NTC deputy foreign minister in tow.

A tense hour of back-and-forthing later, the deputy minister still wanted the plane's cargo turned over to him.

Crocker was willing to let them have the bodies, but as for the six shipping containers, he said, "No way that's ever going to happen."

Remington: "Be reasonable. These people are extremely sensitive when it comes to issues of national sovereignty."

"We're talking about nuclear material that was being smuggled out of the country."

"The trouble is that technically it belongs to the Libyans."

"I don't care who it belongs to. We'll fly this motherfucker back to the States if we have to. Under no condition am I turning it over to them."

The American ambassador, the NATO commander, and the head of the Libyan interim government got involved. Frantic calls were made to the White House, IAEA, and NATO headquarters in Brussels.

At 2 a.m. the Libyans agreed to release the six containers to the temporary custody of the NATO commander until IAEA inspectors could arrive and identify their contents.

Ambassador Saltzman asked, "You happy now, Crocker?"

"I'm a little less annoyed. Any news about Holly?"

"No news is good news."

"Is it, sir? Are you sure about that?"

"I suggest you and your colleague go to the hospital to have your injuries looked after."

Crocker: "Thanks for your concern."

It was half past seven in the morning when he and Mancini dragged themselves through the front gate of the guesthouse. Akil and Davis greeted them at the door, both wearing gym shorts and worried expressions.

"Boss, can I talk to you alone?" Akil asked, the rising sun gilding his face.

Crocker felt too numb to think. He'd been shot up with painkillers, the back of his head had been bandaged, and his wrist had been placed in a hard cast.

Akil: "Brian Shaw's body was dumped in front of the embassy about an hour ago."

The name jolted him out of his stupor. "What'd you say?"

"Brian Shaw's body was found in front of the U.S. embassy."

"Shit..." A sick feeling gathered at the pit of his stomach, then morphed into white-hot rage.

"Attached to his body was a note from the kidnappers."

"What did it say?"

"They're giving the U.S. government twenty-four hours to meet their demands before they execute Holly, too."

With the taste of bile in his mouth, Crocker swallowed hard. "Fuck! I need to find her. Now!"

Akil: "All of us are ready to help, boss. We'll do anything."

Davis: "We're ready to kick ass, but we don't know where to look."

Crocker: "We've got to find out more."

Akil: "How?"

Davis: "When Volman called with the news, I asked him the same questions: Who are the kidnappers? Where are they hiding? He says he doesn't know."

Mancini: "Who do you think does?"

Crocker looked at his boots and the bottom of his pants, still splattered with blood. "Where's Ritchie?" he asked.

Davis: "He went with Volman to some of the militia camps, searching for intel."

Crocker glanced at his watch, then at a big red spider crawling up the front of the house. They had approximately seventeen hours to find Holly. He said, "The two of you throw on some clothes and grab some weapons. I need you to drive me somewhere. But first, call the embassy and find out if Remington's in yet."

"Yes, sir."

He heard the morning call for prayer drift over the wall; heard the children laughing next door. Thought: *Normal life goes on for some people.*

He stepped inside the guesthouse. Splashed water on his face and appraised his ghastly-looking face in the bathroom mirror—his right ear blood encrusted and swollen, lacerations running from his cheekbone to his mouth. He found a bottle of disinfectant in his emergency medical kit, closed his eyes, gritted his teeth, and sprayed it on his face.

He looked older, gaunter, his skin gray and tired. But his blue eyes still burned with intensity.

He grabbed two energy bars and a bottle of water off the kitchen counter, realizing he couldn't remember the last time he had had a meal. Hurrying to the front door, he shouted, "Let's go!"

The neighbor's twin boys were standing outside in their school uniforms and backpacks, waiting for their father. As they drove off, they waved to Crocker, big smiles creasing their faces.

He waved back.

One of the boys shouted, "Have a good day."

"You, too. Thanks." A sob caught in his throat.

Mancini climbed into the Suburban with Davis and Akil. He was ready to come along, too, but Crocker wanted him to stay near the phones in case Ritchie should call with news.

"Okay, boss. Good luck. Signal if you need me to meet you somewhere."

"Thanks, Manny. I will."

Davis: "Where are we going?"

Akil: "I spoke to the watch officer at the embassy. He said Remington's at home and not expected in the office 'til noon."

"Let's go see him."

Davis drove as if demons were chasing them. Fortunately, the streets were mostly empty, and they arrived at the station chief's house in less than ten minutes, tires screeching.

Two Libyan guards outside stood at attention and looked scared. They watched Crocker ring the front gate bell. No answer. He was about to climb over the gate when a thin Hispanic man wearing a shoulder holster came out.

Crocker: "I'm the SEAL team leader, and I need to see Remington immediately."

"I know who you are. He's asleep."

"Wake him."

"I can't."

"Then get out of my way."

Crocker tried to squeeze by. The aide held out an arm to stop him as the Libyans watched.

"He gave me strict orders not to bother him unless it's an emergency."

"This *is* a fucking emergency," Crocker growled, pushing his arm aside and entering.

He knew the house well enough from his earlier stay to locate the back bedroom. There he found Remington sleeping with the curtains drawn and a CD of nature sounds playing.

He yanked open the curtains and pulled the stereo plug

from the wall. The CIA man blinked, rubbed his eyes, and raised himself up on his elbows. Seeing Crocker, he asked, "What are you doing here?"

Crocker shouted in his face, "You forgot to tell me about Brian Shaw."

Remington lay back on the bed and turned away from the window. "I thought we agreed that you were going to let me handle this."

"And you said you were working nonstop and going to keep me informed!"

As Remington turned to look at the clock, an enormous racket echoed from the hallway, sounds of men shouting curses and struggling.

Seconds later the Hispanic aide burst through the door. Davis had an arm around his neck and Akil was in the process of wrestling the man's pistol away from him.

Remington shouted, "What the hell is going on?"

His aide: "Sir, I tried to stop them from entering the house!"

"This is unacceptable! Out of control!"

An angry Remington turned and pointed a finger at Crocker. "I blame you. You're way out of line, Crocker. I'm reporting this to your command!"

"Call the fucking president if you want. You're not doing your job."

Remington grabbed the sat-phone from the night table and started to dial a number. Reconsidering, he stopped and shouted, "Come with me!"

"Where?"

"We're going to see the ambassador."

* * *

Saltzman was pacing the floor with his hands behind his back and his shirtsleeves rolled up. Vivaldi's *Four Seasons* played softly on the stereo. He stopped when he saw the two large men. Said cheerfully, "Come in. Make yourselves at home." Pointed to a silver coffee service on a tray. "Who would like a morning beverage? Coffee or tea?"

The clock on his desk read 9:35. The whole setting seemed absurd to Crocker. Time was slipping away.

Remington ordered his coffee black. The SEAL opted for a glass of water. The men took seats facing the ambassador, Crocker in a straight-backed chair. The red-haired secretary lowered the music volume.

Saltzman said, "I learned as a young attorney filing civil rights cases against the Justice Department to never panic, never lose hope. Things can change in unexpected ways. They often do."

The emotion Crocker held back was almost overwhelming. He wanted to slap them both in the face. Wake them the fuck up.

The ambassador calmly wiped his mouth with a cloth napkin and pushed the tray aside like an actor in a play.

While my wife is suffering and the minutes tick away.

He raised an eyebrow and turned to Crocker. "I assume you heard about Brian Shaw."

Crocker: "What are you doing about that, sir?"

"Shocking and horrible."

Remington: "Leo ID'd the body."

Saltzman: "Animals. Savages."

"I'm here to talk about my wife."

Silence. Saltzman and Remington shifted uncomfortably in their chairs. Tension hung in the air like an electric charge.

"I was getting to that, Crocker," the ambassador said smoothly. "First of all, let's not lose hope. The kidnappers have given us a deadline, but that doesn't mean they'll act on it."

"They did in Brian's case," Crocker countered bluntly. He watched the two officials' faces turn sour, as if he'd let out an awful stink.

"Regretfully, yes. But your wife is different."

"Why, sir?"

"Because without her the kidnappers have no leverage."

Crocker shook with frustration. "Who are they, and why do they want leverage?"

"I'll let Remington answer that."

Crocker waited. Another slow minute passed as Remington crossed his legs, cleared his throat, leaned forward in his chair.

"Remember the three men you arrested at the refugee camp near Busetta?"

"Yes, I do."

"Well, one of them happens to be the half brother of a Tuareg leader named Anaruz Mohammed."

Mention of Anaruz's name put Crocker even more on edge. "I know who he is."

"We believe Anaruz, or people working for him, are behind the kidnapping."

"What led you to that conclusion?"

"Because in exchange for Brian and Holly the kidnappers have been demanding the release of the three men you detained."

The irony hit Crocker hard. He said, "I heard it was gold."

"The gold was just a rumor."

"So Martyrs of the Revolution is just a cover?"

"That's what we've believed all along, yes."

It made sense. Awful sense. Americans had arrested Anaruz's half brother, so he struck back by kidnapping two U.S. officials.

But wait…

"Do you think it's a coincidence that he seized my wife, or does he know she's married to the man who arrested his half brother?"

"I suspect they saw an opportunity to kidnap a couple of Americans, without knowing who they are."

"Where are the three prisoners now?" Crocker asked.

"They're in NTC custody," Saltzman answered. "I made a point of turning the three men over to the NTC. Officials there didn't want to take them at first, but I convinced the NTC that they would improve their human rights profile if they made public examples of them. I pushed hard. They locked the men away and pressed charges. Then Holly and Brian were kidnapped."

"Shit." It was worse than he thought, and it put the onus squarely on him.

"I'm sorry."

"Do you know where the men are being held?"

"No, we don't," Remington answered.

"And you probably wouldn't tell me if you did."

"Crocker, there are big issues at stake," the ambassador said. "Even if we could pressure the NTC to exchange the men for Holly—which we can't, because it goes against U.S. policy—the release of these men would make the

NTC look weak, and that's something we don't want to do."

"I don't give a shit about the NTC, I care about my wife."

"I'm sure I'd feel the same if I were in your position."

"Where does that leave me, Mr. Ambassador? What's going to happen to Holly?"

"Nothing now. I think that eventually the kidnappers will get tired of holding her and set her free."

"You really believe that?"

"Ask yourself this: What do the kidnappers gain by hurting her? Nothing, except to make themselves look like barbarians. We should presume the kidnappers are rational people."

He hated the word "presume" and wished the ambassador hadn't used it. He took a deep breath and asked, "What if they're not reasonable? What if they think killing my wife helps them achieve their goals? What if they think sparing her will make them appear weak?"

No answer.

"Sir, why aren't we out there turning this country upside down to find her?"

"Because it's not an option. The deadline will pass and your wife will still be alive."

Crocker wanted to pick up the coffee table in front of him and throw it out the window. Instead, he gritted his teeth and said, "You're bargaining with my wife's life!"

Remington: "We continue to do everything we can to locate the kidnappers. The more time passes, the more our odds of finding them increase. We're talking about a relatively small country. We've got multiple sources out talking to people from different groups. We're quietly offering money in exchange for information. I'm confident someone will say something that will be useful."

"What have you learned so far?" Crocker asked aggressively. "Where is she being held?"

Remington: "We believe she's somewhere in the capital."

Crocker was on the verge of losing control. "Where, exactly?"

Remington: "We don't know that."

"East? West? South? Along the coast?"

Remington: "We don't know exactly. But once we have actionable intelligence, we'll move quickly."

"Have you examined Brian's body? Did you learn anything from that?"

"Nothing of material value."

Crocker stood, took a deep breath, and said, "If anything happens to my wife, you're both going to have hell to pay. I guarantee that." As he started to walk, his arms and legs shook with emotion.

They seemed to know little, and had given him practically nothing.

"Crocker," the ambassador said as he reached the door.

"What?"

"Don't do anything you'll regret later. The NTC is plenty annoyed with you and your team already."

"Fuck them."

His whole body burning with outrage, he walked past the secretary standing beside the Stars and Stripes, past the marine guard station, and into the dry heat outside. Sunlight glinted off multiple surfaces and stung his eyes. He saw the Suburban waiting and climbed inside, hoping for a few quiet minutes to figure out what to do next. But instead of two men inside, there were four, which confused him.

Then he recognized Volman, leaning over the front seat, sweaty and reeking of garlic, wearing a blue crewneck shirt with snaps at the neck, looking odd, out of place, like he always did. “What’d they tell you?” he asked.

Crocker took a moment to get his bearings. He turned to glimpse Ritchie behind him in the rear seat, with Akil beside him. Davis was at the wheel.

“Nothing, except that they think Holly’s being held somewhere in the city.”

“Where?”

“They don’t know.”

“What’s their strategy?”

“Their strategy is to wait.”

Davis: “Wait for what? Are they insane?”

“They reason that the terrorists won’t carry out their threat, because if they do, they’ll lose the leverage they have by holding her.”

Akil: “What if they’re wrong?”

Ritchie: “Yeah, what if they’re fucking wrong?”

Crocker felt a throb at the pit of his stomach.

Akil: “That’s ridiculous, boss. Stupid.”

Volman tapped Crocker on the shoulder and asked, “Who did they say is behind it?”

“Anaruz Mohammed.”

“Why?”

“Remember those three thugs we arrested at the refugee camp? It turns out that one of them is his half brother.”

“Fuck.”

Volman: "I have a source, someone with his ear to the ground, who is willing to help. He's going to meet us at the guesthouse."

"When?"

"Soon as he gets back into town. About an hour."

"Thanks." A slim ray of hope.

At the guesthouse gate Akil stopped to ask Volman why he was helping them.

Volman said, "I admire you guys and understand your frustration. I also think our policy of refusing to negotiate with terrorists is wrong. I mean, it's fine to say that publicly, because you don't want to encourage them to take our people hostage. But behind the scenes I believe we should do anything, including paying ransom, to get our people back."

The more time Crocker spent with the young State Department officer, the more he liked him. He was an awkward man, but intelligent and with a good heart.

Crocker wanted to go on a short run to clear his head, but he thought it was more important to be ready when Volman's contact arrived. So he lay on the sofa with his MP5 by his side and leafed through a copy of *Sports Illustrated.* One minute he was looking at a picture of Danica Patrick, the next he was dreaming that he was with Holly, lying on a bed in a hotel room. She was reading a magazine with Michelle Obama on the cover and wearing a white cheerleader-type skirt that showed off her tanned, smooth legs. When he reached out to touch them, they felt warm. Almost hot.

She moaned.

"Holly?"

He ran his hand farther up her leg to her thigh, where the skin turned lighter. She moaned again.

"Baby, can you hear me?"

Higher under her skirt he felt a big indentation and stopped. Lifted the dress up. Saw that a big piece of her leg was missing. Little black worms were eating at it.

He gasped, felt a stab of pain in his stomach, and woke.

Crocker lay alone in sweaty clothes. The last time he and Holly had spoken, they'd argued. He remembered it now. She was upset that he'd been spending so much time away from home, leaving her with the burden of dealing with Jenny, who was still adjusting to her new school and being a teenager.

Crocker had asked her to be patient and understanding. She accused him of being selfish and self-involved.

Sitting up, he grabbed the MP5. The clock read 1:44, which meant he'd slept almost four hours.

Holy shit! Why didn't someone wake me?

He hurried into the kitchen, where Mancini was adding sliced red onions to a big batch of tuna-fish salad.

"Where is everyone? What the fuck's going on?"

"Akil and Davis went with Volman. He's trying to pry some intel out of one of the officers at the CIA station."

"When are they expected back?"

"Soon. I'm preparing lunch."

"What happened to Volman's friend?"

"He was delayed but is on his way."

Pushing back a feeling of panic, he stood under the shower with the cast on his left wrist covered with a plastic bag, and let the warm water loosen the muscles in his shoulders and back. He regretted that he'd argued with Holly. Sometimes he forgot how much the team dominated his life. Other men had time to coach their kids' sports team, go on family vacations, do home improvement projects.

He dressed and debated going out and searching the city by himself but instead went out onto the porch and did forty minutes of sit-ups and crunches, despite his aches and pains. He had to find some way to burn off the anxiety and relentless energy that were driving him nuts.

Another half hour dragged by. He picked at the tuna on his plate, feeling he was about to burst out of his skin.

He searched his mind for options but found none, which only added to his frustration. Frustration increased his sense of desperation, which fueled his rage. A vicious circle that made it impossible to think.

"See you later, Manny. I'm going out!" he said, grabbing his MP5 and starting for the door.

"Where?" Mancini shouted.

"To look for Holly!"

"Boss, you don't know the country, don't speak the language."

"So what?"

"Don't you always tell us that undirected aggression is self-destructive? Don't you tell us to think first, be smart?"

He set down the MP5 and took a deep breath. "You're right. I'll call Davis."

He did, on the sat-phone. Davis said he and Akil were sitting in the Suburban outside a café near the embassy. Volman was inside talking to another American—a CIA officer, he thought.

"How fucking long is he gonna be?"

"Don't know. We'll be there soon as we can."

He wished he could turn back the clock. Wished he'd

talked Holly out of going to North Africa in the first place. Wished he'd never accepted the assignment to Libya, even though he really didn't have a choice. Started questioning other decisions he had made in his life, then realized it was a pointless exercise. All he was doing was beating himself up.

He felt an urge to call Jenny. But what would he say? I'm sitting here with my thumb up my ass while your stepmother is about to be executed by a bunch of fucking terrorists?

He tried to imagine what Holly was going through, but that only made him more anxious, so he stopped that, too.

Davis, Akil, and Volman returned at four. All of them sat down at the kitchen table. Volman, out of breath, said, "I learned two things. One, the kidnappers are sticking to their demands—release of the three Tuareg prisoners."

Crocker: "We knew that already."

"The second thing is, there were two cell phone calls from the kidnappers. They've been traced already and turned up nothing, but it might be a place to start."

"Where?"

"You have a map of the city?"

Akil retrieved one from his room and spread it out on the table. "The first," Volman said, pointing to a spot on the map, "comes from a place east of here, between Mitiga Airport and the Belal Ibn Ribah Mosque. The second is a location about four miles southwest of there near the police academy on Al Hadhbah Road."

Davis: "They're relatively close to each other."

Crocker: "Let's go!"

Volman: "We should wait for my friend. He's a Libyan

militia leader—very knowledgeable and savvy. Knows his way around."

"What's his name?"

"Farouk Shakir al-Sayed. His friends call him Farag."

Crocker: "Is he a little guy, young, with big amber-colored eyes?"

"Yeah."

"I think I know him. Dark-skinned, curly black hair that sticks straight up. Weighs no more than a hundred pounds. We fought together at the Sheraton."

"That's him."

"Good."

Crocker felt a little better. Farag was a tough kid, but the optimism his name inspired quickly vanished as they waited longer. Another excruciating hour dragged by, each tick of the clock like a punch to the head.

By 5:40, when they heard a vehicle honking at the front gate, Crocker felt like a boxer entering the final round. And he hadn't even thrown a jab.

"My friend. My brother," Farag said, climbing out of the old Toyota truck and wrapping Crocker in a hug. "Good to see you. You remember Mohi?"

He pointed to a wider, slightly taller young man with short hair who walked with a limp. It was the kid Crocker had given medical attention to after he'd taken two bullets in his hip.

"Mohi. It's good to see you again. You're all healed up?"

The teenager shook Crocker's hand vigorously and smiled. Some of his front teeth were missing.

Farag's face turned serious when Volman showed them the map and explained the situation in Arabic. He looked at Crocker, nodded as if he understood the gravity of what they faced, then glanced at the watch on his wrist and muttered something in Arabic.

"What did he say?" Crocker said.

"Loosely translated: Do not hate misfortune because maybe there is fortune for you inside it."

"I hope you're right."

"I know these areas," Farag said in English. "We go fast."

"As fast as possible."

They climbed into the trucks. Farag led at a breakneck pace in the Toyota pickup with the Americans following in the Suburban. Within minutes Crocker spotted an airport tower ahead.

From the front seat, Volman explained, "This used to be Gaddafi's airport. His compound wasn't far from here. This part of the city experienced the heaviest fighting during the war."

They passed the runway dotted with parked NATO warplanes and ran into a roadblock manned by armed men in black.

Crocker: "Who the fuck are they?"

Volman: "Beats me."

They watched Farag lean out of the Toyota and shout at the men. They shouted back, with a lot of waving of guns and pointing.

Volman started to get out to join them.

Crocker said, "Maybe you should let him handle this."

Volman went anyway.

"Doesn't listen, does he?"

"Acts weird, but he's smart," Ritchie said.

The sun was starting to set, casting long shadows in

the streets. Volman walked back toward them in his baggy pants, shirttail half out.

"We're cool," he said. "It's a ragtag group of volunteers from the neighborhood. They say this area is relatively safe during the day but changes at night. They've experienced a lot of robberies, break-ins, kidnappings, rapes."

"They know anything about a gang of Tuaregs operating in the area?"

"They've heard rumors about a group of thugs stealing cars and shipping them to Tunisia."

"Are they Berber tribesmen? Did they say where we can find them?"

"That's all they know."

Stars were visible in the sky by the time the Toyota took off again in a cloud of dust. One of the men back at the roadblock lifted his AK-47 and fired it into the air.

"What the fuck was that for?" Davis asked.

Volman: "He got excited."

They were in the Bu al Ashhar neighborhood. The Toyota screeched to a stop in front of the mosque, a blue domed structure with a minaret rising from one side. The streets around it were empty. The Arabic speakers in the group—Farag, Mohi, Volman, and Akil—went door to door, trying to elicit information.

The handful of men who were brave enough to answer said they'd seen some strangers in the area but no women, and no one they could identify as Tuareg. Nor could they describe the strangers they'd seen, except to say that some of them were armed.

They took off again and arrived at the second location after 9 p.m. Crocker's stomach was killing him. The area in front of the police academy had also seen heavy fighting, since it was in the vicinity of Gaddafi's heavily armed Bab al Azizia compound and Tripoli University. The academy was dark and its gate locked. Crocker saw no one on the streets, except the occasional vehicle passing on Al Hadhbah Road.

Again the four Arabic speakers knocked on the doors of nearby residential compounds and stores. Most of the latter were closed for the night. One man reported that he'd seen armed men getting out of vehicles beside the fence surrounding a field across the street from the academy.

Farag and Akil went to explore. They came back a few minutes later to retrieve their weapons.

"What'd you find?" Crocker asked.

"Something worth checking out."

"What?"

Akil: "Follow me."

Volman, Mancini, Davis, Ritchie, and Mohi waited beside the vehicles.

The sky glittered like a star-studded crown. A breeze picked up dust and threw it in Crocker's face.

Farag pointed to a place in the aluminum fence where it had been cut and temporarily wired back in place. He undid the wires and rolled the fence aside. "You see?" Motioned for Crocker and Akil to enter.

After he stepped through, Farag let go of the fence so it rolled back into place.

The little Libyan led the way, following a faint trail beaten into the dirt. Past pathetic-looking shrubs and garbage—an old mattress, the twisted frame of a bike, an old sign advertising Canaba King Size cigarettes.

"Where the hell does he think this leads?" Crocker whispered to Akil's back.

Farag stopped ahead of them, held a finger to his lips, and pointed to a spot in the ground. All Crocker saw was a round patch of earth. But when he focused harder in the low light, he was able to distinguish a round cover about four feet in diameter painted the same color as the dirt.

A dog howled in the distance as the three men quietly swung it open. Akil was the first to enter, holding a small flashlight that illuminated metal rungs along the side of a concrete tube.

They descended approximately thirty feet and reached the bottom, where they saw a concrete tunnel about twelve feet high and six wide that extended about sixty feet.

When they reached what they thought was the end, they saw that the tunnel curved left at a ninety-degree angle. The second leg was even longer. There was still no light, but they heard faint, muffled noises and proceeded carefully.

The closer to the end they got, the more distinct the sounds became. Voices at first. A man, then a woman whispering. Then what sounded like two people making love.

What the fuck?

They inched closer. A ribbon of light spilled out of a door ahead to their right.

The sounds of lovemaking grew louder. A woman approaching ecstasy screamed in English, "Harder! Faster! Yes!"

Fingers on the triggers of their weapons, they stopped. Farag pointed to the metal door and tried the lever. It wasn't locked.

He nodded. Crocker nodded back, his heart leaping into his throat.

Farag lowered the lever and kicked the metal door open. Crocker pushed past him and entered with his MP5 ready. His brain picked up thousands of impressions at the speed of light—the size of the concrete room, the source of light, the number of occupants, the presence of weapons.

The second he saw one of them reach for his AK, he started shooting, raking the two men sitting with their feet up on an overturned table. Their bodies shook from the impact, bounced against their chairs, and slumped to the floor. They didn't have time to scream.

But the sound of lovemaking continued. It was coming from a flat-screen propped against the wall, a DVD player on the floor beside it, wires snaking around.

A third man emerged from a room off a dark passageway behind the opposite wall, saw the three armed men and his dead colleagues, and started scrambling down the passage in the opposite direction.

Akil, his MP5 ready, started after him.

Farag reached out and stopped him. "No!"

Akil pushed the hand off his shoulder. "What do you mean, no?"

Crocker: "He's right, Akil. Let him go."

"Why?"

"You'll see."

Akil used the flashlight to illuminate the passageway, which led to a ladder, just as Crocker thought it would.

Crocker removed the radio from his back pocket and said: "Manny, very soon you're going to see an individual emerge from the ground somewhere on the field we just entered."

"Anywhere on the field?"

"Affirmative."

A few seconds later Mancini said excitedly, "Yeah! I see him."

"Good."

"You want me to grab him?"

"No! You and Mohi get in the Toyota and follow him. Don't lose him, and don't let him see you. I think he's going to lead you to the rest of the group."

"Ten-four."

"Don't fucking lose him. It's important."

"Don't worry, boss. That's not gonna happen."

They spent the next few minutes rifling through the contents of the room and bathroom—half-empty bottles of Russian vodka, a box of crackers, several porno DVDs, two Glock pistols, a bag of pistachio nuts, a leather gym bag containing over a dozen cell phones, several grenades, two ski masks. Also a laptop and several thumb drives, which Crocker kept.

He went through the dead men's pockets. One of them had a wallet containing a wad of dinars and pictures of him and his girlfriend. In the other he found a silver amulet like the one he had seen around the neck of the wounded Tuareg tribesman he had tried to save in Toummo.

"I think these are the guys we're looking for," Crocker said. "Let's go!"

They climbed the steps at the end of the tunnel behind the bathroom and emerged in a corner of the field opposite where they'd entered.

They ran to meet Volman, Ritchie, and Davis, who were waiting by the fence.

"The guy sped off in a little dark blue Nissan sedan," Davis said excitedly.

Ritchie: "Manny's on his heels with Mohi. He's headed south."

"Let's hurry!"

They piled into the Suburban. Davis gunned the engine; he'd raced stock cars as a young man and knew how to get the most out of a vehicle—even the bulky, clumsy Suburban they were in now.

Ritchie was on the radio communicating with Manny, then instructing Davis, "Make a right here. Look for a four-lane highway ahead. Get on it going south!"

Crocker sat throbbing on the middle seat, hoping against hope that the man would lead them to Holly.

Manny screamed through the radio, "Turn off at Al Belah Road."

"Ask him how far."

Manny over the radio, "You'll see a stadium on your left."

"How far?"

"You can't miss it."

Two minutes later Ritchie screamed, "There it is!"

Tires burning, they took the turnoff at sixty. Up a ramp, onto a dark, deserted street.

"Where now?" Davis asked.

Ritchie: "Keep going straight. Cut the headlights. Manny says you'll see him parked next to a burnt-out truck. There's one lone streetlight at the end of the block."

Davis: "I see it! Yeah, I see it. There!"

"Stop. Park this thing in the alley."

"You got it, boss."

They slung their weapons over their shoulders, got out, and ran in a crouch behind the few parked cars to where the Toyota had stopped.

Mancini sat in the driver's seat, loading his MP5, stuffing frag grenades and extra magazines in his pants pockets.

"Where the fuck did he go?" Crocker asked, stealing a glimpse at his watch.

"He entered a beat-up building around the block. You can't see it from here."

It was 11:38. His heart sank. They were running out of time.

"Where's Mohi?"

"He went ahead to recon the place."

"Why the fuck didn't you go with him?"

"Calm down, boss. I was on the radio to you."

"Sorry."

"We're gonna find her. I can feel it. We're close. *Fidem tene.*"

"What's that?"

"Keep the faith."

Hearing footsteps approaching, they ducked behind the Suburban and readied their weapons. It was Mohi, out of breath. He pointed as he spoke a mile a minute in Arabic.

"What's he saying?"

Akil: "It's a five-story structure. Two vehicles parked out front. Men are loading shit into them, like they're getting ready to leave. They're moving fast."

"Did he see a prisoner? Were they moving a female prisoner?"

"He says no."

"Fuck!"

"Four large men. No woman. He thinks they're just about ready to split."

Crocker was thinking fast. "Okay. Here's what we're gonna do. Wait. Ask him about the front gate."

Akil: "What about it?"

"Ask him if there is one, and if it's open."

"It's open."

"Okay. Davis—you and Ritchie bring the Suburban around. Position it near the gate so you can block their escape if necessary. Manny, you take Mohi. Climb the wall and take the building from the rear."

"Got it."

"Make sure you've got your radio. Akil and Farag come with me. We're going in the front gate. You guys know what to do. Shoot to kill any motherfucking terrorists. Look for the hostage—my wife!"

"Yes, sir."

"Volman, you stay with the vehicle."

Volman: "Good luck. I hope you find her safe."

Crocker stole a look at his watch: 11:47. Thirteen minutes until the deadline.

He slapped Farag on the shoulder. "Ready?"

Farag flashed back a thumbs-up.

"Let's go!"

They sprinted around the corner, spotted the five-story building, which looked badly damaged, and hid behind the six-foot-high compound wall.

Akil whispered, "Most windows missing. There are some flashlights or other kinds of lamps on the ground floor but no other internal lights."

Crocker heard a car ignition start, then whispered, "Go!"

They turned the corner, weapons ready—a mixture of Glocks, MP5s, AK-47s. Saw two dark-haired men getting into a black pickup. Crocker dropped to his knees and opened fire.

"Not so fast, motherfuckers!"

The men returned fire. Bullets tore into the ground and flew overhead. Crocker scrambled for cover behind the open gate. Heard rounds slam into the metal. Reloaded. Akil crossed to the left side so he could get a better angle. Farag ran inside the compound and hid behind a low concrete wall that led to a stairway at the front of the building.

The dark-haired men directed most of their fire at Farag, to their left. Crocker saw that he was pinned and jumped out from behind the gate to try to pick off the shooters.

Headlights blinded him.

Akil shouted, "Boss! Get back!"

He saw the Nissan sedan speeding toward him on its way out of the compound, its rear tires kicking up dirt. He jumped behind the gate and didn't see Farag rise and toss something in the direction of the pickup. The two men kneeling behind it dove for cover.

Meanwhile, the Nissan fishtailed out, men shouting and firing from the front and back seats. He heard it hurtle out the gate, then brake, followed by the sound of metal smashing into metal and shattering glass.

Automatic fire ringing from the street behind him and in front of him, Crocker had taken two steps into the compound when a big explosion rocked the area in front of the building and threw him back against the wall.

He came to gasping for breath, his head spinning, thinking *Jesus Christ, they killed Holly!*

Everything started to break up inside him, but when the smoke and dust started to clear, he saw that the building in front of him was intact. The pickup lay on its side, and flames were shooting out of the hood.

Akil screamed into Crocker's radio, "Boss! Boss, you okay?"

"What the fuck just happened?"

"Farag threw a grenade."

"He could have fucking warned me," he muttered, glancing at his watch. It was now 11:56. *Four minutes!*

Akil reported, "Manny and Mohi are pinned down in back."

"There's another shooter in back?"

"Roger. Two at least."

"Cover me," Crocker said urgently into the radio. "I'm going in."

He ran in a crouch past the burning pickup and saw Farag finishing off one of the downed men with his knife. He continued through the smoke and ran up six concrete steps into the building, which was a mess—bare concrete columns covered with graffiti, broken furniture, pieces of discarded cloth, plastic bags filled with garbage.

"Holly!" he called.

No answer. Just a hollow echo of his own voice, and gunfire.

Something was burning near the back of the building. Ferocious fighting continued from both the front and back. He ran up a set of stairs to the second floor. Saw mattresses, empty tin cans and bottles. A filthy bathroom with a toilet filled with shit.

Hearing footsteps behind him, he readied his MP5 and turned. Saw two feet through the drifting smoke. He was about to squeeze the trigger when he caught a glimpse of the wild tangle of dark hair.

"Farag! I almost shot you."

"Your wife?" he whispered back.

"I haven't found her, no."

The Libyan pointed to the stairway and motioned upward. "I go."

"Go ahead. I'll join you."

After he finished checking the second floor, Crocker hurried to the stairway, which was clogged with smoke.

Akil shouted over the radio, "Boss, we can't get in. Too much fire on the first floor. Something big is burning, sending up a lot of black smoke. Where are you?"

"I'm on two, on my way up to three."

"Get out before you're trapped!"

"Fuck that."

"The fire's spreading. We've got no way to put it out!"

Crocker continued up the stairs two at a time. At the third-floor landing he heard Farag shout: "Crocker! Mista Crocker!"

"Where are you?"

"Here!"

"Where?"

All he could see was smoke and trash. He hurried to the back of the building and found Farag kneeling near a column. Tripped over a piece of thick rope and saw two backpacks lying on the floor. Another rope led to a digital timer that was counting down in hundredths of seconds—4:01.98, 4:01.97. Small green LED numbers descending fast.

This floor is rigged to blow!

Running out of breath, he reached for Farag's shoulder. "Farag, we gotta get—"

On the other side of the column he saw someone with long hair. He blinked to make sure he wasn't hallucinating. It was Holly! She was taped to a metal chair, with thick silver tape covering her mouth. As soon as she saw Crocker, tears started to fall from her eyes.

"Holly, sweetheart! Oh, my God..."

Farag opened a pocketknife and started trying to cut her free.

Crocker squeezed her arm. He wanted to hug and kiss her, but there was no time.

Emotion coursing through him, he saw Farag struggling with the tape and pushed him away. "Forget it! We're running out of time!"

He handed him his MP5 and picked up the chair with Holly in it. "Let's get the hell out of here! Follow me!"

He ran to the stairway with the chair and Holly in his arms. Thick black smoke curled around their heads. They'd made it down to the landing, eyes and throats burning, when Crocker saw flames shooting up and realized they couldn't get through.

He slapped Farag on the arm and pointed upward. Returning to the third floor, he thought fast. He found the rope, determined that it was long enough, and tied it around the top of the metal chair.

Then he grabbed the radio from his back pocket. "Akil!" he shouted. "We're trapped up here. Tell me, are you able to safely approach any part of the building?"

"The front is the clearest, boss. How come?"

"I'm going to climb out one of the front windows.

Look for me. I've got Holly. I'm going to lower her down."

"You found her? Is she okay?"

"Listen! You grab her and get as far away from the building as you can. The third floor is rigged to blow in less than two minutes!"

"But—"

"Do it! Now!"

He picked her up again and ran to one of the front windows, using the cast on his wrist to punch away what was left of the glass. Black smoke was pouring out of the first- and second-story windows.

He shouted and waved to Akil and Mancini below. They ran and positioned themselves under him.

Crocker wrapped one end of the rope around a water pipe in the corner that ran from the floor to the ceiling and handed it to Farag. He said, "Hold this. Don't let it go. Wait for my signal, then let it out slowly."

The young man looked confused.

Crocker quickly demonstrated what he wanted him to do. "Like this."

"Okay."

With the rope around the chair taut to the pipe, Crocker picked up the chair and lifted it out the window until Holly was clear.

"I love you, baby."

Silver tape still covered her mouth, so she nodded vigorously.

Then, holding on to the rope, Crocker signaled to Farag to give him some slack. The rope burned his hands, ripping the skin off his palms, twisting the bones in his injured wrist.

Gritting his teeth through the searing pain, he watched Holly's head disappear in the smoke. He hoped she could breathe.

After what seemed like an eternity, he heard Akil shout, "We got her, boss! We got her!"

Huge relief. *Alright!*

Quickly pulling up the freed rope, he grabbed Farag by the shoulder. "You're next!"

"No!"

"Hold on to the rope. Use your legs and walk down the side of the building. Like this."

"Maybe."

"You can do it. I'll be right behind you."

"Yes."

He helped Farag out the window, took a deep breath, then climbed out himself. Halfway down Farag stumbled and got caught in the rope. The thick smoke stuck like hot tar in Crocker's throat. He couldn't breathe, but he heard his colleagues shouting. He was too light-headed to make out what they were saying.

Instead he focused on Farag, and climbed down as fast as he could to where he was stuck and hanging by one leg. He was reaching around to try to untangle him when the explosion went off. He saw a tremendous light and felt the oxygen being sucked out of his lungs. As he was flying through the air, he lost consciousness.

CHAPTER SIXTEEN

It was close; but that's the way it is in war. You win or lose, live or die—and the difference is just an eyelash.

—General Douglas MacArthur

HE LAY on his back in the dark, feeling as if he'd been there for years. He couldn't move and was barely conscious. He couldn't even feel his body, aware only of the blackness nestled around him.

Maybe I'm dead and buried. This is what it is.

It was like being stuck in a void, only worse, because part of him was alive enough to be aware of the state he was in.

How long is this going to last... Forever?

He'd deal with it; take what was coming to him, as he always had. Figure out a way to make the best of it, if that was possible.

He kept repeating, "At least Holly's safe."

It made him happy. *I didn't die for nothing.*

More darkness.

After what seemed like hours he heard a sound that was barely perceptible, like a breeze stirring the grass, or a whisper.

"Ka... Ka..."

Or the sound of a bird calling.

"Kr... Kr..."

It took him awhile to realize that someone was whispering his name.

"Crock-er... Crock-er..." Almost like a song.

He tried to respond but nothing came out. So he focused on the sound, and as he did, the darkness around him started to move like a million moths waking up and taking flight. The flutter of their wings tickled his skin and brought it back to life.

"Crocker... Hey, Crocker..." Sharper this time.

As the darkness dispersed, he saw a gray light with touches of green and yellow around the edges. Tried to raise his arm, but it wouldn't move. Tried to raise his head, but couldn't do that, either.

Made out a fuzzy dark object looming over him.

"Crocker. Boss, can you hear me?"

He felt himself blink, which brought him joy. Hope. Slowly, and with great effort, he made out a face with two dark eyes.

"Crocker, can you hear me?"

He blinked again and moved his head slightly.

"Crocker, it's me, Manny."

He blinked one more time and tried to smile. The pain he felt around his mouth and in his neck was welcome. Affirming.

"Crocker, we're in Germany. Holly's here. The rest of the team is back in Virginia."

He smiled slightly.

"Unfortunately, Farag didn't make it."

He winced and shook his head.

"That brave little man saved your life."

He tried to pull himself up.

He heard Mancini say, "His body shielded you from the explosion."

Crocker stopped and sighed. Felt a tear form in his eye.

"I'll go call Holly. She'll want to see you. I'll get her now."

An enormous feeling of warmth and appreciation enveloped his chest and squeezed his heart. He started to weep.

There were no medal ceremonies or parades. Just six weeks of convalescence for injuries to his wrist, lungs, back, neck, head, and ribs. Then another week with Holly on the Eastern Shore of Virginia, where they held each other, rested, took long walks on the beach, paddled their kayaks in the bay, and made love.

Holly wasn't ready to talk about her ordeal in Libya. Though she was okay physically and hadn't been sexually violated, she'd been tied up and forced to witness the torture and execution of Brian Shaw. She said he'd been her friend and colleague, nothing more.

It was difficult, ugly stuff. Both of them understood that the psychological wounds would take time to heal, if they ever did.

Crocker was happy to be alive, but still pissed off.

His first day back at ST-6 headquarters, he was in the team room unpacking his gear and talking to Ritchie about Harley motorcycles when someone summoned him to the CO's office. As he slowly walked across the cement exercise area, teammates came over to congratulate him and shake his hand.

He entered the CO's office with a feeling of pride in being a member of ST-6 but also a sense of resignation. He didn't care what came next. Even if he was going to be forced to retire for insubordination or taking too many risks, Holly and his men were alive. That's all he really cared about. He wished Farag was alive, too. Planned to track down his family and help them somehow.

Captain Sutter rose from behind his desk and shook his hand vigorously. "Congratulations, Crocker. Welcome back."

"Thanks, sir. It's real good to be home."

"We're all damn proud of you."

Crocker started to choke up. "That means a lot to me, sir."

He didn't notice Jim Anders from the CIA until he stepped forward and greeted him, too. "You look rested and in remarkable shape, considering what you went through."

"I'm lucky to be alive."

"Sit down."

Sutter shut the door, then sat behind his desk. Anders popped open his briefcase and removed a yellow legal pad and a file filled with documents. "First," he said reading from his notes, "let's talk about the shipping containers."

"The shipping containers?" Crocker asked back.

"Yes."

He had participated in post-op meetings dozens of times, but today he found it took real effort to retrieve the image of the white 727 and the six rust-colored containers.

"What about them?"

"The team from IAEA just finished their inspection.

They found that those six containers held enough enriched uranium to make at least four five-megaton bombs."

Sutter: "What do you have to say about that, Crocker?"

"Holy shit, sir."

"Holy shit is right."

Crocker recalled that a five-megaton bomb had hundreds of times the destructive power of the bombs dropped on Hiroshima and Nagasaki combined. "That's a lot of enriched uranium," he said.

"A whole hell of a lot."

"That son of a bitch Iranian," Crocker snapped, his anger stirring. "Did he escape?"

"You mean the one you saw meeting with Salehi?" Anders asked, leafing through the stack of documents and locating the one he wanted.

"That's the one."

"You were right about him, too. We've identified that individual as Farhed Alizadeh of the Iranian Qods Force."

"I *knew* it. I wanted to grab him, but I was more concerned about whatever was in those shipping containers leaving the country."

"Understandable," Sutter acknowledged.

Anders: "According to confidential reports we've received from reliable sources, he escaped south and crossed the border into Niger."

"That's the same place he was operating from before. Not far from the Libyan town of Toummo."

"Correct."

"I'm real sorry we didn't get him."

Anders: "We are, too. And you're going to regret it even more when you hear this."

"What?"

"Remember the thumb drives you recovered from the tunnel? The ones belonging to the kidnappers?"

Crocker winced at the memory of following Farag into the concrete room, then nodded. "Yes."

"Based on information we found on them, we believe that Alizadeh was working with Anaruz Mohammed the whole time. We think it's possible he even had a hand in planning, directing, and financing Holly's kidnapping."

Crocker pictured the Iranian's intense, falconlike eyes. "That evil bastard."

"We also suspect he might have been behind the attack in Sebha."

Crocker was fully alert now and ready to fight. "Son of a bitch!"

"Makes sense, doesn't it?"

Sutter: "In a diabolical kind of way, yes."

Anders: "He knew you and your men were in Libya looking for the Scorpion program WMDs, and he needed to either kill you or distract you."

"Where is he now?"

"Somewhere, planning more attacks against the West, probably; looking for more ways to help his country build nuclear weapons. Where that is, specifically, I can't say right now."

"What about Anaruz Mohammed?"

"We expect the Iranians are still going to use him to forward their agenda in Libya and Niger. But he doesn't have enough of a following to pose a political threat on his own."

"That evil fucking Alizadeh has got to be stopped," Crocker concluded.

Anders: “I wholeheartedly agree.”

Sutter: “What would you say if I said you could get another shot at him?”

Crocker leaned forward and said, “I’d love that, sir! I’d thoroughly welcome the opportunity.”

Anders: “Good. Very good.”

Sutter: “Pull your team together and come see me when you’re ready.”

Crocker: “How about first thing tomorrow morning, sir, right after PT?”

In his head he was already explaining to Holly that he had to leave to track down the man who had planned her kidnapping and had helped kill Brian. She was telling him that she’d miss him, but she wanted the bastard punished.

Sutter: “Eight a.m., Crocker. I’ll see you back here.”

“Very good, sir. See you then.”

ACKNOWLEDGMENTS

We couldn't have done this without the hard work, expertise, and intelligence of a whole team of people, starting with our agent, Heather Mitchell, at Gelfman Schneider and a very talented group at Little, Brown led by our editor, John Parsley, and including William Boggess, Theresa Giacopasi, Nicole Dewey, Peggy Freudenthal, and Chris Jerome. Thank you very much.

We also want to express our appreciation to our families for their love and support—Don's wife, Dawn, and his daughter, Dawn; and Ralph's wife, Jessica, and his children, John, Michael, Francesca, and Alessandra.

ABOUT THE AUTHORS

DON MANN (CWO3, USN) has for the past thirty years been associated with the U.S. Navy SEALs as a platoon member, assault team member, boat crew leader, and advanced training officer, and more recently as program director preparing civilians to go to BUD/S (SEAL Training). Until 1998 he was on active duty with SEAL Team Six. Since then, he has deployed to the Middle East on numerous occasions in support of the war against terrorism. Many of today's active-duty SEALs on Team Six are the same guys he taught how to shoot, conduct ship and aircraft takedowns, and operate in urban, arctic, desert, river, and jungle warfare, as well as Close Quarters Battle and Military Operations in Urban Terrain. He has suffered two cases of high-altitude pulmonary edema, frostbite, a broken back, and multiple other broken bones in training or service. He has been captured twice during operations and lived to talk about it.

RALPH PEZZULLO is a *New York Times* bestselling author and an award-winning playwright and screenwriter. His books include *Jawbreaker* and *The Walk-In* (with CIA operative Gary Berntsen), *At the Fall of Somoza*, *Plunging into Haiti* (winner of the Douglas Dillon Award for Distinguished Writing on American Diplomacy), *Most Evil* (with Steve Hodel), *Eve Missing*, and *Blood of My Blood*. His film adaptation of *Recoil* by Jim Thompson, directed by James Foley, is scheduled to reach theaters in 2013.

...AND THEIR NEXT NOVEL

In December 2013, Mulholland Books will publish *Hunt the Falcon* by Don Mann and Ralph Pezzullo. Following is an excerpt from the novel's opening pages.

CHAPTER ONE

"Let us not pray to be sheltered from danger, but to be fearless when facing it."

—Rabindranath Tagore

JOHN AND LENORA Rinehart had just watched their thirteen-year-old son, Alex, dress himself for the first time. It was a special morning. Usually days at the Rinehart house started with a delicate dance determined by their son's moods.

Just because his son was autistic didn't mean he wasn't smart, John Rinehart reminded himself as his shoes met the uneven surface of the slate walk and he punched the electronic button that opened the door to his dark blue Saab 900. His son was exceptional in the IQ department. But his brain's ability to control the warp-speed flow of information, and his emotional impulses, was out of whack. When it didn't work the way Alex wanted it to, the boy got frustrated. And when he got frustrated, he got mad as hell. Screaming, beat-the-shit-out-of-whatever-he-could get-his-hands-on angry sometimes.

Ask him to find the positive difference of the fourth

power of two consecutive positive integers that must be divisible by one more than twice the larger integer? No problem. But little things like buttoning a shirt or fastening a zipper often tripped him up.

Little things... little victory, forty-two-year-old John Rinehart said to himself as he reached across the console between the front seats and squeezed his wife Lena's hand.

She smiled past the straight black bangs that almost brushed her eyes and said, "I credit Alex's new school. It's been a major positive."

"Yes," John whispered back. His heart felt like it might leap out of his chest with delight.

John felt things strongly. Like his son. Sometimes so strongly that it scared him and he, too, had to fight hard to control himself.

His half-Asian wife was the more emotionally balanced of the two. She understood that tomorrow morning might be completely different; that life with a child like Alex was unpredictable at best.

John found it much harder to let go of the hope that his son would one day lead a normal life. He kept looking for a path, or an unopened doorway in his son's psyche, that would lead to that result. Which made sense, because part of what he did for a living as the economic counselor at the U.S. embassy was look for patterns of activity and use them to try to predict future events—Chinese-Thai trade, Bat volatility, Thai-U.S. trading algorithms.

He was a brilliant man who studied the world and saw tendencies, vectors, and roads traveled, like the one he steered the highly polished car onto now into the knot of cars, trucks, motorcycles, and bicycles on what the Thais called Thanon Phetchaburi.

He'd learned to expect the eight-mile ride to the U.S. embassy to take forty minutes because of the traffic, but he didn't mind. It gave him and his wife a chance to listen to music and spend some quiet time together.

This morning he didn't want to think about the embassy where she worked as an administrative assistant in the CIA station. Nor did he want to consider the problems he would deal with when he got there.

Instead he listened as Stan Getz played a smooth, moving "Body and Soul" over the stereo, and he hummed along, feeling unusually optimistic and calm. He even entertained the possibility that when his tour in Thailand ended in a year, he would return to teaching. Maybe even accept the position on the faculty of the University of California, Berkeley, that had been offered to him a little while back. Lena would like that.

The sky above was a murky, almost iridescent yellow. Bangkok was a surreal blend of staggeringly beautiful and disgusting, rich and poor, spiritual and depraved, all living pressed together. He found the yin-yang dynamic of the city fascinating.

Adjusting the air-conditioning, he turned to his wife. "I'm proud of you, darling," he said.

"I'm proud of *you.* And Alex, too."

"Our Alex," he added.

Through the windshield John noticed a battered blue truck squeezing into the little space between his front bumper and the Nissan taxi four feet to the right. He applied the brake, hit the horn, then turned to his wife.

He noticed the way the light highlighted her cheekbones, then glimpsed a motorcycle near the back bumper out of the corner of his right eye. Two helmets, both black with mirrored visors. The driver and rider looked like aliens.

Past the soaring saxophone solo and through the door panels, he heard a metal click. Seconds later the motorcycle roared past, narrowly avoiding a bus.

He was thinking about the first time he had seen Lena standing near the entrance to the Georgetown University library. She was a sophomore; he was pursuing a master's degree in economics.

He remembered how he had stopped to ask her for directions to White-Gravenor Hall, even though he knew where it was. And how when she turned, he was struck by her beauty and the strength and intelligence in her eyes.

John Rinehart opened his mouth to tell Lena how he had felt at that moment. How certain he had been that something important was happening. But before he could get the words out, the small but powerful explosive device that had been magnetically attached to the car's rear fender exploded, tearing through the metal chassis, igniting the high-octane fuel in the gas tank, and causing the car to burst into flames.

John and Lenora Rinehart were dead within seconds. Another eight poor souls riding bicycles and motorbikes in the vicinity also died. Twenty-three were seriously injured.

Before Thai police officials finished their inspection of the site and carted away the wreckage of the Saab 900, a similar magnetic device killed a U.S. military attaché and his assistant in their car a half mile away. That same day, bombs placed by riders on motorcycles killed fifteen more U.S. and Israeli officials in Rome, Athens, Mumbai, and Cairo.

The pain that the bombings caused was incalculable—children denied fathers, wives turned into widows, friends and colleagues left questioning their faith in God.

Alex Rinehart, upon hearing the news that his parents had been killed, retreated inside himself and refused to talk.

That night, 2,410 miles northwest of Bangkok, Navy SEAL Team Six (DEVGRU) leader Thomas Crocker wiped the snow from the goggles attached to his FAST Ballistic Helmet and adjusted the seventy-five-pound pack on his back.

"This remind you of anything, boss?" Davis, his blond comms man, asked in a gravelly voice behind him, little icicles clinging to the half-inch reddish growth on his jaw and chin.

"*The Nightmare Before Christmas*?" Crocker replied as he retaped the straps on his backpack so they wouldn't make noise as he approached the target. His left hand burned from a frigid wind that whistled through the craggy rocks along the ridge in southeastern Afghanistan.

"K2," Davis said, referring to a training climb that Crocker had taken the team on in which a female friend of his had died in an avalanche. Then noticing that his chief's left hand was bare, he asked, "What happened to your glove?"

"Lost it attending to Dog." Dog, aka Timothy L. Douglas, was the new guy who had just completed Green Team. He trudged ahead of them, favoring his left leg and carrying "the pig"—SEAL-speak for the MK43 Mod 0 machine gun, which Crocker preferred to call "the nasty."

Dog, a former middle linebacker from the University of Tennessee, had slipped about a half mile back as they were climbing up the slope and had ripped a foot-long gash in his right thigh, which Crocker had bandaged up.

"I got a spare pair," Davis said, white fog shooting from his mouth and mixing with the condensation around them. He removed a pair of black cold-weather gloves from his drop leg pouch and handed them to Crocker.

"Colder than a witch's tit," the team leader groaned, shaking his exposed hand to keep the blood moving, then slipping the gloves on. "Thanks."

He was leading an element of thirteen men. All SEALs from Team Six, who had been at Jalalabad Air Field, chilling, listening to music, playing video games, reading, sleeping, shooting the shit, when the urgent message came over the radio that Observation Post Memphis (OPM) was under attack. Two things made this significant and alarming: One, the difficulty of the terrain in the middle of the Hindu Kush mountains combined with the blizzard made it impossible to reinforce the post by air or provide it with any sort of air support. People who had been to OPM referred to it as "the dark side of the moon." And two, five operators from Six had been dispatched to the post a week earlier and were now trapped and fighting for their lives along with a dozen marines, several National Guardsmen from Pennsylvania, and a platoon of soldiers from the U.S. Army's 17th Infantry Alpha Company.

As a general rule, when teammates are under attack, you don't sit back at base with your thumb up your ass.

Adding to Crocker's sense of duty in this case was the

fact that one of the Team Six operators fighting for his life in OPM was his running partner Neal Stafford—a former cowboy originally from Waco, Texas, with two wild young boys and a lovely wife named Alyssa, who was his wife Holly's best friend. Crocker's teenage daughter, Jenny, babysat for their kids.

All of this explained why Crocker had sought out the one 160th Special Operations Aviation Regiment (SOAR) helicopter pilot crazy enough to brave the fifty-mile-an-hour gusts and drop them off as high up the mountain as possible, and why they had slowly been picking their way through the snow, ice, and rocks like goats. The 160th SOAR was also known as the Night Stalkers. Their motto: Night Stalkers don't quit.

Coming up the other side—the east side—was out of the question, since the whole Parun Valley, and most of Nuristan Province, was firmly under Taliban control and had been for over a year. Most Americans weren't aware that this part of Afghanistan was called the Islamic Emirate of Afghanistan and flew a white flag with a mujahadeen call-to-arms slogan scrawled on it.

Which begged the question Crocker had been asking himself for hours: What the fuck was OPM doing there in the first place? Someone in Jalalabad had told him that a general had had it built to monitor traffic along one of the most important access roads to Kabul. Another person had told him that Iranians had been seen in the area.

Was OPM monitoring the movement of arms, heroin, Taliban fighters? Where was that general now? Sitting in some warm room with his feet up, watching college football?

Crocker stopped himself. It didn't matter now. All

he cared about were the lives of the SEALs and other soldiers trapped at OPM, and helping to fight back the Taliban assault until the storm abated and rescue helicopters could pull them out.

Judging from the unrelenting ferocity of the storm, that might be a while.

Crocker held up his right fist, indicating to the men that he wanted them to huddle around him. Facing him were twelve grizzled faces caked with ice and snow. Aside from his core five, which included Davis (comms), Ritchie (demolitions), Mancini (equipment and weapons), and Akil (maps and logistics), there were machine-gunners Dog and Yale, an Asian American sniper named Cal, Gabe, Langer, Jake, Chance, and Phillips.

"How you doing, Dog?" Crocker asked over the muffled sounds of warfare echoing up from the other side of the mountain.

"Hurtin' a little and embarrassed, but ready to kick some ass."

"I like that attitude."

As long as Dog was physically and mentally strong enough to set up and fire the twenty-pound gas-operated, belt-fed, air-cooled killing machine (capable of firing as many as fourteen 7.62-caliber rounds per second) that he cradled in his arms, Crocker didn't care how much discomfort he was in. To his mind, pain was weakness leaving the body.

"Refuel. Rehydrate," Crocker barked. "In a few minutes, we're gonna reach the top of this ice cube and enter the shit. I want us all to stick together until I say otherwise. Maintain three-sixty security. Visibility is terrible.

I don't want us shooting at one another. Any questions? Any problems?"

Several of the SEALs shook their heads. No.

Cal spoke up. "This peashooter ain't gonna do a whole lot of good in this weather, boss," he said, slapping the MK11 Mod 0 sniper weapons system he carried slung across his back.

"Manny's got an extra MP7. He'll lend it to you. Right, Manny?"

"A round of beers at the Guadalajara when we get back," Mancini said. The Guadalajara was a popular watering hole close to the SEAL base in Virginia Beach.

"With nachos," Ritchie added.

Crocker said, "Davis, call the post commander. Tell him we're approaching from the northwest ridge."

A marine corporal back at Jalalabad had explained to Crocker that the only possible land approach to OPM was along the northwest ridge, then down rope ladders that had been rigged along the rocks that formed the back wall of the base.

"Roger, boss," Davis responded.

Guys squeezed energy gel into their mouths, wolfed down energy bars, and gulped water from their CamelBaks. Crocker checked his Garmin 450t GPS with preloaded 3-D map of the area and confirmed that they were within four hundred yards of the observation post. Visibility was so bad that he couldn't see more than four feet in front of him.

Davis pointed at him, and seconds later a transmission from the marine major in charge of OPM blared through the F3 radio transmitter in Crocker's helmet.

"Tango-six-two this is Memphis-five-central. I thank

the Holy Father for your assistance. Condition double-red here. Need medevac, immediate support. Taking heavy casualties. Two of our guard stations have already been overrun!"

Crocker thought it was both strange and alarming that Neal Stafford was at the post. Last time he had seen him, he was halfway around the world, tossing a miniature football to his two young sons on the front lawn of his house in Virginia. Now, as he considered how Neal's safety might affect Neal's family and the tender network of relationships and emotions that connected Neal's life to his own, he felt a responsibility to get him out of OPM unharmed.

"Memphis-five-central, we'll soon be approaching along the northwest ridge," Crocker responded. "Alert your perimeter. Is the path clear? Over." He'd been trained to compartmentalize his feelings in order to effectively do his job.

"Tango-six-two, we're under attack from the east and the south. Keep following the ridge. I'll send two men out to meet you. They'll disarm the alarms and show you the way down. Do you copy?"

"Copy, Memphis. Have them whistle. Three short blasts in succession so we know it's them."

"Three short whistles. Copy, Tango. Welcome and Godspeed. Over and out."

Crocker saw the wary look on some of the men's faces and barked, "Be sure to stay alert and stick together!"

"And don't feed the trolls," Akil added.

"You've got the wrong continent," Mancini growled back. "Trolls are mythological beings from Scandinavian folklore."

Akil shook his head. "Are you serious?"

"Yes, I'm serious. When you say shit, get it right."

Crocker had taken a mere twenty steps along the snow-covered trail at the top of the ridge when the first rounds of automatic fire whizzed by, and he shouted to his men to hold fire and take cover behind nearby rocks and boulders. Then the firing picked up and was augmented by a barrage of missiles, mortars, and propelled grenades.

Pieces of hot metal hissed into the snow and ice. Explosions lit up the craggy landscape nearby, but visibility was still limited.

Crocker was high on adrenaline. His mind worked at warp speed measuring distance, speed, and the sequence of information and making calculations. Something was very wrong.

"Should we return fire, boss?" Davis asked, crouched to his right.

"Negative!" Crocker shouted.

From somewhere behind him, Dog muttered, "This situation is double-fucked."

"Double-fucked or not, we'll accomplish the mission." Then Crocker spoke into his headset: "Hold your fire. We don't want to give away our position. Pull back to the other side of the ridge."

He was referring to one they had recently climbed. On their way up, they had followed a snow-covered trail, and now they literally clung to ice-covered rocks as they moved parallel to the ridge. The muscles in their arms and legs burned as they struggled to maintain balance while each man carried roughly one hundred pounds of equipment on his back. Akil led the way, carefully stepping from one toehold to another, in the general direction southeast, keeping his head down to avoid the rock, snow, ice, and hot metal that flew past.

"Tango-six-two, this is Memphis-five-central. Report your position!" screamed the voice in Crocker's headset. "Tango-six-two, report!" The fear in the voice was palpable.

He wished he could tell the major to hold his shit together. Instead he said sternly, "We're proceeding, Memphis-five-central. Over and out."

A large explosion shook the top of the mountain, dislodging an icy boulder that tumbled and hit an outcropping of rock with a large smash and split the boulder in two. A refrigerator-size piece spun in the direction where Dog, Phillips, and Jake were standing.

"Watch out!" Crocker screamed.

The men had little room to maneuver, and there was nothing the other SEALs could do but watch as the big mass of rock glanced off the backs of their three teammates who had pressed themselves against the snow and ice.

Time slowed down. Jake froze, his legs went limp, and he fell backwards. Phillips reached his arms out and caught him. Dog's whole body twisted violently to the left. Crocker saw the acute agony on his face, then watched as the MK43 Mod 0 machine gun flew out of Dog's arms and disappeared into the shower of falling snow.

He didn't even hear it land. It could have ended up hundreds or even thousands of feet below.

Gone. Not that Crocker was worried about the weapon as he squeezed past Mancini, Davis, and Chance, reached for the emergency medical pack at the back of his waist, and looked down at Jake lying on the narrow ledge. His blue eyes were frozen and staring into space as Phillips tried to remove Jake's backpack.

"Don't!" Crocker said.

"But—"

"Don't touch him!"

"Sir, he's breathing but can't speak."

"He's in shock," Crocker replied, feeling along Jake's neck for a pulse and finding that it was higher than normal. He knelt in the snow and carefully reached under Jake's backpack along his back to the place below his neck where the rock had struck. There was swelling and loose dislocated bone under the skin. Damage to some of the vertebrae.

"Tango-six-two, this is Memphis-five-central. Report your position!" the marine major from OPM screamed in Crocker's headset.

Ignoring him, Crocker turned to Phillips. "Help me lay Jake on his side and wrap him in some Kevlar blankets," he said. "He can't be moved. You hear me? Don't move him!"

"Yes, sir. You want me to stay with him?"

The major from OPM screeched again, "Tango-six-two, this is Memphis-five-central. Do you copy? Report!"

"Yeah, I copy!" Crocker barked into his helmet mike.

Panic was dangerous. Phillips touched Crocker's arm and whispered, "Sir, you want me to remain with Jake?"

The sounds of combat had moved farther down the mountain to the approximate location of OPM. The Taliban had stopped directing fire at the ridge.

Crocker waved Mancini over and said, "Manny, go back the way we came. First reconnoiter the ridge. If it's clear, retake it. If there are a number of Taliban there, call and inform me. We can't let the enemy hold that position."

"No, boss, we can't. If so, I believe the base will be surrounded."

"Which will make it real tough for us to fight our way in."

"Roger that."

"Take three men with you, and let me know."

"Got it."

Crocker looked down at Jake again, then Phillips carefully slipped a Kevlar blanket under him. A gust of wind rushed up the side of the mountain, creating what sounded like a wolf's howl.

A voice in his head reminded him that Phillips had asked him a question.

He squeezed Phillips's arm and said, "Yes, I want you to stay with him." Phillips's long, narrow face reminded Crocker of a marine he had served with in Okinawa who fell in love with and married a Filipino prostitute—something that straight-arrow Phillips would never do.

Phillips looked up with calm, intelligent light brown eyes. "You want me to try to monitor his vital signs, sir?"

"Every ten minutes or so, try at least to check his pulse. If it gets below sixty or over a hundred beats a minute, let me know."

"Will do, Chief."

Crocker scooted over to Dog. Dog was leaning against the side of the mountain holding his left shoulder, which was hanging at an odd angle. A rocket whizzed overhead and Crocker instinctively ducked. For a second he forgot he was in Nuristan Province, Afghanistan—the scene of one of his favorite movies, *The Man Who Would Be King*. And throughout history a very dangerous place to be.

Who wants to be king now? he asked himself, looking at Dog, whose head was turned away from Crocker. The Tennessean's thick body trembled. Crocker whispered his name. When Dog turned, Crocker saw tears streaming down the sides of his freckled face.

"Fucking new-guy bad luck," Dog snarled through small gritted teeth. "I'm sorry."

"For what?" Crocker asked, inspecting Dog's shoulder.

"Letting go of the pig."

"Fuck the pig. Bite into this," Crocker said, handing Dog a thick square of rubber he kept in a small plastic bag in his emergency medical kit.

"Why?"

"Bite on it and tell me something: Who was quarterback at UT when you played there?"

"What—?" Dog's answer was interrupted by an unbelievable jolt of pain caused by Crocker, who pulled Dog's right arm away from his shoulder, then forcefully pushed it up and into the socket with a pop.

"ELI-FUCKING-MANNING!"

Happier tears streamed from Dog's blue eyes as he lifted his arm and realized that his shoulder worked again and was close to pain free.

"You're a lucky man," Crocker said in a low voice.

"Thank you," Dog responded, removing the piece of rubber from his mouth, wiping it on his sleeve, then handing it back.

"Grab an extra weapon from someone."

"Right away."

"Let's go kill some fucking Taliban."

Crocker joined Akil at the front of the column. The barrel-chested Egyptian American former marine raised his arm and pointed out a route that he had just explored, which he said would take them along the top of the mountain up to the ridge.

That's when Mancini's voice came over his headset. "Boss, M and M. We've taken the position. All secure. Advise."

"Hold, M. As well as you can, try to protect the northwest access."

"Roger."

"Holler if you see any enemy activity."

"What's your location?" Mancini asked.

"We're proceeding south."

Crocker and the remaining six crossed three hundred yards until they were directly above OPM. They assembled behind a low wall blanketed with snow. Since visibility was still terrible, he blew into a whistle he kept on a chain around his neck three times.

Someone to his right whistled back. He rose with his HK416 ready and tried peering through the mass of swirling snow. He proceeded in a crouch another five feet until he saw a blurry, dark shape standing beside a collapsed stone wall.

"You Chief Crocker?" the voice asked through the wind.

"That's right, who are you?"

"Lance Corporal Novak, sir, of Alpha Company. Welcome to OP Memphis, otherwise known as the House of Blues."